ICED

A NOVEL BY

JUDITH ALGUIRE

Published by New Victoria Publishers Inc., a feminist, literary, and cultural organization, PO Box 27, Norwich, VT 05055-0027.

Cover Art by Ginger Brown

Printed and Bound in the USA
1 2 3 4 5 6   2000 1999 1998 1997 1996 1995

Library of Congress Cataloging-in-Publication Data

Alguire, Judith.
    Iced : a novel / by Judith Alguire.
        p. cm.
    ISBN 0-934678-60-X
        I. Title.

PR9199.3. A368I25   1995
    813'. 54 - -dc20

                                                95-19138
                                                CIP

For Susan: *Sui Generis*

PROLOGUE

This is a hockey puck. It's a hard rubber disk, one inch thick, three inches in diameter, six ounces in weight, shot at incredible speeds by incredible athletes who play the fastest game in the world.

This game, hockey, is played on an ice surface, measuring approximately two-hundred by eighty-five feet. Sometimes the game is played on the river or frozen lake but then it becomes a metaphor for our history as a people and I don't want to get into that right now.

A hockey team is composed of six players—a goal tender (also called the goalie or netminder), two defensemen (hereafter called "defenders"—at least when I'm telling the story), and three forwards called the right winger, the left winger and the center. The goalie defends the net—a contraption four feet high and six feet wide located at each end of the ice. It's the defenders' job to help the goalie defend the net. The defenders do this best by clearing the puck out of their end of the ice and passing it to one of the three speedy forwards. The forwards' job is to put the puck in the other team's net. Sometimes these roles become confused. Defenders score goals and forwards perform a defensive or "checking" role. The intricacies of these role reversals don't matter for our purposes.

The ice surface is divided into sections by red and blue lines and there are rules associated with passing the puck across these lines. But for our purposes that doesn't matter either.

Hockey, in its patterns and rhythms, is often like basketball. Sometimes it's like soccer. It never resembles football.

Hockey is a poetic sport. It doesn't have a violent heart. Hockey, like all sports, is inherently innocent.

Hockey was invented in Canada. It was played here first largely by adult males. Today, hockey is played in many parts of the world. In

Canada hockey is now played mainly by boys. In the United States of America hockey is also played by boys and by men, often in universities, often with the purpose of winning Olympic medals. In Canada the game is geared toward producing players for the National Hockey League. This is where Wayne Gretzky plays. Wayne used to play in Edmonton, but now due to the profit-motivated machinations of the sports world, he plays in Los Angeles.

Canadian and American women play hockey too. So do lots of women throughout the world. We play for love, for the pleasure of each other's company, for the good feelings in our bodies. We play because somewhere on an icy patch in a farmer's field or on an outdoor rink we learned how good it felt to move like the wind, to stop on a dime with a spray of clean white powder off shiny silver blades or release a shot that lifted the puck off the ice like magic and made the net bulge.

There have always been girls who dreamed of playing professional hockey. Eventually, they've had to drop their dreams at the door along with their shoulder pads and black hockey skates.

But not anymore. All that's changed. I'm Alison Gutherie and I'm a professional hockey player.

Announcing, the Toronto Teddies Hockey Club:

Alison Gutherie, player/coach: An aging dyke athlete and all that that implies.

Sharon Sosnoski, defense: The strong, silent type. I wonder what lurks behind those inert hazel eyes.

Pat Carsey, defense: Mother of two. Hockey is the vehicle that could put her up where she belongs.

Carol Gee, defense: Hockey is her escape from a job ghetto.

Julia Martin, defense: Owner's choice from a roller derby—all he saw was the novelty value of a strapping Black Afro-American.

Ingrid Eklund, left wing: "Good play exists where the players are kind-hearted, modest and considerate of their teammates," said Anatoli Tarasov, legendary coach of Central Red Army. If he had added "earthy and wickedly ribald" he would have described our captain, Ingrid Eklund, to a T.

Alice Todd, left wing: Alice is the best seventeen-year-old player I have ever seen. I am acutely conscious of my role in her development.

Chris Young, left wing: There isn't enough tape in the league to deal with this woman's aches and pains.

Molly Gavison, right wing: She was all the joy in the world, a beautiful, natural talent. Then it all went wrong.

Henny Buskers, right wing: The perpetrator of all practical jokes.

Dorsey Thorne, center: I love having her on my team but I'd hate to play against her. She's devastatingly personal in her taunts, sly and quick with the butt end of her stick and a virtuoso in taking the dive.

Lou Frampton, center: My Steady Eddie. Seldom gets noticed but absolutely essential.

Effie McGovern, center: Effie provides a benchmark of sanity in this topsy-turvy world.

Nomi Pereira, goal/right wing: Hockey's only five-foot-five enforcer.

Joy Drinkwater, goal/right wing: Joy is personally gorgeous, flamboyant and rebellious in the most glamorous sort of way. In the net, she's like most goalies—ritualistic, skittish and alone.

Harriett Steele, trainer/equipment manager/bus driver: Harriett plays the role of gruff, no-nonsense trainer to perfection.

Phil Tweddell, owner: Phil would try to sell his grandmother if he thought he could get a few bucks.

Abbreviations

AHL: the American Hockey League.
CCM: a manufacturer of sports equipment.
CFL: Canadian Football League.
CIAU: Canadian Interuniversity Athletic Union.
NBA: National Basketball Association.
NFA: National Feminist Alliance.
NHL: National Hockey League.
OHA: Ontario Hockey Association.
OHL: Ontario Hockey League.
OHRC: Ontario Human Rights Commission.
OWHA: Ontario Women's Hockey Association.
ROM: Royal Ontario Museum.
U of T: The University of Toronto.
WPHL: Women's Professional Hockey League.

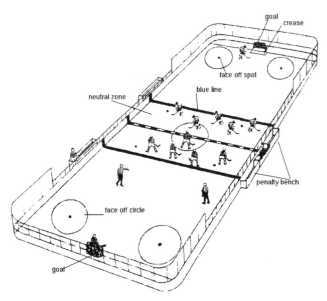

Back check— to attempt to check or cover an offensive player from behind.

Blocker— a goaltender's glove with a flat surface worn on the stick hand.

Catcher— a goaltender's glove with webbing worn on the hand opposite the stick hand.

Charging— Running into the opponent illegally.

Crease— a demarcated area immediately in front of the net. Opposing players may not bodycheck the goalie in the crease. Once the goalie leaves this area, however, she is fair game.

Cross-Check— an illegal play where a player violently pushes another player with the stick where both hands are on the stick and no part of the stick is on the ice.

Crossbar— the horizontal bar at the top of the net.

Dump-and-chase hockey— a style of play that involves shooting the puck over the opponent's blueline and skating in after it rather than carrying the puck in.

Enforcer— a player employed for his ability to intimidate opposing players rather than for his hockey skills.

Five Hole— the area between the goaltender's legs.

Forecheck— to check the opponent in the opponent's defensive zone.

Girdle— a piece of protective equipment designed to protect the lower back, hips, kidneys and upper thighs.

Hat trick: Three or more goals in a single game by the same player. In the old days, fans used to honour the feat by throwing hats on the ice.

Poke Check— a jabbing motion with the blade directed at the puck carrier's stick. The manoeuver is designed to knock the puck loose.

Slot— the area directly in front of the net.

Stand-up Goalie— a goaltender who plays in an erect position rather than in a crouch.

Sweep Check— a checking technique where the stick is swept low to the ice under the puck carrier with the objective of knocking the puck loose.

Zone defense—a defensive strategy where the defenders are responsible for covering an area of the playing surface rather than a particular offensive player.

CHAPTER 1

Being hit in the head with a puck, even one traveling at a relatively pedestrian deflected pace, is no treat. The puck arches and dies, seemingly innocent, but not in its dense inertia. It's what a baseball player would call a 'heavy ball.'

In that fraction of a second before the puck comes to rest, while I'm frozen in position and know there's no escape, I remember the unfortunate pitcher, hit in the face by a screaming line-drive foul as he sat in the dugout, champing sunflower seeds and contemplating the freshness of the new season. Remember the words of his shaken coach: "Hit his face. Square on. Sounded like a ripe watermelon smashing." Remember the scene from *Raging Bull*, what a boxer's nose sounds like when it's broken, splayed amorphously over his face.

I await my fate, knowing that a hand thrown up to protect my face could be broken—and I value my hand more than my nose—and turning the head could mean brain damage. It's too crowded behind the bench to duck. I'm as helpless as a clown in a shooting gallery.

Punk. At the last moment a gloved hand reaches out and bats the puck harmlessly to the ice. The puck dribbles on edge into the corner. The linesman retrieves it and calls the players to the face-off circle.

Nomi Pereira gave me a look of sly satisfaction, then turned away, punctuating her brilliant save—the best of the season in my opinion—by spitting unceremoniously onto the floor between her legs.

Where did I go wrong?

The players were jockeying for position in the face-off circle, giving the linesman a hard time. Fed up, he threw the offending players out of the circle and waved two more in. I slumped against the glass with a sigh. The adrenaline that had sustained me throughout the day had worn off, leaving me feeling as limp as a piece of overcooked spaghetti.

The excitement had begun in earnest when I arrived at the rink over four hours ago. Now, late in the second period of this, the Toronto Teddies inaugural exhibition game, the nerves had started to lose their grip on my guts. For a team that had practiced together fewer than six weeks, whose owner—the forgettable Phil Tweddell— had almost missed the deadline for his franchise payment, we were doing well. Really well.

The shot from the face-off went directly to the goalie. Joy smothered it and the puck was brought back to the circle deep in our end.

I had arrived at Varsity Arena at five o'clock that afternoon, paused briefly at the door to put on my game face, then went directly to the dressing room. The room was going in a dozen different directions. The few players who noticed my arrival smiled and waved. Harriett Steele, our trainer and equipment manager, stood at the door to the training room, taking a critical look at a skate blade. Lou Frampton hovered anxiously at her shoulder.

"Didn't I sharpen your skates after practice this morning?" Harriet asked.

"Yes."

Lou's answer carried a tone of apology. My quiet, steady center never asked for much attention and, consequently, got little. Unlike her fellow centers, the showboating Dorsey Thorne and the irrepressible Effie McGovern—the only person ever to talk non-stop through six weeks of training camp—Lou seemed destined for obscurity.

"And this one still doesn't feel right?"

"Honest, Harriett, I can feel it slipping when I cut."

"O.K., I'll have another go at it." Harriett took the skate and disappeared into the training room.

Lou slumped down on the bench and closed her eyes. She cradled the remaining skate in her lap like a precious kitten.

Skate blades have been known to eviscerate, sever tendons, even slash a goalie's throat. Some kitten.

Harriett's departure with the skate was followed by an anguished cry. Chris Young, the left-winger on our first line, limped after her, bare-footed. "Harriett, I thought you were going to tape my ankle next."

"When I'm finished with this, I'll tape your ankle," Harriett shouted over the whine of the machine.

I dropped a hand to Chris' shoulder to console her. "Problems?"

"It's an old injury. I just feel better when it's taped."

Chris Young was one of those players who remembered every injury she'd had since Novice. The ankle taping was merely the grand finale of her pre-game preparations. She had already wrapped her thigh—hamstring injury from running the hurdles in high school, and taped her wrist—broken when she fell from a treehouse at age six. Chris had applied these wraps so often they had become part of her playing body. Without them, her wrist would fall apart, her hamstring would go into an unforgiving spasm, and the arena would be invaded by locusts and jumping frogs.

My gaze drifted along the bench. Team captain Ingrid Eklund a rangy Norwegian-Canadian with angular good looks sat shoulder to shoulder with Henny Buskers, our slightly goofy right winger. As always, Henny's eyes sparkled with mischief. The two had been following Harriett's trials and tribulations with interest. Ingrid turned to Henny and winked. The wink was taken up and passed around.

"Harriett, I can't find my elbow pads."

"Harriett, my lace broke."

"Harriett, do you have time to massage my iliopsoas?"

The skate-sharpening machine ground to a halt. Harriett appeared in the doorway, her face red under tousled black hair.

"Shut up." She glared about the room, then disappeared back into the trainer's room.

Ingrid looked at Effie. "I think she's telling you to massage your own iliopsoas."

Harriett Steele was not a bad tempered person. The role of gruff, no-nonsense trainer was a role she played to perfection. Our captain, Ingrid Eklund, was very good at helping her play it.

I sat down beside Ingrid. "How are you feeling?"

She put an arm around me, gave me a hug. "Loose. Hell, I gave up thinking this would ever happen for me a long time ago. A rookie at age thirty-three. What a blast."

Harriett appeared in the doorway, dangling a skate in front of Lou with an 'this is it I don't want to hear about your skates until practice tomorrow' look. She gestured wearily to Chris Young. Chris hobbled after her, the limp growing more pronounced with every step.

Dorsey Thorne looked over the top of her newspaper. "Do you think you're going to make it, Chris. Hell, you'd think you were an old

7

woman the way you carry on."

"You'd better hope she makes it," said Henny. "Who else is going to feed you the puck all night?"

Dorsey made a face at Henny.

"Hey, are you sure you aren't reading that newspaper upside down?" Lou piped up.

Dorsey ignored her.

Nobody on the team had much success in getting a rise out of Dorsey. She was much too smug, too self-assured to be bothered by jock needling. And, fortunately, nobody on the team was much bothered by her condescending, caustic remarks. Nobody, except Nomi Pereira.

Right now Nomi wasn't paying any attention to Dorsey. She was sitting on the bench alongside her pal Sharon Sosnoski, champing on her trademark wad of gum and admiring her battered goalie's mask. They made an odd pair—Nomi, little and tough, all elbows and knees and tendons—Sharon, a great bear of a woman. Physically and temperamentally, they couldn't have been more different, but in all things they were joined at the hip.

"Hey, Effie, do you like this?" Nomi held her mask up for the little center to see. "Ingrid painted it for me."

Effie examined the mask uncertainly. "It's great but it doesn't look much like a teddy bear."

Nomi shrugged. "Ain't supposed to. We've got one of those sissy bears on our jerseys. And that's enough."

Effie was not convinced. "It's a good picture. But look at the fangs. They're dripping saliva. The bear looks as if it has rabies."

"That's the way it's supposed to look."

Chris emerged from the training room. Her limp had disappeared.

"Harriett," Dorsey shouted. "You're a bloody miracle worker."

Harriett grimaced. "I know. Now, does anyone here really have trouble with her iliopsoas? Does anyone here know where her iliopsoas is?"

"No," Lou said solemnly.

"In that case you can't possibly have anything wrong with it," Harriett said. "Keep it that way." She dug a 7-Up out of the cooler and sat down on the table in front of the bench.

"Laces?" asked Henny meekly.

Harriett dug into her pocket, found a pair and tossed them to her.

Nomi had put her mask aside. She sat, legs stretched out, head resting against the concrete wall, champing enthusiastically on her gum.

Dorsey lowered her newspaper. "Pereira"—she pronounced the Portuguese name with a broad Spanish accent—"did you see what they said about you in the newspaper?"

Nomi stopped in mid-champ. She eyed Dorsey warily. "What did they say?"

"You'll have to read it for yourself." Dorsey folded the newspaper and handed it to Nomi.

Sharon Sosnoski reached out and intercepted the paper. She glanced at it, then wadded it up and stuffed it into the garbage.

"What did it say?" Nomi persisted.

"Nothing," Sharon grumbled. "It was just the stock report."

Nomi glared at Dorsey. "Shit, I should have known."

"It *was* the hog futures," Dorsey said.

Nomi didn't take the bait so Dorsey sat back, arms behind her head. She seemed inordinately pleased with herself.

"What are you so smug about?" Ingrid asked. "Did you finally get a date?"

Dorsey gave Ingrid a dazzling smile. "As a matter of fact, I did."

"Really?"

"Uh huh. The usher from the Gardens."

"The one with the dreamy eyes?"

"That's the one."

Half the players in the room sighed.

"I happen to know she turned the rest of you down," Dorsey said, adding insult to injury.

Ingrid pounced on Dorsey, wrapping a towel around her head, almost affectionately. "If you're going on a date, I guess you need a shower." She grabbed Dorsey and with Effie's help bundled her off toward the showers.

Joy Drinkwater had been lying on the floor, apparently asleep. All of a sudden, she rolled over and sat up. "I've been in a thousand dressing rooms," she said. "Why should I be surprised they're all the same?"

Pat Carsey, the defender, looked at Joy enviously. "I wish I was calm enough to sleep."

Joy stifled a yawn. "It's an act. Inside, I'm all nerves."

Half the team had joined Ingrid in the showers. I took the opportunity to have a word with the defenders.

"Remember who's in net tonight. Don't be looking for a lot of forward passes. Joy'll be leaving the puck behind the net nine times out of ten. Think about how you'll play it."

Carol winked at me. "It's always nice to play in front of a goalie who stays in the net. With Nomi you have to play goalie half the time—while she's halfway to the blue line or lying on her ass behind the net after being creamed by some forward."

"Shit," said Nomi without malice. "The way you guys handle the puck sometimes, the only way I can count on getting it cleared, is to carry it out myself."

"We've got two good goalies," I reminded. "The point is, always be aware of who's in the net and how she'll react to different situations."

"I'm not hard to play in front of," Joy said. "Just don't pass the puck in front of the net with some hungry forward bearing down on me."

"And remember, no matter who's in goal, if you're checking someone in front of the net, don't forget to lift her stick. It's hard to score when your stick's not on the ice."

Sharon, Carol and Pat, my veteran defenders, listened politely. They realized my elementary reminders were aimed mainly at Julia Martin, a fine athlete and eager student but a novice on defense.

Up until a few weeks ago, Julia had been preparing herself for another season of roller derby. Phil Tweddell practically lifted her off a rink in Minneapolis, reasoning she would have value as a novelty draw—six-foot, three-inch Black woman not being the norm in hockey at any level. Julia had had to pack a lifetime of hockey into the past six weeks.

She leaned forward now listening intently, her eyes bright with anxiety. Julia was a proud woman. She was scared stiff at the prospect of embarrassing herself.

The shower stopped. Dorsey and the gang emerged. Dorsey was dripping wet.

"I hope you like playing in wet longjohns," Harriett said.

"Aw, Harriett, you've got to have another pair around."

"I've got an extra pair in my locker," Ingrid said. "I wore them for practice two days in a row—but they're dry."

"Oh, yuck."

"I've got another pair," Harriett said grudgingly. "If someone mops up the floor, I might be persuaded to give them to you."

The locker room door opened and Alice Todd squeezed into the room.

"Hey, Toddy, where have you been? You've missed all the fun."

"Alison said I could be late."

"Ah, special privileges," said Henny. She was standing in a puddle of water wringing out the mop.

"I had an essay to finish. It had to be in the mail today."

"Essay," Dorsey snorted. "You mean one of those 'what I did on my summer vacation' things?"

"Sort of."

Henny paused, mop poised. "Did you write about training camp?"

Alice shook her head.

"Oh, you should have. You could have talked about how they put down the ice after the horse show and we had to skate through dirt for a week."

"It wasn't dirt," Nomi grumbled. "It was horse shit."

Carol Gee sighed blissfully. "It smelled like heaven to me. After what I'm used to cleaning up, it was a walk in the park." She grabbed Sharon by the arm. "I'm never going back to nursing. Never. Even if I don't make it as a hockey player and end up sweeping the ice for a living."

"You'll make it," Sharon said.

"Maybe I should have written about training camp," Toddy said. "But it's too late. I mailed it."

"So, what did you write about?"

"Doesn't matter."

"Let me guess," Dorsey persisted. "You wrote about your dog: 'My first love—my dog' by Alice Todd."

"Be nice," Pat whispered. "She's just a kid."

"Spoken like a mother of two," Ingrid said.

Pat rolled her eyes. "Speaking like a mother of two...I got a letter from my lawyer today. He was finally able to get a restraining order against Bill. He was bothering the kids at school, trying to find out where I'm living. He's on a tear again. Mad as hell that something good's happened for me."

The dressing room was suddenly dead silent. A slightly resentful silence. Real life had intruded on our grand adventure.

Ingrid broke the silence. "Will the kids be OK?"

Pat nodded. "Bill wouldn't hurt them. Not physically. He's just trying to use them to get back at me. I think he'll stay away now."

"If he doesn't, I'll sic Uncle Walt on him," Sharon said.

When the going got tough, these kids from the North End closed ranks. Sometimes I forgot how close they were and what a small town Kingston was while they were growing up. While Sharon and Nomi were babbling to each other through the rungs of their adjacent playpens, Pat Carsey's future husband, Bill, was probably teasing the family cat or tying a can to a dog's tail. A few years later, at about the same time Uncle Walt was teaching Nomi and Sharon to shoot pucks against the garage door, he was coaching little Bill in Novice. Bill was to advance steadily through the various levels in house league where a number of coaches had a hand in trying to make a man of him. He grew up wild as the wind, a handsome, sullen loner, sufficiently dashing and romantic to turn the head of a seventeen-year-old Pat Carsey. She and Bill were married when Pat was eighteen. A few years and two kids later, Bill's high school drinking problem had become a permanent activity. By the age of twenty-three, Bill Carsey knew he wasn't going anywhere special. Doing booze and drugs and beating his wife helped fill the void.

"If you need any help," Julia said, "don't hesitate to call on us."

Pat squeezed Julia's arm. "Thanks but I think everything's going to be all right now." She glanced around the room. "What's the matter? Did someone die? It's so quiet you'd think we were going to a funeral."

"The only funeral we're going to is for the 'Canes," Nomi said.

"The papers say we're the underdog," Ingrid said. "Do you guys believe that?"

"No way."

"Jim Gough says we can't beat the 'Canes because we don't have enough speed. Do you believe that?"

"No."

"Damned right. We've got Dorsey Thorne and we've got Molly Gavison, the fastest skater in the free world."

Molly Gavison the right winger was sitting off by herself taping a stick. She raised her head to acknowledge the cheers, then returned to her work.

"We've got everything," Ingrid went on. "The best-skating defender, the goalie with the biggest wad of gum."

Ingrid continued, reciting the special attributes of each member of the team, her voice a distant echo in my ears. Molly Gavison, the presence that had been fluttering at the edges of my consciousness, forced itself front and center. And once I had started looking, I couldn't take my eyes off her.

Molly wound the tape along the blade of the stick with practiced precision, brought it toward the heel with a twist of the wrist and snapped it off expertly. I watched as she caressed the stick, smoothing the tape at the edges. I was struck by the beauty of her hands. Simply beautiful—square, with long, perfectly tapered fingers, carefully manicured nails. No rings. Her bare hands were a poignant statement in themselves.

Of all the players on the team I knew Molly the least. Like Julia and Joy, she had been selected by Phil for her celebrity value, a former Olympic speed skater whose checkered career had ended under a cloud of rumor and innuendo. I had heard that she could be difficult and temperamental. I had seen none of that. Her teammates were awe-struck in the presence of this former World Champion. I was struck more by her gentleness and incredible vulnerability. And by her hands.

There are two rules a coach should observe. Never let your players know you don't know what you're doing and never fall in love with your right winger.

Lou Frampton jostled me as she squeezed between me and the table. "Sorry," she muttered.

I was barely aware of her passing, just as I was suddenly oblivious to everything else that was going on around me. I imagined I had violated rule number one from time to time. Now, as I watched Molly Gavison, I realized I was in real peril of violating rule number two.

The room erupted in laughter, drawing me back in. I took a deep breath and grabbed a Pepsi from the cooler.

Four and a half hours later, I took my second deep breath of the day.

Dorsey won the face-off, drew the puck back to Chris and headed up ice. The play was back to Dorsey but she was too well covered. Chris sent a rink-wide pass to Molly who was streaking up the right wing. In the meantime, Dorsey had eluded her check and broke into the slot. Molly laid the puck in perfectly; Dorsey rifled it high on the stick side. The puck rattled off the pipe, hit the goalie in the arm and dribbled to the crease. She flopped on it and held it for the face-off.

The 'Canes won the face-off and started their picture-perfect progression up ice. They were all tall and handsome, resplendent in black and silver, all equipment matching, brand-new and paid for. The Hamilton winger decked Pat who slipped and went down. The winger flipped the puck to the center who fired point blank into Joy's body. Joy couldn't control the rebound; the center corralled the puck and jammed it into the open corner.

Both teams made changes.

I cast a glance toward the visiting team's bench. If that puck with my name on it had been deflected into the visitors' bench, I know what would have happened. Coach Val Warnica would have caught it without missing a beat. The idea that a puck would crease that perfect skull was obscene.

Val looked absolutely stunning as always. Tonight she wore a grey suit, black silk shirt and deep purple tie—the most elegant Amazon in the history of Dykedom.

My outfit for this history-making game consisted of a tweed jacket, fuzzy grey flannels and a white cardigan sweater over a shirt with the pocket buttons missing. I had a wad of gum stuck to one knee, a gift from Nomi who had a habit of sticking her five-sticker on the back of the bench. I had felt reasonably comfortable about my attire when I left home that afternoon, but not beside Val.

Val caught me looking at her and smiled, just enough to reveal the dimple at the corner of her mouth. Then she winked.

I turned away, blushing.

Another face from my past. I knew Val would be here, of course, but I wasn't prepared for the emotions her presence unleashed. The last thing this rookie coach needed was to feel like a tongue-tied schoolgirl around her gym teacher. Val brought back memories—mostly painful, most of which I had hoped I had left behind forever.

I pulled Nomi's gum off my pants and forced myself to focus on the game.

The Hurricanes kept us off the scoreboard until the fifteen-minute mark of the third period when Effie finally squeezed one in from behind the net.

We lost three to one.

After the game Val approached me in the tunnel.

"I'll catch you in Hamilton," she said, and, in response to my blank stare, added, "Copps Coliseum in two weeks. It's a regular season game, Alison."

Her hand was on my shoulder as she talked. Her touch was like fire, her fragrance frankly aphrodisiac. I felt all queasy inside, the way I used to feel when we touched accidentally during high-school basketball games. For a few moments I was sixteen years old, young and skinny and hungry.

Then Val removed her hand and walked away, gobbled up in a small swarm of officials and media people. I stood there, slightly dazed, feeling old and short and frumpy. Finally I made my way to the locker room.

The players were undressing, yucking it up. Helmets and sweat-soaked shoulder pads rolled across the floor. Harriett collected the gear, packed it into the hanging bags, rolled them up and threw them into a heap. Her last job of the day would be to load the equipment into the bus, take it to the Mussyford, unroll the bags and hang the equipment to dry for the morning practice.

I leaned against my locker and thought about Val.

Val was in her final year of high-school basketball when I first met her. I played for rural North Glengarry. She played for urban South Gloucester. I would go home after our games, walk down the long laneway to our farm, moving very slowly because there were chores waiting for me at the other end, and daydream about making love to Val Warnica. We would float together over a pristine white bed, locked together in a splendid embrace, our nipples and crotches tastefully airbrushed. After all these years Val Warnica's breasts remain one of the great mysteries of life.

I could smell the apples on the low-hanging tree at the top of the lane. That's where the dream had to be consummated. A step beyond the apple tree, brother Mike would appear suddenly, striking me none too gently in the chest with a pair of overalls.

"About time you got home," he would say. "It's your turn to feed the calves."

To this day, the smell of frost-nipped apples made my skin prickle.

"Hey, Alison, are you all right?"

15

Ingrid brought me back to the real world. I was leaning against my locker, staring into space. I swayed, slightly off balance. Ingrid said "Oops!" and caught my arm to steady me. I reached automatically for Ingrid's strong shoulders to balance myself and stood there for a moment enveloped in the sweet smell of her female athleticism, a wonderful, clean woman smell.

I hadn't felt so happy in years. I could have stayed in that space forever, but the interviewers, the ones who had swallowed Val, intruded to ask a few questions.

I was the last one to leave the arena. The players had changed into street clothes and escaped out the side door in spite of Phil's injunction to be available to the press. Out in the parking lot, now gloriously alone in the clean fall air, I found my car—that timid grey Datsun—sitting lonely under a lamp in the parking lot. There was a note under the windshield wiper.

Have gone to Stages for a nightcap.

Underneath this someone had scrawled: *Why do you bother locking this car? Who in their right mind would steal this bucket of bolts?*

Who indeed?

Normally I would have appreciated the invitation. But tonight I wanted to be alone. I went home.

Home was a partially renovated low-rise on Gerrard. The team occupied the entire fourth floor—two to an apartment. Phil Tweddell's Dad, Big Frank, had purchased the property with the intention of leveling it and erecting an ugly concrete high-rise. The city thwarted his plans so he turned the apartment into a barracks of sorts. Most of the other tenants were the minions who did the menial work in Big Frank's vast sports empire.

The building had been renovated just enough to keep the property standards people at bay and destroy its 1930s charm. The fireplaces had been boarded up and the hardwood covered with cheap broadloom. What remained were small white boxes with leaking faucets and generations of cockroaches and silverfish. Each apartment had a balcony that no one in her right mind would have ventured onto unless every stick of furniture in the building was on fire. They served, mainly, as receptacles for pigeon droppings and convenient toeholds for second-story persons. One of them also proved functional as a mating area for all the neighborhood cats whose siren serenades could be heard long and loud, far into the night, punctuated occasionally by the sound of Nomi's shoe being fired through the patio door. I knew it was Nomi's shoe because I had spotted her beating the bushes below my window for it on several occasions. The boys on the fifth floor used their balconies to conduct experiments. Their favorite appeared to have something to do with determining the sound a beer bottle makes exploding on the pavement below. Awful.

It was best to keep the windows closed and the drapes drawn around Big Frank's Roach Motel.

My roomie, Joy Drinkwater, wasn't home when I arrived. I made some coffee and slouched down in the easy chair in front of the television. Paused to glance over the news, then changed the picture to the sports channel.

The sportscaster didn't mention our game or even give a score in passing. He was preoccupied with the mop-up of the baseball season. The Blue Jays had won their division but, although we talked a good game, we knew that, once again, they wouldn't make it to the Series. But that was OK. This town had always tolerated losers gladly. I hoped we weren't next in line to catch the fever.

I turned the television off and went back to the kitchen to get a refill on my coffee. I had lived here two weeks now. I wondered as I watched a cockroach slither down a crack in the grouting if this apartment would ever feel like home. That idle thought brought on an unexpected bout of homesickness.

Home for me didn't mean Toronto. Home for me—and most of my players—meant Kingston, that uptight city on the lake, physically a city, psychologically and spiritually a small town. And home specifically was Landlady—her name was Gwen but Landlady suited her better—and her eleven-year-old daughter, Mandy. I've lived with Landlady and Mandy for three-and-a-half years now, since the death, after a long illness, of my one significant relationship. Landlady took me in the way some people take in stray cats. Lured me with food, made life so comfortable for me I no longer had any desire to stray among the garbage cans. Nothing romantic. Just...

I picked up the telephone and dialed half the number. It was almost midnight. Mandy would be asleep, clutching her new official Teddies hockey stick to her still-dormant bosom. Landlady would be yawning now, pushing back her scraggly brown hair, easing off her John Lennon glasses, preparing to put aside *Women's Sport* by Mary

Boutilier. She bought a copy when I announced I had been hired to coach the Teddies—just to refresh her memory.

"The sportsworld, Alison," she said. "Beware. It's a minefield."

I had to admit I was a tad naive about the politics of this particular game. However, I *had* managed to avoid the first booby-trap: I talked Phil out of dressing my team in bloomers and midis. Phil thought this bit of nostalgia would be a nice touch. "Sort of a salute to the history of women's hockey," he said.

I knew his intention was to make the players look less like athletes and more like The Girl Who Married Dear Old Dad. I knew they would take to the idea like a cat to water.

Having said this, I had to admit I would have accepted Phil's offer to coach the Teddies even if he had told me I had to dress like Carmen Miranda for the entire season. The whiff of a locker room had that kind of power over me. Landlady's cooking held a distant second place in my affections. I was shamelessly addicted to both.

Besides, what was the alternative? To spend the rest of my life in academe? Not that I would want you to think I was living in an ivory tower before Phil rescued me. My calling was not that cerebral. I was a teacher of physical and health education; all us old dykes end up there sooner or later. I was a gym teacher, damnit, with nowhere to go. After a while—after you've worked feverishly to extend your basic degree to a master's and have mustered the temerity to contemplate a doctorate—you realize that even admission to the ivied walls will not give you access to the better teams. Most of the plumb jobs in women's sports go to men—men not considered good enough to coach the boys at the college level and certainly not good enough to attract the attention of the professional teams. Please see Rule #113 in the official booklet: a mediocre man will always be a better coach than the best woman.

So, no ivory towers for me. That last year while I awaited Phil's call, I was more like Rapunzel teetering on the edge of her dungeon window while the Women's Professional Hockey League went through months of on-again, off-again negotiations. I had resigned my permanent post with the country school board and worked as a substitute teacher while the would-be moguls thrashed things out. I trekked around to half a dozen area high schools, filling in for teachers away at tournaments, at conferences or indisposed, physically or otherwise. What astonished me about this adventure was that, no matter what the time of year or which classroom I landed in, the topic for discussion that day was invariably Sex Education. I would arrive at my desk to find a note waiting: "Alison, the discussion for today takes in Chapter Eight." And if that wasn't clear enough, one of the students would clue me in: "We're doing Chapter Eight today, Miss Gutherie."

I rapidly developed a reputation for being something of an expert in the field. Those who possessed minds of the filthy sort—namely my old Principal Mr. Hamilton—passed a rumor to this effect. The rumor made its way to the students who came to the conclusion I lay somewhere on the continuum between Dr. Ruth and Xaviera Hollander. They awaited my arrival eagerly, particularly one young lad called Gerald who took extensive notes and leered suggestively whenever I entered the room. I was certain he spent his time in study hall, fiendishly transferring these notes into a handy pocket-sized notebook for easy reference during his forays to lonely lanes off County Road 4.

But that was history now. I had finally made it. I was big time, free of Gerald and his sort of adolescent sex fantasies—or so I thought.

I drank my second cup of coffee and toyed once more with the idea of phoning home. Going on one by now. Too late, too late.

I took out a notebook and jotted down my thoughts on the game: Pay special attention to Lauren MacDonald (The big Hamilton center had ten shots on goal tonight); encourage Chris and Molly to take more shots on goal (They're too quick to give the puck to Dorsey); Hamilton goalie Karen Ives is great. Her weakness—and it's not glaring—is the low glove; work with Julia on the roll check; find a suitable gum receptacle for Nomi (I'll never get that Doublemint out of my pants).

I put the notebook aside. When I was a little kid on the pond, never in my wildest dreams did I imagine that I would, one day, coach a professional women's hockey team. I could pretend I was scoring the winning goal in the Stanley Cup play-offs; I could pretend I was Terry Sawchuck stopping the great Rocket Richard on a break-away. But when I left that patch of frozen water in the field, the dreams had to stay behind.

True, Aunt Maude did her best to make the dream come true. She chopped off my hair and registered me for the team she coached, recording my name as "Al". Since she coached every team I played on until I was twelve, this little deception was a cinch. Girls weren't allowed to play on boys teams in those days. Aunt Maude wanted me to play hockey and she didn't want to waste my time or hers in a pro-tracted—and at that time, probably futile—battle with the Ontario Minor Hockey Association.

By the time I was twelve, I had discovered that playing with girls was a lot more fun than playing with boys. During high school I caught on with a team sponsored by the local feed store, proudly wearing the Checkerboard Square across my flat chest until I gradu-ated.

Then it was on to Queen's University's School of Physical and Health Education and a spot on the women's hockey team. Hardly the big time, although the uniforms were pretty spiffy.

After university, I caught on with a team in the newly formed Women's Industrial League. I met some real tough dykes in the Industrial League and learned a whole new language, including some words for certain parts of the female anatomy I was sure were never meant to be said out loud.

I had a year of college eligibility remaining when I enrolled at Queen's McArthur College to study for my teaching certificate. I elected, however, to stay with East Frontenac Cement. The caliber of play was much better in the Industrial League, and by that time, I was accustomed to having my body appraised and no longer blushed at speculation as to how I might perform in bed. When I finally left East Frontenac, it was to play with the Yellowjackets, the premiere wom-an's hockey team in Eastern Ontario. I played with this great team for five years, during which time we won two Provincial championships and made the finals at the Nationals.

I retired from the Yellowjackets at age thirty, telling my surprised teammates—and fooling myself—with the explanation that I was slowing down and it was time to "hang them up". The real reason? Domestic pressure. My partner, Gail, thought the game took too much away from our lives. She blamed hockey—softball too—for the rough patches in our relationship.

Since the break-up of my relationship with Gail, I've coached a bit, played some too, but at a drastically different level. Certainly my previous coaching experience—I coached mainly small kids with big hearts but wobbly legs—was not the stuff that should have earned me the position of head coach with the Toronto Teddies, a job which dozens of hockey woman across Canada and the United States would have killed for. Phil Tweddell hired me for reasons that had nothing to do with his perceptions of my merit, reasons that like my truncated relationship with Gail had a bittersweet edge.

I went to the window, feeling restless and ill at ease, the way I always felt when I allowed myself to think about Gail. After a three and a half year struggle, I had developed a certain emotional accommodation that if not rewarding at least permitted me a modicum of psychic comfort.

Now even that modest accommodation seemed in jeopardy. With my life entering a new phase with its attendant upheaval, it seemed entirely appropriate that Val Warnica should appear on the scene to rob me of my last shreds of complacency.

Val Warnica was a life-long lesbian—a bright-eyed, elegant, sophisticated, cocky lesbian. She had recognized my sexuality before I did. At least she resurrected it from the back burner, holding it up to me, laughing and gently taunting. It was an "I know what you are" sort of laugh. In those brief, fleeting moments together on the court in high school—and later on the ice—I was a proud, almost swaggering lesbian. Scared too. Because I didn't know what I would have done if she had called my bluff. I was a country kid, physical, unsophisticated, lean and awkward, all knees and elbows. And she was tall and dark and willowy with deep grey eyes that sparkled and turned my tongue and legs to mush.

Now I was forty years old, an aging dyke athlete and all that that implied. I'd like to think I'd gained a measure of worldliness. But Val Warnica still had the power to leave me tongue-tied. She revived in me, a piece of myself that existed a long time ago—a muddled place of hope and exquisite pain. Seeing her tonight reminded me of how different were the paths we'd taken. She'd arrived at this point in her life unscathed, still reveling in the power of her sexuality. I'd arrived in a different way. How could I tell Val I had grown tired of the game? That for the last three-and-a-half years I'd let my sexuality die, replaced it with Mandy's companionship and Landlady's homey ministrations? That if it weren't for this redoubtable friend who dragged me along kicking and screaming, and a sports crazy eleven-year-old, I might have turned into the walking dead?

I went into my bedroom, turned the light out and sat in the dark, staring at the wall. Joy came in a few minutes later and went straight to bed. After a while I struggled out of my clothes and lay down.

I told myself I was comfortable. I'd found my niche where I could exist without tearing my heart out. I didn't want to want anything again.

Except to go to sleep. But even that modest wish eluded me. The apartment was too quiet. The silence depressed me. The bed felt strange. The fact I had chosen a single, highlighted my acceptance of my condition.

Val Warnica...I was too old for hero-worship. I was definitely too old to feel teen-aged pain.

CHAPTER 2

Show time. Wednesday night. Our opponents for the evening were the O'Brien's, a nice team of young players, mostly college kids, graduates of the University of New Hampshire and Northeastern—Canadian women lured south by hockey scholarships.

The O'Brien's were owned by Jack O'Brien, a sportsman of the old school. Jack—like the Shortt family who owned the Hurricanes—had bought the team because he loved hockey. Making money was not on his list of priorities. The O'Brien's were his pride and joy.

For some inexplicable reason, Jack had hired Connie Siebart to coach his team. The O'Brien's deserved better. Connie was a woman who had dutifully played the role of hockey mother for years, getting up at five every morning throughout the winter to ferry her four sons to and from the rink. Connie was a *real* woman, the least woman-identified woman I had ever met, a woman who gained praise in the male world by being the kind of woman men think a woman should be. I assumed she got the job because she had coached Jack's grandkids at some point. Jack's sentiments always seemed to take priority over good sense. In honor of her initial encounter with the Teddies, Connie wore a skirt, blazer, fluffy blouse and spike heels. Her hair was strictly '50's bouffant and she wore an appropriate amount of make-up. She looked askance at my cords and pullover.

Nomi Pereira's family had come down for the game. They sat in the third row, directly behind our bench. I was surprised they had come, knowing that Nomi's hockey success was nothing but failure in the eyes of this immigrant family that had sent a son to college and a second daughter into an upwardly mobile marriage. Nomi, on the ice with her friends, living out her childhood dream, represented the old life, the North Side working class they had worked so hard to escape.

Papa Pereira was certifiably insane. I had had some experience with him back home in the Senior Women's League where he had a habit of sitting directly behind the players bench, pelting his daughter's coach with empty pop cans. In one instance, he had shown up at the rink wearing nothing but a red tie and patent-leather shoes under his London Fog trench coat. Tonight, fully clothed, he contented himself with making rude gestures and screaming "filthy lesbian" in Portuguese.

"Let me know if he starts collecting pop cans," I told Harriett.

More loathsome than Papa was a small group of O'Brien supporters who sat to the left of our bench and sang a rousing chorus of "Things Go Better With Coke" when Molly stepped onto the ice.

"Old rumors die hard," Harriett murmured. "Nice support for a national hero."

At the end of the first period we were down two to zero. The players seemed distracted, withdrawn.

"OK," I said, "what's happening?"

I got a lot of sighs and a few blank stares.

"We played like shit," Nomi volunteered. She bent down to adjust one of the straps on her pads. "That shot from the blue line shouldn't have gone in."

I nodded. "We've had a few distractions. This crowd is not as polite as the one in Hamilton. So, what are we going to do about it?"

"Shut them down," Dorsey grumbled. "And shut them up with a few goals."

"Right. Let's take the crowd out of the play. And let's take the O'Brien's out too. Sure, they're good players; they wouldn't have been offered sports scholarships if they weren't. But, frankly, we're beating ourselves. We're not playing our positions. On that last goal, we had three players chasing after the puck carrier. Nomi didn't have a chance. So play your position and forecheck, forecheck. Harass them in their own end. If you put some pressure on those young defenders, I guarantee they'll cough the puck up pretty regularly." I stopped to let that sink in. "Another thing…how many shots did we get on goal in that period?"

"Six," someone said. Lou said, "Seven."

"Six, seven shots. We can do better than that. Make their goalie do some work. She's had enough time out there to knit an afghan."

They all laughed. End of speech. I dug a soda out of the cooler and made my rounds.

"Molly, don't be afraid to take a few more shots on goal. You and Chris have done a good job getting the puck to Dorsey, but you've had a couple of good chances yourself. Dorsey's not the only player on the line who can score.

"Julia, don't let them have the front of the net. Lean on them. Lift their sticks.

"Toddy, don't wait so long on your passes. Effie's doing a good job, breaking her checks. Just lay it in where you think she's going to be. Nine times out of ten, she'll be there."

The buzzer sounded.

Dorsey's goal from the opening face-off took the crowd out of the play. The second, five minutes later, silenced Papa Pereira. Papa showered me with a collection of paper cups and serviettes in full view of a security guard. Then he too was out of the play.

The Teddies went on to win, five to three.

I stood at the door to the dressing room, murmuring "good play" to each player as she passed by, tapped a few helmets, felt the excitement and satisfaction. Dorsey got the hat trick and was named first star. Molly, who had a goal and two assists was named second star.

"Well done," I said.

Dorsey gave me a high-five. Molly smiled and slipped past me, head down.

The dressing room was alive with good-natured ribbing and jock talk. The players attacked the post-game pizza with enthusiasm.

I stood back for a few minutes to soak in the frivolity, to try to fix these moments in my mind. We had just won our first game as a team. Someday down the road, I would want to remember.

The *Citizen* carried an interview with Connie Siebart the next morning. According to Connie: "It's very important the girls act like ladies. Who wants to see tough, masculine women play hockey?"

The Buffalo fans, apparently. They came out in droves to see their team kick our asses all over the ice. Coach Bill "Mauler" Mason stood behind the bench yelling "Hit, hit" throughout the game. His experience as a defensive lineman was painfully obvious. The Belles were a team of large players. They had been instructed to lay on the bodies.

The Teddies, who had just come off two light-hitting, fast-skating games, were temporarily stunned. The only thing that slowed the Belles at all was Sharon Sosnoski who proved virtually impossible to move off her feet.

The game ended in a three to three tie.

The traffic had been heavy in the crease and Nomi had taken a battering.

"I thought some of those shots were coming right through my catcher," she said afterwards. She paused to spit into her towel. "I took so many shots off my chest, my tits are sore." She looked at her breasts disdainfully as if they had betrayed her. "I took one in the stomach too. I thought I was going to puke."

Nomi had a string of bruises running along the insides of both arms and legs. She showed them to us with indifference.

There was a brief silence, then the players sighed in unison.

"That big dyke used to play in the Border League," said Nomi finally. "She's got a shot like lead. It's heavier than anybody's, except maybe Sharon's."

> Dateline: Toronto
>
> Subject: *Sharon Sosnoski, defenseman, Toronto Teddies.*
>
> This twenty-five-year-old plumber from Kingston, Ontario, was rookie of the year in the Eastern Women's Hockey League and played well enough to be named to the first all-star team every year thereafter. She's a stay-at-home defenseman of the old school who blocks shots, quarterbacks the play and clears the puck flawlessly. For this campaign, she's joined by her long-time defensive partner from the Yellowjackets, Carol Gee.

> Private Diary;
>
> *Sharon Sosnoski is a big, solid, tow-headed kid with a deceptive layer of baby fat over smooth hard muscles. She's the kind of kid everybody has on her ball team—the strong, silent type, the type that tends to disappear after age thirty. Too much fast food, too much booze, too many unanswered dreams. It all catches up.*
>
> *Sharon is bright but she's not a scholar. She's hockey*

smart and mechanically smart. She learned the plumbing trade from her uncle at an early age. She's in business with him now—Sosnoski and Sosnoski, Plumbing and Heating, Inc. Sharon's uncle dotes on her. Calls her "Butch". He's not trying to make a comment on her lifestyle. It's just that he always wanted a son and he would have called him "Butch".

Sharon is slow to anger. On the ice her checks are legal but inexorable. Like being hit by a slow-moving freight train, opposing forwards say.

Sharon is a woman of few words. I often wonder what lurks behind those inert, hazel eyes.

CHAPTER 3

With the exhibition schedule completed, I was eager to get away for the weekend. Unfortunately, I had to work Saturday morning. Phil had committed me to serve coffee and sign autographs at the grand opening of Pop Goes The Weasel's new Keele and Sheppard outlet. In return for this appearance and a few other advertising gimmicks, Pop had agreed to provide free laundry service for the season.

The promo, mercifully, finished at noon. I returned to the apartment to pick up my bag.

"I wish you could come with me," I said to Joy.

"Me too."

Joys parents were coming to town for the weekend. They had tickets to see the Royal Winnipeg Ballet at the O'Keefe.

"They think women's hockey is a cultural wasteland," she said. "Imagine that." She gave me a hug and a little kiss on the corner of my mouth. "Take care."

"You too," I said as the door closed.

I tapped hopefully on a few other doors as I made my way to the elevator, just in case someone was inside, pining for a ride to Kingston, to the train station or points east.

I stopped at the door to the apartment Effie shared with Molly. I knew Effie had left the night before to spend the weekend with her husband, Joey.

Strains of music seeped from under the door. I was certain I heard someone moving about inside. I knocked softly, waited, then knocked again.

If Molly was at home, she apparently had no desire to open the door.

I drove to Kingston alone.

Landlady had to attend a benefit for victims of the Afghan War that evening. Mandy and I ordered a pizza and settled in front of the television set to watch the Blue Jays play Oakland—the second last game of the regular season.

"Remember when we were there?" said Mandy. She pointed to two seats about ten rows back to the left of the Blue Jays dugout, peering into the bank of blurred faces as if she expected to see us there, frozen in time like a pair of doomed astronauts.

"I think I want to play shortstop," she said.

Last week she wanted to be a pitcher.

"Or maybe third," she said.

"Play short," I said. "Good shortstops are always in demand."

She looked at me suspiciously. "Do you really think I'll play, Alison? *Really?*"

"Of course, you'll play," I said.

"Mom says she doesn't know. She says baseball is regressive, repressive and patriarchal."

She got mixed up, stumbled over regressive and repressive.

"If you're good enough, you'll play." I stared at the ugly green carpet. If this were 1947, the Blue Jays would have to field a team of pitchers and catchers, Black men being conspicuously under-represented in these prestige positions. In spite of this, Black men were still less discriminated against than women. It took them just over a century to break the color barrier in baseball. We women had been at this game since the dawn of time and still couldn't field an umpire.

Mandy measured my expression. "Do you think you'll be in the NHL soon?"

"No."

She hesitated, surprised at the indifference in my voice. "Don't you *want* to be?"

"No."

"Why not?" She sounded almost cross.

Because I don't want to live in a man's world. Because I like the way women play the game. "Because we're better."

She sighed, the way she did when her mother's rhetoric and my optimism seemed out of touch with her daily reality.

"Play on the girls' team," I said in answer to her unasked question. "The best players are on the girls' teams."

I had breakfast with Landlady and Mandy the next morning. *The*

Sunday Star carried a story about my appearance at Pop Goes the Weasel along with a grainy black and white picture of me with a coffee pot in one hand and a sour expression on my face. *She's cute and she plays hockey too,* said the caption.

Landlady read the story without comment, but when Mandy left the table to get dressed, she said, "So, you poured the coffee."

I mumbled something about promotion. "All athletes do that sort of thing," I said.

"Next thing we know, they'll have you nude and spread-eagled on the hood of a sports car," she said. "Sex sells women's sport. Isn't that the prevailing wisdom?"

"Jim Palmer advertises underwear," I said.

"The difference between Jim Palmer showing his balls and you showing your ass just about sums up the status of women in our society."

She said the words calmly but I knew she was boiling inside. I've never heard Landlady say "ass" before, certainly never "balls".

She tightened her grip on the sports section. "Jim Palmer could pose nude and still be less exploited than you pouring coffee. She read the story again, shaking her head. "Toronto Teddies…well, I suppose we should feel thankful they didn't call you the Toronto Twats."

I sank into the travel section, defeated.

"Sportsworld," said Landlady with sympathetic triumph. She handed me a clipping she had conveniently stashed in her hip pocket.

> Dateline: Toronto
>
> Subject: *Girls Playing With Boys* by Jim Gough
>
> Perhaps I'm a male chauvinist, but in my opinion, the Ontario Human Rights Commission has gone too far in its ruling that Justine Blainey can play for a male hockey team—a bona fide member of the Ontario Minor Hockey Association no less. The problems, of course, are obvious. Sooner or later, one of the girls will get hurt, whereupon we'll hear a hue and cry for rule changes designed to protect the weaker sex. And where will this leave the game? Emasculated, I say. Secondly, the ruling will lower the level of play throughout minor hockey. Coaches will be under pressure to include girls regardless of their ability, effec-

tively denying boys with greater skills the opportunity to play for the best teams. And that simply isn't fair.

Thirdly, let's remember that minor hockey in Canada is not about health and good fun. It's about producing players for the NHL. And we all know that a woman doesn't have a snowball's chance in hell of making it to the Big Show. And even if the new Women's Professional Hockey League succeeds—and that is highly doubtful—it will always be bush league, unable to offer opportunities to more than a handful of the girls whose hopes have been raised by the Human Rights Commission's ruling.

Stick to tennis and golf, ladies. That's where the money is. And, frankly, don't you think a pretty face is wasted in a hockey helmet?

Dateline: Toronto

Subject: *Girls Playing With Boys, Rebuttal* by Mary-Beth Jones-McAlpine.

The recent ruling by the OHRC is a significant step up for the sporting women of Ontario. No longer will it be possible to deny girls entry to the upper echelons of junior hockey simply because they are girls…

Dateline: Toronto

Subject: *Girls Playing With Boys. No Way!* by Faye Surgenor

The OHRC's decision to let girls play hockey on boys' teams is hardly the great leap forward liberal feminists like Mary-Beth Jones-McAlpine would have us believe. A woman operating in a predominately male environment will have little impact on the way hockey is played in North America. Women playing with men are likely to be coopted, used to validate male systems and values. Women playing together have opportunities to change the game, to eliminate the brutality and return it to the game of finesse it was meant to be. The newly-formed Women's Professional Hockey League has an unparalleled opportunity to make this happen. I, for one, will be watching with interest. And with some skepticism. Coaches like Alison Gutherie have been weaned on the myths and values of patriarchal jockdom with its emphasis on aggression and performance quantification. They are seldom feminists.

I put the clippings aside with a nervous cough. "I'm a feminist," I said. "What does Faye Surgenor want? Is she one of the ones who wants us to do away with referees and umpires and just do what comes naturally? Is she one of the ones who thinks winning is anti-feminist?"

"The sportsworld," Landlady repeated smugly. "It's a minefield, Alison." She nodded sagely and disappeared into the international news.

CHAPTER 4

The last few weeks had been a struggle—hassling over contracts, fighting for decent equipment and ice time, lugging equipment back and forth. We practiced at the Mussyford in North York but played our games in cramped old Varsity Arena downtown. But we had made it through in one piece, the payroll had been met with unexpected alacrity and we were preparing for our first regular-season game.

On Tuesday morning I snuck into the Mussyford at eight o'clock, a full hour before the players were scheduled to arrive for the morning practice. I laced on my skates, took a bucket of pucks and went out onto the ice. I took a few slapshots from the blue line, hit the net on every one. I moved in, taking some wrist shots from various angles, watching with satisfaction as the puck rose a neat six inches off the ice and rippled the back of the net. I nudged a puck from the net and set out up ice.

I was no longer Alison Gutherie, forty years old and as rusty as an old spike. I was Doug Harvey, legendary defender for the Montreal Canadiens. I broke past my own blue line with Butch Bouchard trailing. I had Elmer Lach, Rocket Richard and Toe Blake up front. Gordie Howe tried to give me an elbow but I evaded his check and got off a perfect pass to Elmer. Elmer took a shot on goal; Rocket got the rebound and fired it past a sprawling Harry Lumley.

Between the roar of the Forum crowd and the face-off I metamorphosed into Jean Beliveau, the huge, graceful Montreal center. Jim Morrison of the Leafs tried to tee me up but my long arms allowed me to reach around him and get a shot on Eddie Chadwick.

I raised my arms in victory and circled the net. A smattering of applause drifted down from the bleachers.

"Way to go, Alison." Soapy, the janitor, leaned on his broom, clapping.

I lifted my stick to acknowledge the cheers of the crowd, and streaked back up ice. I faked a shot from my forehand, then shifted the puck to my backhand and cut for a shot from an absurd angle.

The puck disappeared. Sharon Sosnoski stole the puck with a nifty sweep check. She charged past me, crunching the ice with her size eleven skates. Her shot on goal rang off the goalpost and ricocheted off the boards to center ice. I corralled it and held it there.

Sharon coasted past me.

"Sorry, coach. I hope I didn't ruin your fun."

"Go on with you," I said.

Soon all the players were on the ice. I leaned against the boards and watched. The cool haze from the ice encircled my ankles and soon I was lost in the sights and sounds of the game. The puck boomed resonantly off the boards, plopped into the loose mesh at the back of the net, dribbled off Nomi's pads with a dull punk-punk and danced off Joy's toeboots with a brisk tap-tap.

Ingrid Eklund drifted past me, shifting the puck from her stick to her skates, kicking it back to her stick, making something difficult look incredibly easy. Ingrid Eklund, my old teammate from the Yellowjackets. I wasn't ashamed to admit I got a little misty-eyed watching her, remembering her at eighteen, in her rookie year, raw and aggressive. Reckless. Now, at thirty-three, she had lost a step to the younger players, a deficit she more than compensated for with her intelligence, her sense of where the play was going.

"Good play exists where the players are kind-hearted, modest and considerate of their teammates," said Anatoli Tarasov, legendary coach of Central Red Army.

If he had added, "earthy and wickedly ribald" he would have described our captain, Ingrid Eklund, to a T.

I watched Ingrid with appreciation and some guilt. I was thrilled I'd been able to snare her for my team. I wanted to forget that I had lured her away from a secure government job with its perks and generous pension and turned her ten-year "marriage" with partner, Lise, into a weekend affair. If the WPHL failed, Ingrid would lose more than most. I consoled myself with the knowledge that, on another level, Ingrid had already realized her dreams—a job she loved as illustrator with the Ministry of Natural Resources and an untouchable ten-year relationship. For many of the players, the WPHL was the last chance to realize their dreams, dreams they had had since childhood, never dared express and even now were reluctant to articulate for fear they might jinx them.

Ingrid took a shot at the net, collected another puck from behind the net and headed back up ice. Dorsey Thorne swept by. Hotdogging. She cruised in on the wrong wing, unleashing a shot on net. Effie McGovern scurried, rushing the net like a frantic rabbit, and dumping the puck high on the stick side with a nervous hyperkinetic yip. Sharon Sosnoski drifted in casually, banking a shot off the end boards. The wood groaned. Joy winced and twitched her catcher in sympathy. Pat followed Sharon to the net, picked up the rebound and tossed the puck apologetically to Joy's blocker.

The players continued to circle, taking a shot on net, picking up a new puck and heading back up ice. Nomi turned away a half-dozen shots in quick succession. Finally, Dorsey Thorne looped one in over the blade of the stick. She circled the net, laughing.

Nomi shook a fist at her and spat on the ice. "Do it again asshole and I'll–"

Dorsey wheeled at center and churned down ice on the opposite wing. She faked high and blasted a low riser through Nomi's pads. Nomi ended up in the net on the seat of her pants. Dorsey banged her stick on the ice in delight. "Hey, got you again, Pereira."

Nomi popped up like a jack-in-the-box, swinging her stick at Dorsey's skates as she cruised across the net. Dorsey fell to the ice and rolled over, laughing. Nomi was on her in a flash. "Show me up again and I'll ram my stick up your cunt."

Dorsey said something I couldn't hear. Dorsey rolled Nomi over and pinned her to the ice. Nomi took a swing at her, but Dorsey just laughed and ducked.

I had no idea what Nomi said but Dorsey stopped laughing. They were suddenly very still, talking quietly, nose to nose.

The practice had stopped. The players stood, leaning on their sticks, watching. You could have heard a pin drop. Then Dorsey jumped up, hauled Nomi unceremoniously to her feet and skated away.

I blew the whistle. "OK, everybody warmed up? We're going to work on some two-on-ones. Dorsey and Molly, you've just done some nice work to create this advantageous situation. Sharon, you're the lone defender. How're you going to play it?"

"Go for the player with the puck and stay on her."

"Right, she'll either have to shoot from a bad angle or pass. You'll create a one-on-one with the goalie and the goalie should have the advantage."

I let Sharon demonstrate the play, then sent Chris out to join her line. "OK, three-on-one. The lone defender—Sharon in this case—plays between the player with the puck and the center. The goalie, Nomi, has to be ready to defend against whoever has the puck. Unfortunately, the opponent should always score on the three-on-one. But, back it up. What went wrong here? How'd they end up with a three-on-one?"

"Somebody fucked up," Nomi said.

"Right. We had too many players deep and lost control of the puck; we weren't covering our checks; half our team fell down at the same time. Something pretty gruesome. Sufficient to say, the best way to play a three-on-one is to prevent it from happening."

We worked on the plays for about an hour. I watched and made notes. Some I would take up with the whole team, others I would discuss with individual players privately. Players like Dorsey, Sharon and Ingrid required very little coaching. Julia Martin needed a lot. Alice Todd was the best seventeen-year-old player I have ever seen. I was acutely conscious of my responsibility in her development.

And then there was Molly. I watched as she broke down ice, defying space with those smooth, effortless strides. I was aware that Phil had acquired Molly for reasons that had precious little to do with her playing potential. Molly was no stranger to the game of ice hockey but like Joy and Julia she was here strictly for her celebrity value. While not as good a stick handler as Chris Young and not a natural scorer like Dorsey Thorne, she was undeniably the best skater in the league. Her speed alone was disorienting, making defenders hesitate about playing up, begging opponents to chase her, drawing them out of position and making it easier for Dorsey to get in the clear. Not afraid to go into the corner for a loose puck, I noted. A race for the puck? No contest. I sighed and shifted my sights to Carol Gee. Good player, using limited natural skills to their absolute potential. Perhaps I could help her develop more mobility. Goalies: two different styles. Nomi wanders more than I would like but that's the way she plays; that's the way she keeps herself in the game. Both goalies communicate well with their defense.

Molly evaded a sweep check. Like Dorsey, Molly looked as if she had been born on skates. But unlike Dorsey who seemed to attack the ice, Molly wooed it with whisper-quiet strides. I shook my head. Time to blow the whistle.

"OK, folks. I want you to line up facing the north goal—one behind the other. Moving laterally...back and forth five times, then hit the showers.

Most of the players groaned. No one particularly liked this drill except Dorsey who looked very good doing it and loved to show off. By the time they had completed three laps, Ingrid and Henny were doing their laps in time to a badly sung version of 'Can-Can' and generally goofing off.

"Shut up," Nomi yelled. "You're making me get my feet mixed up."

The players left the ice, one by one. I was left with Julia and Pat, doing my own soft-skate shuffle.

"Hey, coach," Soapy yelled from the top of the bleachers. "Telephone."

There was a call waiting—a very drunk, angry call. "What are you bitch dykes doing with my wife?"

No one had ever talked to me this way before. I recoiled in horror. Felt a kind of fear I had never experienced. "If I knew who your wife was..."

"Patty, Carsey—if she's still using my name." He paused. "Now listen up. You tell her to get her ass home here or else. I'll get a court order, have her declared unfit. I'll take the kids. I can do it to."

"Just a minute now..."

"I know she's screwing around. Don't try to tell me any different. Out fucking around, leaving the kids for somebody else to look after. What do you think of that..."

"I think if you call here again I'll have you arrested." I slammed the phone down before he had a chance to reply.

Pat was cruising by the bench when I returned to practice. I called her over.

"I just fielded a call from your husband," I said.

She looked away. "I'm sorry. I didn't give out the number."

I gave her the gist of Bill's message. "I think he was drunk."

"He's always drunk. That's his excuse. When he's drunk he can say or do anything."

I confessed I'd hung up on him. "I hope I didn't make the situation worse."

She bit her lip. "What happened was Ray, the guy who drives the Zamboni, took me out for a drink and gave me a lift home. I invited him in for a drink. Bill called when I was in the washroom and Ray picked up the phone—wouldn't you know. That's all it was. I wouldn't do anything at the apartment—not with Toddy around."

I nodded.

"I asked my lawyer to start divorce proceedings," she said. "I guess he got his letter today. That's probably what set him off again."

"Can he do what he says? About the kids, I mean?"

"No. The kids are safe with Mom. She's one woman he's afraid of."

"What about you?"

"I'm not afraid of him." She said this in a resigned way.

Her expression told me why she wasn't afraid of Bill. She knew what to expect. Figured that whatever happened couldn't be any worse than what had happened before. I compared the defeated look now on her face with the smile she had given me the day I told her she had made the team and felt sick at heart for the difference.

I didn't know what to say. Having grown up in a home where my Dad never said an impolite word to my mother, I was somewhat naive about certain realities. Even my brothers-in-law and brother, male chauvinists that they were, were nonetheless unfailingly courteous to my women relatives.

"Let me know if you need any help," I said finally, although I hadn't the faintest idea what I would do if put to the test. She smiled and said, "Thanks." But I knew she smelled my fear, sized me up correctly as a paper tiger.

I knew Ray, the Zamboni driver, a quiet, decent man in his mid-thirties. He was also a strapping big man who had once boxed successfully for the Cabbagetown Club. I had been aware for some time that Pat was dating him and found their relationship a tad unlikely. Pat, although not well-educated, was a bright woman with a quick, eager mind. I couldn't imagine how nice but plodding Ray could hold her interest. It occurred to me now that Pat might be keeping Ray around for the same purpose some people keep big dogs—protection. If that was the case, I felt bad for both of them.

"Get an unlisted number," I said. "I'll tell Soapy not to accept any calls from him."

"OK." Her eyes drifted hungrily over the ice, like someone taking a long last nostalgic look at a cherished vista. "I don't want to cause you any trouble, Alison," she said. "If he keeps it up, I'll have to go back."

Julia had come over to the bench. Out of the corner of my eye, I saw her stiffen. "You won't do anything of the kind," I said.

"If he comes around making threats… I can't let Toddy in for that. She's just a kid."

"We'll call the police."

She gave me a smile, patted my arm affectionately and skated away.

"The police don't come until it's over," a voice behind me said.

Before I could reply, Julia opened the gate and slipped past me into the dressing room.

Pat had her home phone number changed. Over the next three days, Soapy intercepted a dozen calls. Then the calls stopped. When we hadn't heard from Bill for two days, I considered the problem solved.

Three days later, at two o'clock in the morning, I was awakened by what sounded like a tree being hit by lightning. I got out of bed and ran into the living room.

Joy met me there in bathrobe and slippers. "What was that?"

"I don't know."

We opened the door cautiously and looked out.

For once Phil's penny-pinching heart had saved us. The solid-oak door to Pat's apartment had not been replaced during the renovations. The baseball bat Bill Carsey wielded had dented it but left it otherwise unscathed. The blow had also reduced the bat to a handle with an evil-looking eighteen-inch splinter.

Pat, wisely, had not come out of her apartment.

"What the fuck." Nomi straggled out into the hallway, followed by a sleepy-eyed Sharon. Ingrid was the next one out. She assessed the situation, reached inside the apartment door and pulled out a nine iron.

Bill Carsey turned and thrust the broken bat handle toward Ingrid.

Pat had witnessed the scene through the peephole. She opened the door, leaving the chain in place. "Stop, I'm coming out."

"Just a moment." A quiet voice broke the silence. Julia stepped out of her apartment, wrapping her robe around her. She paused and very deliberately tied the belt into a neat bow. "It takes a lot of courage to beat up a woman, Mr. Carsey. I hope you have sufficient courage to take on all of us." She nodded toward the group that was forming around her.

Bill hesitated.

Julia took one step forward. "I suggest you leave," she said. "And if you have any thoughts of coming back at a more opportune moment—here or elsewhere—I should advise you I'm teaching your wife judo and a number of other martial arts."

Bill hooted with contempt, then he turned on his heel and left, tossing the bat against the wall.

Pat came out into the hall and gave Julia a big hug. The small crowd melted away.

"Come on," Julia said to Pat, "I'll make you a nice cup of tea."

I had the feeling Bill Carsey would never bother us again. The number of women he feared had just mushroomed.

CHAPTER 5

We played our first regular-season game at home October 15 against the London Lambs.

The Gardens was sold out. It was a black-tie affair, an event with the atmosphere and trappings of a charity gala. Many of the people who attended did not ordinarily watch hockey. The Prime Minister was there; the Minister of State Responsible for the Status of Women was there—a man since the Prime Minister was apparently unable to find a woman qualified for the job. The Minister of Amateur Sport was there. Everyone who wanted to be seen and take advantage of free, positive television coverage was there.

Yes, Virginia, we were on television, if not coast to coast, at least across the province and upper New York State.

The players took their pre-game skate, then filed back into the locker room. Harriett stood at the door, waiting expectantly as the players passed by.

"Everybody skates OK?"

"Perfect, Harriett."

"Anybody need extra tape?"

"Nope."

Harriett snapped her bag shut. "Great. We should have the season-opener every night."

"Shit," said Nomi, "did you see all those cameras out there?"

"And all the bigwigs in the box seats," Ingrid added.

"What do you think the Lambs are wearing under the sweats?" Chris wondered.

Carol made a face. "Probably those sexed-up Cooperalls they wore in exhibition. God, can you imagine having to wear something like that?"

"I'll bet all those politicians got in free," Pat said. "We'll never see them again."

"I say, good riddance," Chris chimed in.

"Don't worry about the cameras and the politicians," I said. "And don't worry about the Lambs. From what we saw on the game tapes, they can't play hockey. They're also small. Lay off the body; you won't need it. This is your first real game as professional hockey players. Relax. Enjoy the experience. But play your best. Remember, you represent the dreams of thousands of woman hockey players across Canada; you embody the dreams of thousands who played the game for years with no where to go. You're the link that connects Bobbi Rosenfeld with that little girl who leans over the boards to get your autograph."

"Who's Bobbi Rosenfeld?" Toddy whispered.

Nomi shrugged. "Probably some old dyke jock who played hockey a million years ago."

Before I could confirm or deny this rumor, the buzzer sounded.

It was time. An usher was at the door to line us up for the player introductions. Nomi first; Harriett last.

I heard Nomi's name called faintly, then Sharon's, Carol's, Pat's and Julia's.

The murmur started up the line and gradually worked its way back.

"Jesus," Dorsey said.

I leaned forward and tapped Ingrid on the shoulder. "What's going on?"

"They're wearing figure-skating outfits," she said.

"Like Brian Orser's?" I asked hopefully.

"No, like Katarina Witt's." She winked. "I presume they intend to destroy our concentration."

The line edged forward.

My name was called.

Ingrid had not exaggerated. Katarina Witt would have felt right at home in a Lambs uniform. The tutus were white and sparkled with silver spangles. The necklines plunged to reveal ample bosom. The outfits were complete with white skates, and matching shin guards and gloves—white kid, encrusted with rhinestones. The Lambs weren't wearing helmets. The league didn't require them.

"I have never faced so much cleavage in a public place," Joy murmured.

"Dangerous," muttered Harriett. "Disgusting."

I imagined Mandy watching at home, squealing with derision and tying herself in knots around the footstool.

The Minister Responsible for the Status of Women presided over the ceremonial face-off. The team captains exchanged logos—a mangy teddy in a hockey uniform for a dancing lamb with strategically placed fans. Ingrid snickered and hid the lamb in her armpit.

The anthem was played.

As the last note died away, Perry Hartschorn, the Lambs' coach, crossed the ice to shake hands. Perry played for the Edmonton Mercury team that won gold at the 1952 Winter Olympics. He coached for many years in the OHL without getting a call to the promised land. He looked embarrassed by his new assignment.

"Good luck, Alison," he said. "I hope it works out."

Harriett was checking out the first-aid kit behind the bench. "I hope they have a good trainer," she said. "Someone's going to get hurt."

I watched nervously as the puck was dropped. I knew my team would do well. But I couldn't bear to see fifteen women disgrace themselves before twenty thousand people and countless others on semi-national television.

Seconds after the puck was dropped, it was obvious the Lambs couldn't play with us. They were fine skaters and handled the puck reasonably well. They were good athletes after all, something one was apt to forget when faced with a woman dressed like a Las Vegas show-girl. They were intimidated by the very idea of a collision, though, and coughed up the puck with great regularity whenever a Teddy moved in to stick check. By the end of the first period, the score was four to zero. It would have been more lopsided but the Teddies were too embarrassed to turn it on.

When the buzzer sounded to end the period, the Teddies charged for the dressing room. Harriett followed, shaking her head.

"They shoot the puck like pansies," Nomi said. "I could beat the whole team by myself." She threw her stick toward the corner. It hit the side of the bench and clattered toward the floor.

"I'll bet they're freezing their butts out there," said Pat sympathetically.

"Those outfits are an affront to the dignity of every woman in the league," said Julia.

"You couldn't pay me enough to go out there, dressed like that," added Effie.

"I can't believe Perry Hartschorn would let them play that way," said Joy bitterly. "He should know better."

Ingrid put her hands on my shoulders and looked me square in the eye. "Alison, tell me they're going to change into real uniforms during intermission."

"Somehow, I doubt it."

"What the hell," said Dorsey. "They have nice asses."

Henny threw her towel at Dorsey. Dorsey laughed. "I don't know about you," Henny said, "but I don't like being part of a freak show."

The other players murmured assent. I held up my hands.

"Look," I said, "I agree with you. The uniforms are a disgrace. The Lambs shouldn't even be in this league. The reality is they are here and we have a game to play. We have an obligation to play it the best we can."

"It's hard to play your best against a team like that," Effie said. "It's hard to play at all.'

"Right, but if we don't play, we jeopardize the future of the league; we'll just be giving ammunition to the types who say women are too sensitive to play this game. Don't forget, owners come and go. Ed Rybak won't be around forever."

"Yeah," said Joy, "what can you expect from a guy who made his fortune from strip joints?"

"Well, if they come out on the ice naked, I'm not playing," Chris said.

"Agreed." I waited for a moment for the room to settle. "I want you to go out and play so well that the fans don't even look at the Lambs. I want them to leave the arena tonight talking about how well the Teddies played, not what the Lambs wore."

I received a few nods of assent. Henny got up and turned the television on. Pip Blackburn was talking about the Lambs' uniforms.

"They look OK," Pip was saying. "They're figure skaters, eh? They're used to wearing that stuff. But I'm sure glad the Teddies are wearing regular uniforms because I'd hate to see Big Julie Martin in a tutu."

Henny turned the television off.

My brother, Michael, and his wife Denise came down for the game. My parents didn't make it. Dad couldn't leave the cows—his real children. He did call before the game to wish me well. Those few fumbling words, drawn from the depths of his shy heart meant more to me than having him front row and centre throwing bouquets. My mother got on the phone and added her congratulations, effusive in her genuine country way. In her hard life, what mattered was being able to bake bread from scratch and preside over the birth of a calf. What I was doing was luxury and suspect. I accepted her value system.

Michael and Denise took me for a drink afterwards. Perry Hartschorn, still looking edgy and embarrassed, joined us.

Denise was delighted for me. We lived in different worlds but she had a generous spirit. Michael wanted to be delighted but couldn't quite pull it off. "Who would have thunk it," he said for the tenth time. "My kid sister, a professional hockey player."

Riding alongside his congratulations and threatening to overtake them was his jealousy. A mere woman had achieved something he had lusted after all his life. Although I was his kid sister by only fifteen minutes, this accident of birth was something he could hold over me when all else seemed lost.

Michael and I were fraternal twins who, given the right haircuts and clothing, could easily have passed as identical—part of the reason Denise was so fond of me and, sometimes, so confused.

Denise smiled. Her eyes told the story: She had the patience to humour Michael through his petty insecurities and incredible vanities. Michael was small for a man, certainly too small to have made it in professional hockey with his very average skills. I had the feeling he blamed me for his small stature—we're both five-feet-eight—was convinced I had taken something from him in the womb. He compensated for this imagined inadequacy with a machismo, bordering on misogyny.

"That college game is what got Alison the job," he told Perry.

Perry shrugged.

Denise smiled and shook her head. Normally Michael doesn't like to be reminded of this old prank. But now that I was successful, he was anxious to take some of the credit.

Michael was about to tell the story of the trick he played on his old coach when he played intercollegiate hockey at the University of Western Ontario. He always came off looking better in the story when he told it.

Denise who had heard the story a hundred times, sat back, her eyes glazing over. Perry who knew the story only from newspaper accounts, leaned forward.

"So, coach—old Henry Jerkface—said I played like a girl. So, I figured I'd show him what a girl really plays like." He paused for a moment to let the anticipation build then launched into the story.

My version was slightly different.

I was staying at Michael's apartment that weekend. My team was in London to play a hockey game against the Fillies, the female counterpart to the Mustangs. The fact I went along with Michael's insane prank showed I was a lot more adventurous in those days.

"Alison was visiting me that weekend," Michael said. "Her team was playing the other girls' team. So, we were sitting around, shooting the bull, and it came to me: This was the perfect opportunity to show old Henry what a girl plays like. It went smooth as silk, didn't it, Alison?"

I nodded.

"I got her an extra pair of pants and stockings. Had her wear my roomie's old raccoon coat. Told her to hang out in the hall near the locker-room door. Then when we were about to go out for the third period, I told old Henry I had diarrhea and had to hit the crapper. As soon as the coast was clear, I snuck Alison into the locker room, gave her my helmet and sweater and laced her into her skates. Out she went. I told her to keep a towel wrapped around her neck and keep her mouth shut. The idea was—just before the game ended—she was to mumble something about having diarrhea and beetle it to the dressing room. Then when Henry and the guys came in, I'd be sitting on the crapper, nice as you please." Michael paused and gave me a disparaging look. "It would have worked too if Alison hadn't got knocked on her can and had her lip busted. There was blood all over the place. The trainer ran out, got a good look at her and the jig was up."

Perry laughed.

"Michael got kicked off the team," Denise said.

"Yeah, but I didn't care that much. It was the second last game and we weren't going to make the play-offs anyway. It was kind of disappointing, though. I would have loved to have sidled up to old Henry when it was all over and said: "Hey, guess what, coach?" He stopped, smiled to himself for a moment, then said, "I suppose I should have expected he'd notice something. I mean…after all…even thinking I was sick…"

Translation: Sooner or later old Henry would have noticed I wasn't playing up to form and gotten suspicious.

The truth is someone did notice something was different.

"I knew something was wrong," Michael's linemate told the press. "I've never known Michael to get that much zip on his passes."

Michael dismissed the remark at the time.

"The guys were just joshing me," he said.

I knew they weren't. I've always been a better hockey player than Michael.

I've always been the better hockey player but Mike always got the opportunities, the advantages. The boys, regardless of skill, got the best equipment, the lion's share of precious ice time, the bulk of the community's support. More important, they were given the privilege to dream, unimpeded by reality. This—the chance to play professional hockey—was my vindication. I wasn't surprised Michael didn't jump for joy when he heard I had been hired. I was living his dream—a dream he regarded as his by divine right—and he resented it.

I could not deny the truth, however. I did owe my hockey success to Michael. Without his insane prank, I never would have become a local legend. And without this status, Phil Tweddell would never have hired me to coach the Teddies.

This then was my claim to fame and the ultimate irony. I had played hockey for thirty years, some of it bordering on the spectacular. I had been hired to coach the Teddies, though, because I once played eight minutes at left wing for a fifth-rate men's collegiate team and had my lip busted.

"Too bad you didn't get a better team," Michael was saying to Perry. "What'd you do? Get all the last picks?"

I flushed. Perry looked at me nervously. I turned to Michael. "Do you know what makes me really mad about tonight?"

Michael shook his head innocently.

"The uniforms are bad enough. But what really sticks in my craw is that there are hundreds—probably thousands—of women out there who have earned the right to play in this league. But they didn't get the chance because a moral degenerate filled fifteen roster spots with a bunch of women who never touched a hockey stick before." I turned to Perry. "You've been around a long time. Doesn't it bother you that you've been saddled with a team that doesn't have a hope in hell of winning a single game?"

Perry sighed. "I've been around long enough, Alison, to know you've got to run the horses you're given."

Michael gave Perry a broad wink. "And you've got a great stable of fillies."

"I don't have the energy to get into that one, Michael." With that I said good bye to Michael and Denise at the bar—Michael well into his cups, Denise jingling the car keys suggestively—and went home.

The apartment was dark save for a dim light over the television set. I was about to go to my room when a voice said, in a slow drawl, "Hello, Alison, heavy date?"

Joy was lying in the dark, stretched out on the couch, dragging leisurely on a cigarette. The light from the lamp lit up her hair like a new copper, brought out the delicate colors of her skin. Joy always reminded me of England—bright splashes of apples and peaches against fine bone china.

I told her where I'd been.

She made a face. Joy knew Michael well. He tried to hustle her when we were roomies. "I came straight home," she said.

I knew something was bothering her. Sitting alone in the dark, contemplating the meaning of life was not Joy's style. "What's up?"

"I made the mistake of going out the front door," she said. "I got mobbed by media types. Did they want to know about the game, about the WPHL? My thoughts on being a rookie at age thirty-five? No. All they wanted to know about was Robby. Have you talked to your ex-husband? How does he feel about this? Have I talked to him? I wouldn't talk to him if he were the last person on the planet. How does he feel about the WPHL? He's probably ready to shit. He's afraid they'll ask him about it and he'll have to swallow his hostility and say something nice—so as not to destroy his heavily sponsored, all-Canadian-boy, Johnny-Canuck-at-the-bridge image."

"What did you say?"

"I smiled and said I hadn't talked to him, but I was sure he wished us well." She grimaced. "I know he hopes we'll fall flat on our faces. But I didn't want to open a can of worms."

That too was unusual. Joy was an expert at thrust and parry, delivering the telling blow with her quick rapier wit. "He'll say something nice for the press," she said. "He'll be patronizing, of course—just enough to be obvious but not enough to incur anyone's wrath. He's got the best PR men in the business on his side. They'll tell him what to say." She butted her cigarette and immediately lit another.

I got a cup of coffee and sat down in the chair opposite her.

"There are things I *could* have said…" She sighed and shook her head. "But, I told myself: 'Joy, let it go.' There were enough questions at the time. Don't get them into that: 'Why did a little girl like you, mess up with a great guy like Robby Boyle—I mean, he scored fifty goals last season and was honorary chairman for Hoof and Mouth Disease. It would have taken some kind of slut to fool around on poor old Robby.'"

Her words echoed *The Groupie: Biography of a Sport's Marriage*. Robby had come off looking like a prince in this piece of trash, an innocent from the Prairies, preyed upon by a big-city woman who used him to gain access to the big time and its endless supply of strong, masculine bodies. Trash or not *The Groupie* made the best-seller list without a peep from Joy and a "no comment" from Robby that showed plenty of comment—that he was still wounded and above lowering himself to such sordid debate. He made no effort to defend Joy; she made no effort to defend herself, although the book was a mishmash of innuendo, gossip and unattributed quotes. I couldn't ask her about it, was ashamed to admit I had a copy of it at home, tucked into the back of my closet out of reach of Mandy who eagerly gobbled up anything with a hockey player on the cover.

A shadow crossed her face, then suddenly her expression lightened. "Remember the old days?"

"Sure."

Joy lived with me for a couple of years while I was working for Parks and Rec. She was eighteen when I met her, mature beyond her years, infinitely more sophisticated than myself. We played hockey and soccer and softball on the same teams. She was a fun roomie, a crackerjack athlete and an all-around Sweetheart of Sigma Chi. We spent many long hours, talking about our love lives—hers plentiful and conventional, mine not and not.

She poured another scotch without getting up. "Want one?"

"No thanks."

The bottle was half-empty. It was full when we left for the game. Joy wasn't even slurring. But then she had always been in command of her booze. It showed itself only in the sleepiness around her eyes and a slight slowing of her speech. Sexy.

"Michael and Denise," she said with a half-smile. She rested her teeth gently against her lower lip. "And I thought you'd met someone."

I shook my head.

"How long has it been since Gail?"

"Three and a half years."

It was her turn to do some internal head-shaking. She didn't ask any more questions. Lay back and closed her eyes. We sat in silence, quietly sharing the shame we felt over our failed love lives.

Joy fell asleep after a few minutes, exuding a not unpleasant aroma of expensive scotch. I watched her. One small hand swept back a lock of hair—even in sleep, expertly arranged—from her forehead. A sixty-dollar haircut, one of the perks of her old, richer life she had hung onto. The scotch remained clutched in her hand, balanced against her abdomen. I eased it from her grip, stared at it for a moment, then sat back sipping slowly.

We all had things we desperately wanted to hang onto. Being with Joy reminded me of that. When nothing remained, all the years were wasted years, a swath cut through your life like the path of a thresher through a field of ripe wheat.

Seven and a half years. And what did I have to show for them? Memories—all of them bad. The night Gail left me was etched on my brain as indelibly as words carved in stone.

She left me by telephone, the cowards way out, without revealing her whereabouts. I remember running all over town in the pouring rain, checking out her favorite haunts, mad with grief, my face a raging river of cold autumn rain and hot salty tears. Knowing it was a mistake. Knowing we could fix things, if only we could talk. And all the time I was sloshing around in rain-filled loafers, she was tucked away safe and snug with her therapist.

She phoned me a few days later to tell me she was cured. Her therapist had explained I was an aberration, a way station between a bad marriage and a glorious future as a heterosexual woman—with her therapist, of course. Another sinner returned to the fold, her sexuality reclaimed. I didn't even put up a fight. What did I have to fight with? I was one dissenting voice against a whole straight world set up to validate her decision.

"She left you for her therapist," Landlady had said with a snort. "She must be insane."

I topped up the scotch as I considered my losses. Seven and a half years as a sporting woman—Gail didn't approve of sports, said she felt jealous of the spell the locker room cast over me. So, I retired early, played sporadically at a level far below what I was accustomed to. I lost touch with my best friends. Financially, I lost my shirt. But it wasn't the monetary loss that overwhelmed me. It was the specter of shared accomplishments, dismantled, thrown to the wind. But the worst loss was seven and a half years of my life that could be reclaimed only through pain.

What did I gain? Knowledge. How to live from dawn to dark without giving in to despair. How to ignore the calendar, pretend certain days didn't exist. How to convince myself that what I had—work and platonic friendship—was enough. Truth. Don't play house with a straight woman. And never put yourself in a position where you could be hurt again.

That was what I had given up seven and a half years of my life to learn.

I should have felt grateful. Others had given more.

I finished the scotch, sat for a while, watching Joy. She slept peacefully, the easy, relaxed sleep of the gently sedated. Sat for a while longer and stared at the wall.

Knowledge and truth. I've paid a queen's ransom but, once again, I felt that familiar confusion and urgency. Fight it, I told myself.

I took the glass to the sink, rinsed it and went into my bedroom.

I was in the middle of writing on my mental blackboard five hundred times when sleep mercifully claimed me.

You will not get involved again.

Dateline: Toronto
Subject: *Teddies Butcher the Lambs* by Jim Gough
Alison Gutherie's Teddies played like knights in shining armor last night. There was chivalry in every fiber of those brown and gold jerseys. Playing against a team without enough padding to save a fly from a fly swatter, the Teddies stayed away, declining to lay as much as a finger on the hapless Lambs. The Teddies put on a fine display of individual and team skills. They were simply too good for a team of figure skaters with limited hockey experience.

Perry Hartschorn, accustomed to coaching in the OHL, surely the most brutal arena in hockey, found the game, admittedly, a little odd. "Sure my team might have played better in full gear," he shrugged, "but uniforms aren't my decision." Mae Naesmith, a pretty little right winger for the Lambs, admitted some of the girls felt a little uneasy about the paucity of protective gear. "But, we're figure skaters, for Pete's sake!" she exclaimed. "We've fallen in dangerous situations before. Don't you think it's possible to fall doing a number with the Ice Capades and be cut with another skater's blade? Besides," she added, "most of the teams in the league have no intention of hurting anyone. The Teddies? Well—they're teddy bears." Another player said, "We're just proving you don't have to be masculine to play hockey." But a player who refused to be identified had other thoughts: "These (the uniforms) are insane," she said. "Someone's going to get hurt."

What the hell! They sure were cute!

Dateline: Toronto
Subject: *The Principle of the Thing* by Faye Surgenor
The score last night was seven to zero but both teams lost. The game should not have been played in the first place. The London Lambs, a team of ex-figure skaters trained from childhood to "sex it up" for the sake of artistic impression, seemed equally willing to "sex it up" for future gate. Alison Gutherie should have taken no part in this charade for the Lambs are the antithesis of everything that is desirable in women's sports. With their skimpy star-spangled outfits, the Lambs announced to the world that their real goal is not to play hockey but to pander to the fantasies of the macho male spectator. We play hockey, they say, but we're sexually exciting, we're still available to men.

Alison Gutherie should have forfeited the game.

Dateline: Toronto

Subject: *We've Come a Long Way* by Mary-Beth Jones-McAlpine

Last night the Toronto Teddies played the London Lambs in the first women's professional hockey game to be played in venerable Maple Leaf Gardens. We've come a long way. Sure, compromises were made. Compromise is indeed the magic ingredient in progress. There are those like Faye Surgenor who feel Alison Gutherie should have forfeited the game as a matter of principle. But Alison was right to stay. By staying to play she'll return to play another day.

The newspaper hit my doorstep at seven a.m. At nine, I was sitting in the reception room outside Phil's office with the relevant section tucked under my arm. Mrs. Toop, the wicked witch of the west—for this century disguised as Phil's secretary—sat at the desk, ignoring me as she opened the morning mail, slitting each letter with deadly accuracy with a gold embossed Frank Tweddell Sports Enterprises letter opener.

Finally, Phil's door opened. A preppie in blue blazer and grey flannels sauntered out. A few minutes later, the intercom at Mrs. Toop's elbow buzzed.

"Mr. Tweddell will see you now."

Phil was ensconced behind his desk, an enormous kidney-shaped affair that even the Prime Minister would have had trouble justifying. The walls behind him were covered with sports memorabilia, most of it football and boxing, most of it, I assumed, purloined from his father and older brother. A picture of a pubescent Phil wearing a soccer uniform, receiving a handshake from his father held the center position. Big Frank looked as miserable at age forty as he did today. Phil, minus the cheesy little mustache, didn't look a day older.

Phil raised his head to acknowledge my arrival, giving his trademark red suspenders a weary tug. He had rolled his sleeves to the elbow to give me the impression he had been slaving since dawn. "Sit down, Alison." He whipped a paper from the thin stack to his right and studied it intently. "I'm glad you came by," he said before I could open my mouth. "I've been going over your purchase requisition.

What's this about eight red and eight blue sweatshirts?"

"It's hard to run an effective scrimmage when every player is wearing a different color."

"Oh," he said grumpily. "And what about the tires?"

"Every tire on the bus is as bald as a cue ball. It seems the Catholic School Board didn't replace them before it sold you this piece of junk. Do you know we're the only team in the league that uses a school bus?"

Phil frowned. "A bus is a big investment. If we show something in the books later on…well, maybe we can talk new bus. Maybe." He threw the purchase requisition back onto the stack. "So, what's up?"

"You were at the game last night."

"Of course."

"And?" I tossed the newspaper onto his desk.

"What's your point?" He glanced at it briefly and set it aside. "Faye Surgenor likes to give you a hard time, doesn't she."

"I'm talking about the Lambs uniform, Phil. What are you going to do about it?"

He looked at me, perplexed. "What in hell do you expect me to do about them. They're regulation."

"You've got to be kidding."

"The rules state that every player must wear shoulder pads, elbow pads, shin guards, chest protector and kidney pads. Helmets are optional."

"Phil, that 'protective gear' they were wearing was white kid leather, studded with rhinestones. I could have slit it open with a fingernail."

"Nonetheless, the stuff met the letter of the law—whether you like it or not."

"Did you like it, Phil?"

"Hell, Alison," he said crossly, "they looked all right. They're figure skaters after all. They're used to performing in that sort of thing. Besides, they really don't *need* wads of protection. Nobody's going to get hurt. Those girls can't play hockey. You know it; I know it; everybody knows it. Nobody's going to lay a hand on them. Your players didn't go within three feet of them last night."

"No, they didn't. But what if one of them had taken a puck in the shin. Accidentally. It's not always possible to predict where the puck's going."

He slapped his hands down on the desk, clearly annoyed. "Oh, come on, Alison. None of the girls shoots that hard."

"Do you really believe that?"

He looked at me, shifty-eyed. "Sure, I believe that."

"Then you wouldn't mind coming down to the Mussyford and standing in the net in your business suit while Sharon Sosnoski takes a few shots at you."

He stared at me, long and hard. "That's ridiculous. I'm the owner. I've got to maintain some semblance of decorum."

"If you were really interested in decorum, you'd file a protest with the governors about a bunch of woman playing hockey, half-naked."

He didn't blink an eye. "As I've said, the uniforms meet the requirements. Besides, the Lambs are good for business. They attract interest."

"Do you really want that kind of interest?"

"At this stage of the game, you take what you can get." He whipped the purchase requisition off the stack, signed it with a flourish. "There you go, new sweatshirts and new tires." He paused, pen poised. "And, Alison, thank your lucky stars you don't have an owner messing around with your uniforms."

I left with the distinct feeling I'd been bribed.

CHAPTER 6

Detroit. Motor City. Home of another of the Original Six. I couldn't stop smiling as the bus rolled off the expressway. Detroit. Great hockey town. Gordie Howe, Ted Lindsay and Sid Abel played here, spinning out their magic in the old Olympia where the fans threw everything on the ice from ink wells to live guinea pigs.

We weren't scheduled to play at the Olympia, of course—the old arena was torn down years ago. Nor would we get as much as a foot in the door of the Joe Lewis Arena, the latest temple to machismo. Our game against the Dynamos was played out at the Aero, a sterile chunk of concrete in the suburbs.

The Dynamos were coached by Pierre Deschamps, a modest farm boy from St. Hyacinth. As a player, Pierre was a tenacious plodder but he was a great favorite of the Detroit fans in the '50s. The Dynamos, a team hand-picked by Pierre, paralleled his mindset. The players were less talented than the Belles but infinitely better coached.

Joy started in net. She had selected this game to try out a new face mask, an elaborate device designed for maximum shock absorption. The mask stuck out about three inches, resembling a cross between Darth Vadar and a cowcatcher.

"One can never be too careful," she said.

Joy had a phobia about losing her teeth. She'd played hockey for twenty-five years with a figurative hand in front of her mouth. I watched as she fussed about in the crease, smoothing the ice. Joy Drinkwater was personally gorgeous, flamboyant and rebellious in the most glamorous sort of way. In the net she was like most goalies—ritualistic, skittish and alone.

The game was a grinder—methodical, close-checking, bone-wearying. We won two to one. The Detroit player assigned to check

Molly took one step in the wrong direction and Molly was gone. She swept up ice, faked a shot on goal, then dropped the puck back to Dorsey who had the open net. The play was picture-perfect. I saw Pierre Deschamps' eyes widen in surprise.

There were two-hundred-and-twenty-four miles between Toronto and Detroit—four hours travel time going down, an eternity coming back. By the time we had showered and stowed our gear, it was late and Harriett, now tired, drove at a snail's pace.

It was in the dusky recesses of the bus that the players got to know each other. They moved from seat to seat, played games, told jokes and engaged in serious conversation.

Molly secreted herself away in the gloom at the back of the bus and slept, stretched out on the long bench seat. During the game she was alert, vigilant, almost hyperkinetic, always moving. Afterwards, she seemed to deflate, like a balloon with the air suddenly let out.

Julia sat by herself tonight, staring out the window. She was always serious and intense in her immensely soft-spoken way but tonight she seemed down.

"I was born here," she said as I slid into the seat beside her.

I strained my eyes, peering off into the darkness.

"Not right here," she corrected. "This is the suburbs. I was born in the inner city. Here, the kids have a few things."

She looked at me. I nodded and she went on.

"Most of the kids I grew up with are still there," she said. "When I went away to university, I had it in my mind I would return and save everybody. But I didn't. The minute I had a job and was making a decent salary, I moved my family to East Lansing. This is the first time I've been in Detroit in years." She paused.

"It must have been quite an honor to be recruited by Louisville," I said.

She nodded. "Oh, yes, it was great. All the attention. Being the big star. I can't say it prepared me that well for the real world, though. You would be surprised at how few jobs are available to a woman with a psychology degree—especially a Black woman who is taller than most of the men doing the interviews."

"Is that when you started roller derby?"

She shook her head.

"No, I didn't get into roller derby right away. I worked at

McDonald's for a while. Then I got a call from the Chicken King asking me if I wanted to play with King's Diamonds."

"What's King's Diamonds?"

"It's a basketball team that plays out of Birmingham. The South's answer to the Harlem Globetrotters. Strictly bush league."

"Better than McDonald's, for sure."

She rolled her eyes.

"Only slightly. I was the only woman on the team. Most of the men were OK but the King was rough. I was a draw, a novelty. The plays were scripted to include little games ripe with sexual innuendo. The boys would pass the ball between my legs. The referee would admonish them and so forth." She stopped, embarrassed. "I did it because I loved playing basketball and I was paid a decent wage. Oh, it was all nonsense during the game but the game we played in practice was real basketball. It was good."

"How long did you play for King's Diamonds?"

"Almost three years." She paused with a short laugh. "Then the Chicken King lost me to the Taco King in a Superbowl bet. I went from Julia Martin the swarthy sex queen to Big Julie Martin the roller derby queen. They asked me to gain weight. I gained weight. They asked me to bump. I bumped. I was in roller derby almost five years. Then I got the call from Phil Tweddell. He had heard of me through a business associate. I knew what he wanted me for. Still, it took me all of three seconds to consider his offer. Mind you, I liked roller derby. But hockey is my opportunity, my last chance."

"What do you mean?"

"I mean it's my last chance to be a real athlete," she said quietly. "I may not be making as much money as I did in roller derby but this is a chance to play a respectable sport that respectable people come to watch. I want to be a real athlete. I'm tired of being a spectacle." She paused, then said, "I want people to remember me as a sporting woman not as an Aunt Jemima who used to roller derby. Phil Tweddell is going to get a lot more than he bargained for."

We talked for almost fifty miles. Then Julia fell asleep and I returned to my seat.

I wanted to talk to Molly but she was asleep. Molly, I imagined myself saying, I could make you a sniper, a great goal scorer, better than Wayne Gretzky, perhaps almost as good as Dorsey Thorne. That seemed a perfectly innocent coach-like approach. Molly was sleeping soundly, though, stretched out on her back, vulnerable, breathing rather noisily. Her forehead was moist. The little spikes of blonde hair along the front were dark with perspiration. I tried to take a deep breath. It caught, shallow and painful. I had been staring at Molly throughout the course of my thoughts and would have kept staring but, suddenly, Dorsey who was sitting directly ahead of Molly opened her eyes and looked at me rather strangely. I smiled and turned around in my seat.

Gradually the conversations trailed off and the bus was silent. I dozed off only to be awakened a few miles later. I heard Harriett say indignantly, "If I find out who did that, she'll walk the rest of the way to Toronto."

Apparently someone had hit Harriett in the back of the head with a zip-lock bag full of water as she stopped the bus at a crossroads.

There were a few chuckles, a nervous laugh and some muffled grunts. Finally everyone settled down and the bus was silent once again.

CHAPTER 7

Three days after our triumph in Detroit, Phil held a cocktail party for the team. The event was not intended for our pleasure, nor had it been arranged because Phil particularly liked spending an evening with a women's hockey team. The party was strictly business—please see "promotional obligations" in the fine print—an opportunity for us to meet the sponsors, a group of small businessmen who had forked over a few dollars for the privilege of having their advertising displayed on the boards during our home games.

The players, ravenous from practice, ate everything in sight, devouring the delicate canapes as if they hadn't eaten in weeks. Phil's wife looked on, appalled. By the time we were through, there wasn't a thing left on the table but a few pieces of wilted lettuce and a dozen olives with the pimento missing.

I put on my best face, smiled for Mr. Pop Goes The Weasel, feigned an intense interest in the goings on at Mr. Smoothie Shock Absorbers, and posed for pictures with every member of the Teddies Booster Club. And, out of the corner of my eye, I watched Molly.

She hung at the edges of conversation, polite but remote, the smile on her lips threatening to break through but never quite making it. At one point her eyes met mine, for one fleeting moment, then pulled away. My head, heart and lower parts went through a quick, messy wrestling session.

I couldn't believe this timid, awkward kid was the owner of the body and soul that produced such artistry on the ice night after night. *Molly Gavison steps off the ice and turns into a pumpkin.*

I left the party early, went home and took out some old films I had cadged from a sportswriter buddy. Molly Gavison skating for gold at the World Championships. Three short years ago. Molly gliding into a victory lap, effortless, like a shadow on air. Molly talking to the reporters, twinkling with quiet ebullience.

The flick faded into the men's five-thousand. I turned off the VCR, took out the tape and sat still, holding it in my hands.

Was that all there was?

The die was cast. Once, you'd allowed a thought to enter your head, you were doomed. I went to *The Star* morgue late the next afternoon, telling myself I was acting like a coach—albeit a sneaky, cowardly coach. I had convinced myself I had to find out about Molly Gavison for "the good of the team". I had to know what motivated her, what made her tick. And, naturally, I couldn't come right out and ask her. After all, I had no legitimate reason to probe into her personal life. Her game performance left little to be desired. I had no evidence that her reticence created problems for her teammates who appeared to accept and respect her obvious preference for solitude.

No. I had a more compelling reason for avoiding direct confrontation: I was just plain chicken. I was convinced that any attempt to establish a dialogue with Molly more intimate than the most mundane game/practice exchange would result in the revelation of feelings I earnestly desired to keep under wraps. And once the genie was out of the bottle, I had grave doubts about my ability to coax her back in.

I sighed as I plunked myself down at the table in front of the microfiche reader. Personal cowardice aside, the ethics of the coach/player relationship were dicey. We've been berating male coaches for years for using their position of power and trust to seduce impressionable young athletes. The situation, we've been told, was particularly loathsome when there was a fifteen-year age gap.

The Star morgue was full of stories about Molly Gavison. They told me very little I didn't already know. Molly Gavison had been an accomplished speed skater who won Olympic medals and World Cup titles. Her parents had been accomplished speed skaters who also won medals and championships. Her younger sister showed great promise. She would, in all likelihood, be an accomplished speed skater and win Olympic medals and championships. The stories ended abruptly about one and a half years ago. One brief piece suggested booze was the problem; another hinted at recreational drug use. These allegations were denied indignantly by Molly's parents, in absentia by Molly and routinely by the athletic bodies concerned. Fellow athletes said:

"She drinks. So what? A lot of us drink more than we should sometimes. Drugs? No way! Nobody does drugs. Not in this sport. Drugs weren't an issue at all. That sort of rumor always goes around when an athlete retires unexpectedly."

One short piece caught my eye.

> Molly Gavison retired from speed skating today at age twenty-three. Those of us who care about athleticism should pause to mourn her departure. For Molly represented something seldom seen in the stern world of international sport. She loved the game; she was a happy warrior—generally brilliant, frequently irreverent, always entirely likable, flamboyant on the ice, surprisingly shy and deferential one-on-one. She took the competing seriously always gave the game her best—but never the winning and definitely never the medals. She was accomplished and bright. She knew there was more to life than a skating oval and she reached for it.

The story read like an obituary. I checked the by-line. Dale Yalden.

"Yeah, Dale's still around," one of the guys at the sports desk told me. "He's a stringer. He covers the scene in the 'burbs, some minor sports in the city. Softball and the like."

"Have you got his phone number?"

"Sure, but you're more likely to find him at Willard's on Dundas. He's the bartender."

Willard's was a spanking new neighborhood bar—clean and bright with light wood paneling and dozens of athletes grinning from autographed pictures. It had a large-screen television, a dart board, shuffleboard and pool table.

The fellow behind the bar was short, stocky and mustached—a frustrated jock. I sat down on a wooden bar stool and ordered a Blue.

"Dale Yalden?"

He looked at me, eyebrows raised. "Yes, I'm Dale Yalden."

I held out my hand. "Alison Gutherie."

"Sure," he said with a smile. "I thought it was you."

"You look familiar too."

He shrugged. "A face in the crowd. You've probably seen me hanging around the high-school track meets, minor hockey, whatever. I'm a sports junkie."

"Me too."

"Congratulations on your new job," he said. "I hope it works out."

"What do you think?"

"It's got a chance," he said. "Provided the owners don't get too greedy."

"Yeah." I ran a finger along the rim of my beer bottle. "Dale, Molly Gavison's on my team. I've just finished reading a piece you did on her for *The Star*."

He pulled the towel from his shoulder and gave the bar a quick rub. "I've written about her a lot," he said brusquely. "Two years ago would have been the last thing I did, I imagine."

"I heard you were working on a book."

He grimaced. "Yeah. Well, I abandoned the project. On second thought, writing the life story of a twenty-three-year-old seemed a little premature."

I nodded.

I settled into my beer. He leaned on the bar, staring past me.

"What's she like? I mean, from the perspective of someone who's known her from way back when?"

He looked at me, surprised. "Molly? She's a good kid."

"What happened to her? Why did she quit?"

He gave me a quick, hostile stare. "I don't know why you're asking, although, I suppose you've heard all kinds of crap." The hard look in his eyes turned wistful. "You want my opinion? Molly was a good kid. A lot of world-class athletes aren't very attractive close up. They don't have the time of day for you unless they think there's something in it for them. They're hard, driven people. They've got one thing on their minds—domination. To win at any cost. Molly wasn't like that. She was a breath of fresh air. Whether you were with *Sport's Illustrated* or the local rag—she treated everybody the same."

"Why did she quit?"

He turned sullen again. "Who knows? Motivation, I guess. It's hard to stay motivated year after year." The tone in his voice told me he knew how lame his words sounded.

"How far did you get on the book?"

"Seventy-five pages. Double spaced."

"I'd be interested in reading it."

"I don't even know where it is anymore. Excuse me." He paused to pour a jug of draft for the foursome at the shuffleboard.

The Westminster chime over the bar struck the half-hour. The dart teams began to trickle in. Dale was busy, slinging jugs of draft and topping up the bowls of peanuts and pretzels, the ever-present bar towel slung over his shoulder. He stopped by my seat long enough to say, "Alison, good to see you. If I don't catch you again this trip, drop in again."

A few days later, I found an envelope in my mailbox, containing seventy-five pages of double-spaced manuscript. *The Golden Girl* by Dale Yalden. Draft One. I leaned against the mailbox, scanning the pages.

Mary Margaret Gavison—eldest in a family of four. Father, Austrian, mother, Finnish. Born in Montreal. The chronology took me up to Molly's sixteenth birthday, then finished abruptly.

There was a brief hand-written note clipped to the last page. I held it up to the light, squinting to decipher Dale's handwriting:

> *She was all the joy in the world, a beautiful natural talent. Then it all went wrong.*

CHAPTER 8

A few days later we were at the Copps Coliseum, losing to the Hurricanes before a very respectable crowd of eight thousand.

Val Warnica wore a navy-blue pinstripe suit, matching tie, white shirt and soft grey fedora. She had a white handkerchief in her breast pocket and smelled like wild roses before a stiff ocean breeze.

"I'm going to have to give you a rain check on that drink," she said ruefully. "I've been nailed for a radio interview. I can't refuse. It's a big show locally."

She was standing six inches from me as she said this, her eyes roving up and down my body like a happy spider.

A slightly dykey Ingrid Bergman.

"I'm sorry," I said.

"I suppose you're going to tell me you came down on the team bus and are, therefore, without your car."

I nodded guiltily.

"Of course, I could always drive you home," she continued, smiling. "Or, if it's too late, you could stay over."

I balked. She watched me, her eyes piercing, the left corner of her mouth dimpling in amusement.

I was saved by Harriett. "Everybody's on the bus, Alison."

"I'll be right along."

Val smiled and shook her head. When she smiled her nose wrinkled. "Coward," she said. "You got away this time, Alison Gutherie. But I'll get you in Toronto. That's a promise."

Harriett's eyes were fixed on the ceiling. She was trying to let on she wasn't listening. Val turned on her heel, Fred Astair-like, and, still smiling at me over her shoulder, slipped away.

We had a record of six-two-zero after our first eight regular-season games.

To celebrate our success we treated ourselves to dinner at La Bomba, a restaurant owned by one of Phil's sporting buddies. La Bomba had given us coupons for free beer and fifty per cent off everything on the menu. The maitre'd whisked us away to one of two small party rooms at the back and immediately sent a waiter with a cooler of Labatt's Blue. Obviously he had had some experience with sports clubs.

Dinner was excellent. La Bomba himself came in, got our autographs and sent along another cooler of beer. La Bomba was a defensive lineman for the Tiger Cats in his previous life. He didn't know quite how to approach us at first and was delighted to find he could talk to us "man to man" about football and hockey. He seemed to understand something about our predominant sexual orientation. Obviously, I was one of the boys. He talked about "the girls", some species apparently wholly different from mine.

The beer flowed freely. Joy got smashed for the first time in years and spent most of the evening, feeling Sosnoski's biceps. Sharon handled this familiarity with the benign splendor of a lion being pestered by playful cubs.

Nomi and Dorsey got into an arm-wrestling duel that seemed to go on forever and have no objective other than shredding ligaments and rupturing tendons.

"I think it's their way of making love," Ingrid commented dryly.

Julia nursed a Dubonnet and fell into an earnest conversation with Henny.

Molly sat at the edge of the group, talking to Pat. Pat left and was replaced by Effie. I had been waiting, building up enough nerve to approach Molly and engage her in a conversation more normal than the usual on-ice tutorial and locker-room banter. But by the time I had marshaled my courage, she was gone.

Effie was sitting by herself, happily eating pretzels. I slid into the chair recently vacated by Molly.

"Did Molly leave?"

"Yeah, I guess so," said Effie in her tremulous, high-pitched voice.

I paused for a moment, then in my best coachlike manner, said, "So, how are you and Molly getting along? Is she a good roommate?"

"Sure, Alison. She's great. She's really neat and quiet. She likes to listen to music. I think she sleeps a lot. She spends a lot of time in her room anyway."

"Do you talk much?"

Effie laughed. "Oh, Alison, I always talk. You know that. I talk her arm off." She sobered, then said, "Yeah, she talks sometimes. A little."

"Does she talk much about her family, her friends?"

Effie shook her head. "No. I don't think she gets along with her family. Except with her younger sister. Who does anymore? She never seems to get any mail and nobody calls."

"Does she ever talk about speed skating?"

"Just about what her sister's doing. I think it's just so much water under the bridge for her. She doesn't even have her medals anymore. I asked to see them because I've never seen a real Olympic medal before. She said she lost them. After I'd asked about the medals, I heard she got kicked off the team for using dope. I felt bad about asking." Effie paused to take a sip of wine. "But no matter what, you know, she's a great athlete. Everybody's kind of in awe of her. The Olympics and everything. Cortina, Oslo, Lake Placid. Sometimes when I see her skate, I get goose bumps. None of us will ever do what she's done. We'll never get up so high. This hockey is a big deal with us. She's good about it. She never says anything to put us down but you know she's fallen. I mean, you've got to figure for her this isn't the Ritz."

I nodded. "Yes, I guess that's true."

"Oh yeah," said Effie after a brief pause. "She has a hamster called Sam. There she is all day on her little wheel, going around and around. She's kind of cute though." She frowned, then said, "If it wasn't for Sam the room would look dead. It's all white like a hospital room. There's nothing lying around. No clutter. It looks like a room where somebody isn't planning to stay long."

I waited but Effie didn't volunteer any more information. She sat looking at me a little nervously as if I were conducting an inquisition.

I asked about her husband. "How's Joey?"

"Oh, Joey's fine," she said with relief.

Harriett, Lou, Chris and Carol were playing bridge. Lou kept throwing in her hand and saying, "It's a lay down," much to everyone else's consternation.

Ingrid, Pat, and Toddy were at the shuffleboard. Toddy was too young to drink legally but that beer in her hand was definitely hers. I put the beer in the back of my mind for future exploration.

Actually, I didn't have to worry too much about Toddy, a mature kid who conducted herself well on and off the ice. There are plenty of professional athletes—some of them men in their thirties—who don't conduct themselves half so well, who appear to need a great deal of guidance to get through their relatively uncomplicated playing lives. Toddy, on her own for the first time, encumbered with a full load of high school credits, did very well indeed.

At eleven-fifteen Nomi and Dorsey were still arm-wrestling.

"Best out of fifteen," I heard Nomi say.

I watched their faces angry and strained. Obviously the game had long since passed the point of pleasure. I walked over to the table, put a hand on their clenched fists and said very quietly, "I think that's enough."

Dorsey got up abruptly and left. Nomi sat, staring at the table, clenching and unclenching her right fist.

"Do you want a ride home?"

She nodded, not looking at me.

Ingrid and Toddy joined us. Ingrid took the keys from me and slid into the driver's seat. I didn't argue. I went to bed and fell asleep promptly. Drinkwater stumbled in around one.

> Dateline: Toronto
>
> Subject: *Nomi Pereira, goal/right wing, Toronto Teddies.*
>
> This twenty-five-year-old was born in Canada of Portuguese parents. Her family runs a deli and catering business in Kingston.
>
> This woman is a stand-up goalie who uses her stick with enthusiasm. "If you let them hang around the crease, they think they own it," she says. Even goes after her own defenders when they obstruct her view. "I only clip them on the boots," she'll tell you. "Tell them to get their asses out of the way. Doesn't hurt much and it gets their attention," she says without apology.
>
> Nomi left high school after grade ten. "School's not for me," she says. "It's a waste of time." She seems

bright but not interested. She works in a small factory in Kingston that makes cement moldings. She's small—five-five, one hundred and fourteen pounds—but she can toss a bag of cement around with astonishing ease. "I like working with my hands," she says. She plays hockey in winter and softball in summer. She catches for pitchers like teammates Sharon Sosnoski and Henny Buskers. She loves sports passionately but resists sentimentality. When you ask her why she plays she says, "What else is there to do in a dump like Kingston?"

Dateline: Toronto

Subject: *Private Diary*

Nomi Pereira is a tough, scrawny dark-haired kid with brown eyes that wander when you talk to her and swim with suspicion. She plays goal with gusto, chews gum furiously and spits a lot.

In practice and in games, she bickers at Sharon constantly and slashes her on the back of the skates when she backs in too close to the net. Nomi comes from a family of educated people, although she didn't do well in school. Her high-school guidance counselor told her mother she'd probably find her niche as a domestic.

Nomi's relationship with her family is clear: They're ashamed of her. Her relationship with Sharon Sosnoski is less so. They're a pair—Mutt and Jeff, Laurel and Hardy—they move and breathe together. They've been friends since childhood but never lovers. People who knew them way back when say the little one was always in trouble and the big one was always bailing her out. They've engaged in a kind of bonding that is usually available only to men. It's beautiful to see and a little scary. As they grow older it's becoming harder for Sharon to bail Nomi out. There's a toughness setting into her that even Sharon may not be able to save her from.

I hear their conversations, catch snippets when they don't know I'm around.

"Are you going out tonight?"

"Yeah."

"Where to?"

"Don't know yet."

"Watch your wallet."

"Yeah, sure."

"Call me if…"

"Yeah, yeah."

"You know the colors on the subway."

"Yeah. Stop acting like a fucking mother hen."

End of conversation. Stamps out. Audible sigh.

Dateline: Toronto

Subject: *Dorsey Thorne, center, Toronto Teddies.*

This five-foot-five, one-hundred-and-twenty-pound bundle of dynamite centers the Teddies best scoring line.

Dorsey—that's her mother's maiden name—was born in London, Ontario twenty-four years ago. She played intercollegiate hockey at Queen's. She's a natural hockey player, a compact wiry frame propelled by piston-like legs. She skates as naturally as most people walk and stickhandles with the best of them. Best, as far as the Teddies are concerned, she's a sniper in a line-up short on offense. Add this to competitive zeal and this fine center spells all-star, MVP and all sorts of good things.

Dateline: Toronto

Subject: *Private Diary*

Dorsey's parents are very comfortable, middle–upper-class people with all the amenities. Dorsey's mother wanted a debutante. She forced Dorsey to take piano lessons and ballet which she hated with equal vigor. Dorsey rebelled, refused to practice, sat on her hands and disrupted the classes. In desperation, her mother struck a deal. Dorsey was allowed to play softball and hockey, provided she continue the piano and ballet lessons. Dorsey plays the piano woodenly but on the ice her music is as pure as a single note on a French horn. Dorsey's parents produced a fine athlete.

She would have excelled at any sport.

She's physically "cute" with close-cropped dark-brown curls, brown eyes, long eyelashes, smallish nose—slightly upturned. She hates her nose. Hides her feelings behind macho swagger and an indecent mouth.

I love having Dorsey on my team, but I'd hate to be an opponent. She's bought into the macho image in ways that are less obvious but more troublesome than Nomi. I'm amazed at how quickly she can size up an opponent's sensitive spots. She's sarcastic and devastatingly personal in her taunts, sly and quick with the butt end of her stick but quick to cry foul and a virtuoso in taking the dive. I think she has a real mean streak.

"She likes to wiggle her rear end around the ball field," says Ingrid. "Gets a lot of the women pretty worked up. I've seen fights over her. She just laughs and walks away. She thinks she's too good for most of them."

Dateline: Toronto

Subject: *Private Diary, Pat Carsey—Update*

Pat Carsey has broken off with Ray after a brief but intense dating period. Ray is hurt and bewildered.

"I thought she respected the fact I wasn't all over her all the time," he said. "Now I don't know what she wants."

"I don't know," Pat told me. "I guess I expect more now."

CHAPTER 9

The Buffalo Belles made their first trip to Toronto on a dark, blustery afternoon in mid-November. I drove up to the side door of Varsity Arena just in time to see the team arrive. I sat in my car as the players filed off the bus.

Bill Mason certainly had a big team. The players looked even larger and more imposing bundled up in their parkas and Sorels. The Belles management had deliberately chosen players for size. The shortest player on the team was five-nine. The hometown fans called the team, affectionately, "The Bulls".

I went into the dressing room and shucked my coat. The players milled about in various states of undress, most of them in longjohns, although a few had made it into girdles and shoulder pads. Dorsey examined the curve of her stick, looking for the infinitesimal adjustment that would give her perfect touch. Harriett bent over the skate sharpener while Toddy peered critically over her shoulder. The others were playing cards, chatting, hanging out. The players were jocular in a nervous way. A win tonight would move us to within two points of the Hurricanes. They also knew they were about to take a beating. Games with the Belles left us sore for days.

Joy was scheduled to start in goal. She had another new face mask. This one resembled a cross between Darth Vadar and a cowcatcher with a cow in it.

"Don't take any in the head," Nomi advised. "This team's got shots that can take your head off from the blue line."

Joy looked at me and shook her head. "I had a dream last night," she said. "I felt something loose in my mouth. I reached in and pulled out a piece of jagged, white bone. I reached in again and pulled out another piece, then another and another. Finally, they were all gone. I had pulled out all of my teeth."

I've never known an athlete who worried about her teeth than Joy. Why she had chosen to be a goaltender was beyond me.

"It's a bad omen," Joy said glumly.

"Don't worry," said Julia. "We'll discourage the Belles from entering your crease."

Julia considered it a point of honor not to use her large size to intimidate opponents. However, she had grown increasingly impatient with the antics of a pair of Buffalo players who enjoyed hassling our small goalies, firing at them point-blank after the whistle, hooking their skates out from under them while the official's back was turned.

"I used to worry mainly about being hit by the puck," Joy said. She sounded totally miserable.

Joy's equipment was spread out on the floor around her—thirty pounds of it. It had to go on in a definite order. That was another of Joy's obsessions. Nomi, on the other hand, grabbed whatever appealed to her.

"Lately, I've started to worry more about being run over," Joy continued. "Since they started anchoring the nets with magnets, no one worries about crashing into the posts. Everybody was so concerned about the players getting hurt on the pipes. Nobody worries about the way the goalies are getting knocked around."

"Give them a lick with your stick," Nomi shifted her wad of gum to her left cheek. It bulged obscenely. "Just above the tendon guard is good or right over the ankle bone."

Harriett threw an extra bottle of smelling salts into her bag.

Varsity Arena was packed—another capacity crowd. Teddies games were camp in this venerable collegiate arena. We stepped out onto the ice to a chorus of cheers and a barrage of small, stuffed bears.

Bill Mason's team was in fourth place behind Detroit. The Lambs, still clutching their skimpy outfits to their bosoms, languished in the basement. The O'Brien's held down a comfortable fifth, one point behind the Belles. The O'Brien's were a good team but Connie Siebart's REAL women preaching had demoralized the players. It was one thing to be coached by a sexist male, quite another to be coached by a sexist female. Women expect more of each other.

Bill Mason had obviously come to the erroneous conclusion that to defeat the Teddies he had to neutralize Molly. He'd instructed his defense to double-team her, ride her into the boards and bump her—hard.

This strategy was, apparently, designed to discourage Molly from going into the corners and to intimidate her into passing the puck prematurely. The plan failed miserably. Molly continued to dig and held the puck until the last possible moment. In the meantime, Dorsey was left uncovered in the slot.

"Are you all right?" I asked after one particularly brutal assault.

She nodded quickly and slid down the bench to sit beside her linemates.

I dug my hands into my pockets to keep from slapping myself. *Of course she's not all right, you idiot. Those two Goliaths just sandwiched her so hard her helmet flew off. Butt-ended her too. She had to crawl ten feet to retrieve her stick.*

Julia went into the corner, pushing the other players aside to get at the puck. The Belles pushed back to no avail. Julia found the puck and kicked it back to Pat.

Pat took a quick look, faked a pass to Lou, then sent a long pass to Nomi who was flying up the right wing. The puck tipped off Nomi's stick into the corner. Nomi streaked in after it, followed by a six-foot Belle defender. There was a brief skirmish, then the defender fell suddenly, clutching at her midsection. Nomi jumped away. Bill Mason was up on the bench, screaming at the referee.

I pounced on Nomi when she came to the bench. "What was that all about?"

"Nothing."

"Did you butt-end her?"

"She fell."

I didn't press further.

The unspeakable happened at the five-minute mark of the final period. The Belles were pressing hard, trying to put a dent in our three-goal advantage. Julia had positioned herself in front of the net to defend against the pass out from the corner. The Belle forward made a nifty move to get away from Pat but tripped as she made her move to cut in front of the net. She pitched headlong through the crease. The blade of her stick caught Joy's face mask, wrenching it up and back. Her skates became entangled in Julia's. Julia fell backward into Joy, knocking the face mask away with her elbow. Joy fell into the net.

Julia fell on top of her. The net toppled over the whole mess.

Joy lay very still for what seemed forever, the net, big Julia Martin and the Belle forward on top of her. The players swarmed around. Harriett ran out, pushed everyone aside and knelt beside the heap.

I pushed the gate open and started out onto the ice. A linesman grabbed me and pushed me back unceremoniously. He must have thought I intended to start a fight, perhaps attack Bill Mason. I was too shocked to resist. I stood at the boards, ashen, my heart thumping wildly. I had a death grip on Lou Frampton's shoulder.

Finally, after what seemed an eternity, Joy twitched. Harriett and Julia helped her to her feet. She stood there, wobbly and disoriented, blood streaming down her chin and onto the pristine white jersey with its adorable brown teddy.

Harriett said something to Julia. Julia began to shake out her sweater. The players gathered around, got down on their hands and knees and began to search the ice. Finally one of the Belles scooped up something and handed it to Harriett. Harriett took the object and wrapped it in a towel.

Joy was herded quickly past me and into the dressing room.

Dorsey was the first Teddy to skate over to the bench. "She lost a tooth," she said, trying to hide a guilty little grin. "Wouldn't you know!"

The linesman grabbed a towel, sponged the blood off the ice and dumped the sticky towel back into our laps.

"Split lip," Dorsey said. "I imagine she'll have a shiner too. She's lucky she's alive. Big Julie landed right on her head."

Julia felt terrible. Having vowed to serve and protect, she had unwittingly become the instrument of the fate Joy most feared, dreamed about and agonized over ad infinitum.

Within seconds, Harriett appeared at my elbow. "I'm sending her to the General," she said, then disappeared back into the alley.

Decision time. Nomi would be going into the net. That was a given. Next, I had to select one of the defenders to take Nomi's spot on the wing. That left one person to fill the fourth defensive slot—me.

In the Stanley Cup final of 1928, New York Ranger coach Lester Patrick—forty-four years old at the time—went into the net when goalie Lorne Chabot was injured. In those days, teams didn't carry spare goaltenders.

"I'm going in to play goal, fellows," Patrick said. "Check as you've never checked before and protect an old man."

I didn't say anything nearly as memorable. I merely said, "Carol you're moving up to right wing."

I followed Nomi to the dressing room. Fortunately, league rules on injury placements allowed me a reasonable amount of time to suit up. Nomi changed into her goalie gear quickly and watched solemnly as I pulled on the jersey with the big Number 2 on the back—for Doug Harvey, of course.

Nomi took her place in the net. I joined Sharon.

I felt rusty and out of shape but mostly I felt frightened. It's amazing how much terror can build as you stand behind the bench and watch and imagine. Mason must have told his players to check and hit me hard. They did. Much harder than necessary. After the first few hits, though, I became inured to the pain, settled down and played decently.

Nomi managed to get three penalties for slashing in the final fifteen minutes, paying the Belles back for their attacks on me. She deserved several more.

After the game I said, "Nomi, I appreciate the fact you want to look after me. But I don't want you doing that again. I can take care of myself."

She looked me square in the eye. "Shit," she said, "they were making hamburger out of you."

I stopped by the General to pick Joy up. Sharon, Toddy and Nomi accompanied me.

"Hairline fracture of the socket," The oral surgeon said. "Right here." He pointed to a bottom incisor. "I replanted the tooth, cleaned things up. She'll be out for a day or two."

Joy had been signed out. She'd been given some Demerol, however, and was as wobbly as the Scarecrow from Oz. She was also semi-delirious and babbling from the effects of the potent analgesic. We found her leaning against a water cooler while the nurse searched frantically for a wheelchair.

Sharon scooped Joy into her arms and headed toward the door. Nomi, Toddy and I followed.

Sharon put Joy in the back seat of the Datsun and crawled in beside her. She dutifully fastened Joy's seat belt, then put a large arm around her to steady her. Joy babbled like a lunatic and tried to kiss

Sharon. Sharon put on her gruff face and tried to ignore her. After a time Joy stopped babbling and fell asleep against Sharon's shoulder.

By the time we arrived at the apartment, Joy was snoring. Sharon carried her in and deposited her on the couch.

I made a pot of tea and stretched out in a tub of hot water to nurse my aches and bruises.

Joy came to around midnight. I gave her a cool drink and gingerly applied a little vaseline to her cracked and crusted lips. She laughed and carried on and choked on bloody saliva and made no sense at all. She was feeling no pain.

Finally, she calmed down. I folded three thick towels across her pillow and put her down for the night. She fell asleep again around three.

The next morning Joy was as sober as a judge. She came into the bathroom while I was having a shower, rubbed a hole in the mist on the mirror and looked at her reflection squarely.

"My God," she said in the cold light of day, "I hope no one saw me this way."

Her left eye was deep purple, black and bulging. Her lips were swollen and crusted with dried blood. Her nose and chin were scraped and gouged.

"Everyone at Varsity Arena, everyone in the emergency room at the General, three old drunks on the corner of College and University," I said. I didn't mention that her picture was on the front page of *The Star*. She would find that out for herself shortly.

The players cleared out of Toronto *en masse* that weekend. Sharon and Nomi were headed to Montreal to see the New York Rangers play the Canadiens. Most of the players, though, were headed home.

I was going home too. Always the last to leave, I dawdled, waiting to say good bye to everyone before they cleared out. I had a full car this time—Pat, Toddy and Carol. They were already in the car, eager to go, teasing me about stopping at the first exit for a Big Mac.

I loaded everybody and everything, then went inside to get my valise.

Joy was dressed and packed, sitting on her suitcase, waiting for her parents and grandparents to pick her up.

"I need to be pampered," she said, "and not seen."

Joy's lip was healing well. The eye, though, remained sore and angry-looking.

"I would have thought the swelling would have been out of your eye by now," I said.

Joy shook her head. "It's par for the course," she said. "I should know," she added calmly. "I've had enough shiners in my time."

I knew from her expression she hadn't received all of them playing hockey. My jaw must have dropped three feet. "You mean..." I was standing in the hallway with a valise in my hand and three impatient friends in the car downstairs. What could I say? "You mean..." I stammered again. I didn't know how to finish. I felt sick and angry.

Joy came to my rescue, grabbing me quickly with a little hug and kiss. "Have a good weekend," she said.

She ushered me out of the door before I could say another word.

I spun out into the hallway, feeling a trifle giddy. Someone had turned the light out. The only illumination was a faint sliver of light from under the door of Molly's apartment. I paused at her door, listening. I could hear music, very faint music, Sibelius, I think. *Finlandia.* I edged closer, my lips parted, barely daring to breathe. The music disappeared into soft footsteps. The steps came nearer and paused. I stiffened. The steps receded. Silence, then a squeak, the squeak of a small wheel on an ungreased axle, a tiny animal on a treadmill, doing her own thing, divorced from the rest of the world.

I turned and hurried down to the car.

"It's about time," said Pat as I emerged into the daylight.

Pat was happy—for Pat, almost euphoric. She was full of plans for bringing the kids to Toronto for the Christmas break.

"We'll go to the game, of course, and the zoo. They've never been to a zoo in their lives. I'd like to take them to the museum too, maybe the planetarium. The best news is, I don't have to worry about Bill spoiling anything."

"Good," I said. "He's leaving you alone."

She laughed. "He's in jail. Got drunk and went after a police officer with the broken end of a beer bottle. Funny, he used to come after me with broken beer bottles all the time. They never put him in jail for that."

I basked in Pat's excitement as we meandered along the 401. Pat had changed dramatically over the past few weeks. The pale, hangdog look was gone. Gone too was the nervous skitter. She'd slowed down, relaxed. She moved with purpose, spoke clearly, slower. She laughed.

Her eyes too. It was obvious Pat liked being an athlete. She also liked living with a group of women.

We pulled off the 401 at Port Hope to let Carol off. She was spending the weekend with a "friend".

Pat talked. Toddy and I listened. She was trying to talk Toddy into taking up a trade.

"But I want to be a hockey player," said Toddy with typical teenage rebelliousness.

"This is for after you're a hockey player," Pat said. "Get started on something in the off-season and you're all set. I always wanted to be a mechanic. I've always been good at fixing things up. I even had everything lined up at one point. Talked a guy with a little garage into taking me on as a helper. Bill screwed that up, of course. He couldn't stand the idea of me being able to do something he couldn't. I guess he was ashamed of being a janitor. Nothing to be ashamed about. I never put him down because of it. It's a hell of a lot better than what he is now—a drunken bum." She reached out and playfully ruffled Toddy's hair. "This, Alison, is a good kid," she said. "She's going to make something of herself, aren't you, Hon? She isn't going to run off and get married like a fool at eighteen." Pat shook her head. "Hell, Alison, I could kick myself. I've got the kids. They're worth it, of course. But what a damned fool I was."

"Pat," I said, "you're only twenty-six years old."

"Some days I feel like a hundred." She laughed, then said, "Well, you never know. Maybe I still have a chance. Maybe I'll turn out to be a mechanic after all."

We dropped Toddy off at a nice brick house down a long laneway at the edge of the urban-rural divide. Mom was waiting. A curtain dropped as the car crunched to a halt in the driveway. Alice's mother existed in a constant state of nerves, certain the big city would corrupt her daughter.

I left Pat at her mother-in-law's rambling white vinyl-sided house on the north side and went home to Landlady and Mandy.

Landlady made a pot of tea and got out the pumpkin bread. She then gave Mandy some money and sent her to the store for milk.

"Don't forget, Alison," Mandy called to me before she left. "I've got a game at four."

I had completely forgotten. I said I hadn't.

"You realize," said Landlady when the door closed, "Mandy

believes she'll play in the NHL one day."

I shrugged. "Maybe she will."

Landlady smacked her lips lightly. "Mandy's coach wants her to play on a girls' team," she said. "She thinks it would be a mistake to try out for the Bobcats. She thinks the coach would treat her miserably. He'd feel compelled to accept her. She's made the all-star team each year. She's clearly better than the majority of the boys in her age-group. Doris feels he would take her to deflect criticism but would do whatever necessary to persuade her to drop out."

"What do you want?"

Landlady knit her brows. "I want her to be able to do what she wants to do," she said. "I don't want her to give in to the idea that certain routes are unavailable to her because of her sex."

"The girls' teams are every bit as good as the boys' teams," I said. "Kids of that age are the same in size and ability."

"That's not the point. I don't want Mandy to grow up learning to avoid situations because males may try to intimidate her, whether it's with presumed superiority, ribald remarks, coarse language, or sheer physical size. I don't want her to be afraid to try." She stared at the table for a moment, then said, "If the route to the NHL lies through the Bobcats, I don't want her defeated at the first step."

I tried to smile. "Maybe she'll be the first woman to play in the NHL then," I said. I felt rather sad.

I accompanied Mandy to her game. Afterwards I took her to Tim Horton's for hot chocolate and donuts.

"Your Mom tells me you want to try out for the Bobcats," I said.

"Jay and Herm are trying out," she said. "I'm better than they are."

"The girls' teams are just as good," I reminded. "Nomi and Sharon and all those women played on girls' teams. Don't you think Nomi's as good a goalie as Pete Peeters? And Nomi plays right wing too. Pete can't do that."

"Yeah." She looked at me sulkily. She knew what was coming next.

"I played with both," I said. "I liked girls' hockey better. I was a better hockey player in the girls' league. On a girls team you'll get more attention from the coach, more playing time."

"I want to play in the NHL," she said stolidly.

"Why?"

"Because it's the best."

"Better than the WPHL?"

She hung her head.

"We play a different game," I said. "I like to think we play the game the way it was intended to be played. I like to play a game where a good small player can still be a hero."

She didn't say anything, just hung her head. Maybe she didn't believe me. Maybe she thought Nomi and Sharon and I had had to settle for second best, that in our hearts, in our wildest imagination we hoped our performance would miraculously lead to a tryout with an NHL team.

"I want my picture on a hockey card," she said finally.

CHAPTER 10

The Hurricanes were coming to town. We held a light practice in the morning, took a leisurely swim and went home at lunch to rest and prepare.

Joy was already home when I arrived, bouncing around the apartment, looking totally appealing in an over-sized white T-shirt, khaki fatigues and black Reeboks. She'd tossed together a light lunch—devilled eggs on a bed of romaine lettuce, a carefree handful of asparagus tips, and a side dish of smoked salmon, topped with fresh dill. Joy was feeling normal again. Her mouth had healed and nothing remained of her goal-line collision but a pale yellow moon under her right eye.

"Lunch will be ready in five," she said.

I stood at the counter and watched as she reduced a lemon to transparent-thin slices. It was lovely having Joy as an apartment mate. She was a great cook, raised her own fresh herbs in window planters. I compensated for my culinary illiteracy by doing the housework, something Joy hated and for which I, without a modicum of creativity, was ideally suited.

"That's it," said Joy. She popped a ripe olive into my mouth and gathered up the tray.

Whenever I sat down to one of Joy's elegant meals, my heart went out to Nomi and Sharon. Nomi survived on toast and marshmallow brooms and looked deathly pale most of the time. Sharon consumed large quantities of fast-food hamburger, fries and pizza and lifted weights three times a week to keep the extra calories in muscle. Their apartment was, however, immaculate. They cleaned rigorously twice a week. I knew they did because twice a week boots and mats appeared in the hallway outside their slightly ajar door and I could hear Nomi bickering at Sharon as she scrubbed and directed the cleanup effort simultaneously. Sharon lifted enormous pieces of furniture to accommodate Nomi's obsession for waxing and polishing in the deepest, darkest corners, held Nomi up on her shoulders to dust inside the light fixtures and over the windows. They were a great team.

I shared my thoughts with Joy.

"Speaking of Sharon," said Joy absently, "I think I'll ask her to check out our kitchen sink. There's water leaking around the faucets."

I nodded. Sharon did most of the plumbing repairs on our floor. It was nice not to have some condescending male disturbing our tranquillity.

Lunch left me sleepy. I would have loved to have had a nap. Unfortunately, I was due downtown to preside over the opening of a new health club—another promotional obligation.

"I guess I have to go pour carrot juice," I said.

Joy was buried in the newspaper. "What time will you be home for dinner?"

"About four-thirty."

"I have a beautiful cheese, zucchini and tomato casserole in the refrigerator," she said. "I'll put it in the oven as soon as you get home."

I said "great." Joy accompanied me to the door and helped me into my coat. I almost kissed her good-bye.

I arrived home at four-thirty. Sharon was just leaving our apartment, toolbox in hand. I must have startled her. She flinched and immediately turned crimson.

I laughed. "It's just me."

She muttered something about seals and washers and disappeared into her apartment.

Joy was putting the casserole into the oven as I walked in the door. She was wearing a bathrobe. She gave me a dazzling smile, and said, "Hi, dinner'll be ready in twenty minutes." So saying, she disappeared into the shower.

I followed her into the bathroom and tried to share my experience at the Heather Club between bursts of water. She kept saying "Hm" and "really" but I knew she wasn't paying attention to a thing I was saying.

The game against the Hurricanes was our last before Christmas. Phil had planned a big party for us and our opponents at La Bomba afterwards. Phil had intended to be there but at the last minute something came up. He did send Mrs. Toop by the dressing room to give each of us a one hundred dollar bill. She stuck her hand through a crack in the door, extending the envelope stiffly, eyes averted.

"Bonus for a good year," she said, relaying the message.

Buoyed by the wave of appreciation, we won the game three to one. Joy was superb in goal. Dorsey got the hat trick.

Val was waiting for me in the runway after the game.

"Don't you dare tell me you won't be at the party," she said.

"I'll be there."

"Good." She took my arm, a little smile playing around her lips. "I wanted to make sure you wouldn't escape this time."

I muttered something inane. Her touch warmed me and scared me.

She smiled again and said, "Should I call a cab?"

It occurred to me then I couldn't remember if I'd driven to the arena that night.

"I have my car," I said. I was guessing. Fortunately, I was right.

Phil had not stinted on the party. The food and drink were plentiful and sumptuous. He'd even hired a DJ with a decent selection.

After dinner Val mixed. I sat, my chair tipped against the wall, and sipped my liqueur.

Nomi was involved in what appeared to be a rather heavy discussion with the Hurricane goalie. Although Nomi was not noted for her elegant use of language, her counterpart seemed fascinated. I watched them for several minutes. Dorsey seemed fascinated too. She stood a few feet from me, leaning against the bar, sipping a beer and watching them, her eyes a bewildering mixture of anger and disdain.

"I've done many things," Julia told a Hamilton forward, "but I could never bring myself to box. I would never want to hit at someone, to deliberately attempt to hurt someone."

My eyes drifted casually toward Molly. She was surrounded by a group of star-struck Hamilton forwards. I looked away.

Ingrid asked the DJ to play a tango. She grabbed Henny and dashed about the room in an exaggerated version—rose clenched between teeth, dizzying dips, dramatic pirouettes. Soon most of the room joined them. The party was taking off.

Molly was alone temporarily. Our eyes met uncertainly. I had almost gathered the courage to ask her to dance. But fate intervened. A tall, good-looking Hamilton defender beat me to it. I watched them dance very close. The Hamilton player pressed, whispering persuasively, urgently. I saw a terrible look in Molly's eyes, hungry and vulnerable. They danced the next dance and the next. I stared now, absolutely without restraint, my heart bouncing against my chest like a basketball in a fast dribble.

The music ended. The Hamilton player had not let go of Molly's hand. She said a few words in a low voice. Molly nodded and stared at the floor. They left together. I looked down at the table, dazed. Molly's over-the-shoulder gaze swept the room as she paused at the door. I caught a glimpse of it as I looked away.

Val returned to me with a gentle tap on the shoulder. "There," she said, "now that I've been perfectly ingratiating to everyone, perhaps you'll dance with me."

The DJ was playing "Shadowland". Val took me in her arms. Val was a regular Valkyrie, an Amazon of the highest order. Everything about her was elegant and sensuous from the fiber of her clothing to the fragrance of her body. I stole a glance about the room. The eyes of two women's hockey teams were upon us.

"They're watching us," I whispered.

Val steered us deftly into a small corridor that led to a longer corridor that led to the women's washroom.

"Now they can't watch us," she said. She stared into my eyes for several long moments, then said, "Walk me home."

"All the way to Hamilton?"

She laughed. "No. I have a room at the Royal York. I'm catching an early flight to Montreal. I have to be up at four or some such obscene hour." She winked and tweaked my cheek. "Let's sneak around to the lobby, grab our coats and blow this joint. Nobody will be the wiser."

We left my car at La Bomba and walked the few blocks to the Royal York. It was the witching hour—midnight on a very crisp, clear night. Val held my hand and talked in a velvet whisper.

"On the prairies the stars would be as big as the streetlights," she said. "Bay Street's a long way from home for a little girl from Moose Jaw."

She caught my expression as she said this and laughed. Val was hardly a little girl from Moose Jaw. Her Anglo-Montreal mother had seen to that. First, private school in Toronto—Bishop Strachan—then Sainte Jeanne d'Arc, then proletarian South Gloucester High School thrown in to give her an appreciation for the common folk. Val and her hockey were sophisticated and cosmopolitan in the Montreal fashion. They had very little in common with the sun-burnt, stick-thumping hockey of the great flat plains.

I told her this and she laughed again.

Val's room at the Royal York was bright and cheerful and full of expensive luggage, gold jewelry and clothing. While I stood, mildly agog, in the midst of this careless opulence, Val called room service and ordered a carafe of coffee and a bottle of cognac—Remy Martin XO.

"They must pay you well to coach the Hurricanes," I said as she brought the cognac to the table.

She shook her head. "Old money," she said. "The best kind. Inherited wealth."

She poured the cognac into a brandy snifter, cradling it gently in her hands for a few moments before passing it to me.

She looked at me, beaming. "I'm glad to see you, Alison."

"I'm glad to see you too."

"It's been a long time."

"Yes."

She paused, then looking straight into my eyes, said, "I'm sorry about what happened to you. I hurt for you when I heard."

I nodded.

"Seven and a half years," she murmured. "God, that's a long time."

"Yes."

"She must have been very disturbed."

"Yes, I think so," I said quickly. "Still is, I guess."

"Has she left town?"

"Yes, thankfully." I took a long drink. The cognac burned my palate and brought tears to my eyes.

"Thankfully," Val repeated softly. She paused, then said, "Has there been anyone else?"

I assumed she wasn't inquiring about the one-night stands I'd indulged in while wallowing in despair and booze in those painful weeks before Gwen salvaged me. "No," I said.

"You don't sound so sure." She looked at me over the rim of her glass, her eyes sparkling. "You're interested in someone," she said, amused.

I felt suddenly very hot, as if I, like the brandy, might vaporize and flame if someone put a match to me. "No," I said. I felt miserable as soon as the words came out of my mouth, as if I'd betrayed someone. I hesitated, then in a small voice said, "Yes, I guess I am."

"Is she nice?"

"Yes."

"Cute? I mean, sexy." Val was teasing. Her eyes were laughing.

"I think so."

"You seem hesitant. What's holding you back?"

"A lot of things." I thought of Molly and the defender and felt even more miserable.

She must have seen the pain in my eyes. She smiled very gently and squeezed my arm.

I took another swallow of the cognac. "What about you?" I asked boldly. "Anyone special?"

She nodded a little sheepishly and set her glass aside. "She's a cellist with the Montreal Symphony. She's the one I'm flying off to see."

"Have you known her long?"

"A year or so," she said. "I met her at the University of Saskatchewan. She had brought her string ensemble to entertain the troops in our cultural wasteland. I've been pursuing her somewhat indifferent self since then."

"What's she like?"

Val laughed. "A temptress," she said. She put one hand to her breast, dramatically. "Cleopatra with a cello. A snob—almost a snot. Totally anti-jock. Abhors the odor of the locker room. Is absolutely repelled by sweat. Can you imagine? To us old jocks it's an aphrodisiac. In spite of that she's quite a dish as well as a terrific strain on my long-distance phone bill and frequent-flyer card."

"It sounds serious," I said.

She raised her eyebrows. "Don't say that. It makes me nervous. You're talking to the world's most confirmed bachelor after all."

"Maybe that's what I should be." My words sounded as bitter as I felt. I drained my glass.

Val laughed, a nice clear gleeful laugh. "No, it wouldn't suit you at all. You're definitely the marrying kind, Alison."

The brandy snifter was dangling rather precariously from my fingers. She moved over beside me on the couch, easing the glass from my hand. She put it on the table, then draped her arm around me, pulling my head down to her shoulder. The cognac had relaxed me well beyond the point of protest. Besides, her shoulder felt very comfortable and her body smelled wonderful.

I was awakened sometime later by Val kissing me lightly on the lips.

"Alison," she whispered. "I think I should take you home."

"What time is it?" I snapped upright.

"Just after two. Come," she urged, "I'll walk with you to your car, then drive you home."

"I'm sorry. I shouldn't have drunk so much."

"There's nothing to be sorry about."

She got my coat and helped me into it. Her hands brushed my breasts as she pulled the coat around me and buttoned it.

I walked back to the car in a haze. Val held my hand. I could feel her fine kid gloves through the pedestrian fabric of my woolen mitts. She drove me home, parked the car, walked me right to the elevator door and pushed the button. She said good night, drawing me to her gently and kissing me softly on the lips. Her lips were warm and sensually pliant. I felt embarrassed, knowing mine were chapped and dry. She drew away from me, her eyes sparkling.

"Merry Christmas, Alison."

"Merry Christmas." I backed into the elevator, watching Val's enigmatic smile until it was cut from view by the closed doors.

I didn't realize for a full minute the car wasn't moving. I blushed and pushed the button. I could imagine Val standing in front of the elevator, laughing.

Joy's bedroom door was closed. That was unusual. I washed my face, then went into the kitchen and got a can of root beer. I took the soda to my bedroom and sat down on the bed, feeling very sober and lonely.

I thought of Molly. I imagined her even now in bed in the arms of the Hurricane defender. I lay very still, alert to every gasp and crackle the building made, my eyes wide and staring into the void.

I fell asleep around three-thirty.

I woke at seven with a desperately full bladder and stumbled to the bathroom. Under the cover of the flush, I heard the apartment door open and close.

I surmised with chagrin, Joy had brought a man home. She had never done that before—not even in her randy, insensitive teen-age days.

I felt betrayed. I was filled with revulsion.

Joy's door was open when I came out of the bathroom. I tried to pass by without glancing in but she called out to me.

"Alison."

I stopped in the doorway. "Hi," I said a little stiffly.

Joy was sitting up in bed, propped up on two large pillows, the blanket pulled up just above her breasts. She looked so small and soft and comfortable, my whole body ached.

My discomfort must have shown because she asked, "Are you all right?"

I nodded.

"Are you going back to bed?"

I nodded again, then seeing a flicker of disappointment paused and said, "Did you want a cup of tea?"

"I'd love a cup of tea."

I made the tea good and strong, and brought it to Joy on a small tray with a glass of milk. I handed her the cup and sat down on the bed.

Joy took an appreciative sip. "That's good," she said. She looked a little tired around the eyes, soft and happy too.

I didn't know what to say. I stared into my tea as if I expected the wisdom of Solomon to rise from the dregs.

"I'm in love," Joy said.

I took a sharp breath. "Oh," I said weakly, "that's nice. Who's the lucky guy?"

"Sosnoski," she said.

While I choked on my tea, she stared dreamily off into space. "She undressed me," she said. "In the kitchen, no less. Carried me to the couch and went over my body as if it were a fine racing car. Then she swept me up—I mean swept, as if I were light as a feather—brought me to bed and made the most passionate love to me."

"Sosnoski," I blurted out between wheezes.

Joy nodded. "She's so big, so incredibly soft. I finally know how

Jessica Lange felt with King Kong. It was like being made love to by an enormous soft pillow." Joy sighed. "Imagine, Alison, your breasts engulfed by giant mittens, the softest, warmest most sensuous...," her voice trailed off.

I took a deep breath. It was exquisitely painful. I turned my head away, my cheeks flaming with embarrassment "Joy," I said feebly, "don't do this to this woman."

She looked at me in surprise. "Do what?"

"Use her to satisfy your curiosity, your sense of the outrageous, whatever."

"You don't understand," she said quietly. "I really care for Sharon."

"But you're straight."

"No, I'm not."

I stood up, my head spinning, my face going through all sorts of contortions. Joy patted the bed, beckoning me to sit down again. When I did she snuggled up beside me, holding onto my arm as if she was afraid I might bolt. I sat there, leaning into her at an awkward angle, stiff as a mannequin.

"So," she said, "aren't you going to ask me the obvious? Like why did I marry Robby?"

"Why *did* you marry Robby?"

"I don't know." Her brow wrinkled. "I guess I didn't do a lot of soul-searching in those days. I thought getting screwed silly by the biggest jock on campus was where it was at." She grimaced and squeezed my arm. "I know, I know. I did a lot of that, Alison—even though I had an orgasm every time Jennifer Lawless brushed against my arm. I was Joy Drinkwater, after all, the home-coming queen. I was used to being...normal. I told myself it was a phase I was going through. Still, I knew it was a mistake to marry Robby. I went up the aisle, screaming 'no' in my head. But what could I do at that point? My parents had put out a fortune for the wedding. My friends were thrilled. Everybody was so excited about playing their part in the great heterosexual drama."

I shook my head. By the time I was thirty I was convinced I could spot a lesbian at one hundred paces. Another of my cherished myths shattered. I was about to say that or something equally tasteless when Joy interrupted. She didn't need my response. She was telling her story of a life within a life. I was merely a sounding board.

"I get sick thinking about it now," she said. "About the physical part. Of course, I was so horny in those days I could have made it with a broomstick. And, there was all the excitement—being part of the team, getting so much attention. I was living vicariously through Robby. It was as if I had made it to the NHL myself. Afterwards, when things started to feel wrong, I kept saying: Hell, Joy, you married the wrong man, that's all. All it will take is the right man to get rid of those nagging little whispers in your brain.' I just couldn't get used to being different. I fought the idea as long and as hard as I could. I didn't even like the word 'lesbian'. It sounded…dirty." She paused. "I'm sorry, Alison."

"It's OK."

She was quiet for a moment, then said rather proudly, "Then something happened. I fell in love with a woman. She was the wife of one of Robby's teammates. It was love at first sight. It all seemed very romantic, but in retrospect, it was a real backstreet affair. Together when the guys were on the road, separated when they were home—worse, together as a foursome. Playing the little wifey. It really does make me sick when I think about it." Her grip on my arm tightened. "Then one night we got caught. Robby came home unexpectedly. He'd got into a barroom brawl in St. Louis and hurt his hand. Of course nobody knew about that. The team enforcer took the rap. Nothing happened at first. Robby just took a long look, then stormed out." She paused and swallowed hard.

I waited.

Joy crept a little closer to my side. "The night the team got back to town, Robby showed up. He had my lover's husband with him. They'd already 'looked after' my girlfriend. Now they were going to look after me. Robby pushed me into the bedroom and ripped my clothes off. Then he tried to rape me. At first I thought, what the hell, I've had him in me a hundred times. One more time doesn't matter." She shook her head. "Then I got mad. I said: 'No way!' I brought both fists down hard on his nose. Splayed it all over his face. He swore at me and slugged me in the eye—very hard. Christ, that hurt. I kneed him in the crotch. He rolled off the bed and started to retch. I went out into the living room and told his buddy to scrape him off the floor and get him out of my sight. You should have seen the expression on his face. Robby was out of action for two weeks. He told everybody he'd been rolled in an alley by a bunch of Hell's Angels. I wanted to charge the son of a bitch but my lover talked me out of it. She didn't want any scandal. She asked me to go along with whatever Robby and her husband wanted.

"Robby's lawyer called eventually. They agreed not to compromise my lover. Robby, of course, wasn't all that keen on letting anyone know he had lost his wife to a woman. I agreed to say I was having an affair with another man and he hit me when I told him I was leaving him. I was given a lump sum, under the table—fifty-thousand—in recognition of my years of service as it were. I had to agree to relinquish my claim to everything else. There were all sorts of wild rumors going around—I think Robby and his lawyer started most of them. They made me out to be an out-and-out prostitute, that everybody on the team had had me, that I'd offered myself to practically everybody in the Smythe Division. One of the stories was that I had starred in a hard-core porn film. There are people still looking for that one."

I hung my head, too embarrassed to look at her. I had heard the rumors, some of them more sordid than she could have imagined.

"What happened?" was all I could manage.

She took a deep breath. "Well, when the initial excitement subsided, I got in touch with my lover. We met at a little coffee shop in Victoria, would you believe, across the water and far away. She said it was over. She'd just come to say good bye. I guess the…violence she'd gone through had destroyed her feelings for me. What could I say? What had happened hadn't exactly set us up for a great life together."

"No, I guess not."

"About a year later, she got a quiet divorce and moved to Montreal. She's from Montreal originally. She got involved with the lesbian scene there. I hear she's in a nice relationship. Anyway, I lost her. I lost everything. My government contract wasn't renewed. I guess I wasn't considered a great asset in the PR field. They offered me, instead, a minor administrative position with the Department of Motor Vehicles—working out of a basement in Prince George. Later they transferred me to another basement in Vancouver."

The bastards! "Why didn't you let me know. I could have helped someway. At least I could have given you a shoulder to cry on."

She shrugged. "I think I was a little bit afraid you'd turn against me."

"But why?"

"Sometimes lesbians act strange when their straight friends turn out to be gay. I didn't want to put any strain on our friendship. I knew

I'd tell you sooner or later...then I met Sharon." Joy stopped, smiling. "I couldn't believe it. I was shocked. I never thought I'd be attracted to a woman like Sharon. Big butchy dyke! I thought I was strictly the model/stewardess type. But one look at Sharon and that was it. It wasn't easy mind you. I tried the subtle approach. Nothing. Then I said, 'What the hell'. I threw myself at her like a bankrupt whore. Got sloppy drunk at La Bomba and felt up her biceps. The day she came to fix the sink, I put on my bathrobe and leaned over her as she worked. She just stared straight ahead and kept talking about seals and washers. I had her check everything in the apartment that even remotely resembled plumbing. Christ, Alison, I'm embarrassed to think what I did. I spent too many years in the straight world, playing games. Finally I swallowed my pride—my stupidity—and asked for her. And it worked."

I gave her shoulder a self-conscious squeeze. "I'm sorry I wrecked things by going to the bathroom."

Joy smiled. "You didn't wreck anything. I don't think she had any intention of being here in the morning when you woke up. I think she was embarrassed at the idea of confronting you directly after bedding me."

"I'm really glad for you," I said.

She looked at me for a long moment, then said, "I know you left with Val last night."

I nodded, then shook my head as she quizzed me with a raised eyebrow. She grimaced.

"She's a nice woman, Alison. She's obviously fond of you."

"She's fond of a lot of women." I shrugged and said quietly, "I'm fond of her too. But trying to have a relationship with Val would be like being Mrs. Casanova."

"Something purely sexual then," she said.

I shrugged. "I don't want a fling."

"It's been three and a half years, Alison. That's a long time."

I thought of Molly lying in the arms of the Hamilton defender, perhaps even now engaged in a playful tussle of the morning after kind. I imagined Molly naked, laughing, then, breath quickening, in the throes of orgasm.

Joy looked at me quizzically. "What's the matter?"

"Nothing." I yawned stiffly. "Just tired."

"Why not go back to sleep? I'll wake you at noon for lunch."

"Can't. I've got to shower and pack. I promised Pat and Toddy we'd be on the road by ten."

I sat with her while she finished her tea, a thousand thoughts going through my mind, searching backwards for something I had missed. The only thing that struck me was that Joy never broke a date with a woman friend to go out with a man.

"What are you thinking about?"

"Nothing." I got up with a sigh. "Just that you picked yourself a winner."

And that was the truth.

I took a quick shower and packed. Pat called at nine-thirty to see if everything was on schedule. She and Toddy were packed and champing at the bit.

Joy got out of bed to see me off.

"Have a nice Christmas, Alison," she said. She melted into my arms like a small soft kitten.

"You too," I said. I hugged her again.

I stepped out into the hall, closing the door gently behind me. Everyone was either gone or in the process of going. Julia was catching a bus to Detroit. She dropped her suitcase to give me a big warm hug. Harriett was driving her to the station, then heading off to Ajax. Carol was waiting for her younger sister to pick her up on her way through from Guelph. They would drive to Kingston together. Lou and Henny and Ingrid were driving down home together. Ingrid's nifty Saab was parked ahead of my battered heap. Dorsey was catching a train to London at noon. Effie and Joey had taken a flight to Brandon, Manitoba that morning. They would spend the holidays with Effie's family.

Faint music came from under the door of Molly's apartment.

I ran down the steps into the lobby. Pat and Toddy were waiting by the mailboxes, surrounded by a mountain of suitcases and packages. On impulse, I threw the keys to Pat and said, "Pack up, Patty. I'll be back in a minute."

Ingrid was just getting out of the elevator as I rushed back through the door, looking relaxed and sassy in a Nordic sweater, blue jeans and cowboy boots.

"Meet us at the McDonald's for breakfast," she called to me as we passed ten feet apart. "Hey, it'll be the last time I see you before

Christmas."

"OK."

As an afterthought she came back, took me in her arms, kissed me very firmly on the lips, grinned and said, "Merry Christmas, Alison. I'd probably get arrested if I tried that in a hamburger joint."

I pirouetted into the elevator.

The music was still sifting from under the door of Molly's apartment. I knocked tentatively.

Molly opened the door almost immediately. She was wearing blue jeans and a black T-shirt several sizes too large, slipping low to one shoulder to reveal the line of her collarbone.

"Hi," I said uncomfortably, "I'm just heading out. I wanted to wish everyone Merry Christmas before I left." I was having trouble keeping my eyes off the collarbone.

"Thanks." Her smile was enigmatic. She stepped aside hesitantly. "Would you like to come in?"

"Sure," I said shrilly, "just for a minute." I had visions of Pat and Toddy fretting in the car below.

She wandered off into the center of the room. I followed. We stood there for a moment, gazing at the balcony. Neither of us seemed to know what was supposed to happen next.

"Can I get you a drink?" she asked suddenly.

I demurred. "No, no thanks. I just stopped to say Merry Christmas and to see if you needed a ride anywhere—bus, train, airport."

She was staring at the floor, one hand resting against the back of Effie's old easy chair. I was struck again by the beauty of her hands.

"Thanks," she said quickly. "That's very kind of you. But it's OK. I'm staying here."

"Here?"

I must have looked as shocked as I sounded because she added. "Here in Toronto. What I mean is, my family is coming here."

"Oh," I said, relieved. "Will they be staying here at the apartment?"

"No, a hotel. They'll get a suite. That's what they usually do."

I nodded. "Good, that sounds good."

"Yes." She continued to stare at the floor, her face reddening. Finally, after an uncomfortable silence, she said, "Would you like to see Sam?"

"Sure."

The room she led me into was as surgically stark as Effie had described. Sam's cage, however, was bright and lively, decorated with red and green bows and pine cones. Molly had placed a small Christmas tree within her line of vision. Sam looked fat and sassy and quite indifferent to what were obviously loving preparations.

"Sam is an old friend of mine," she said, apparently feeling an explanation was in order.

I put my finger against the cage. Sam stood up on her hind legs and wrapped both tiny paws around it, her nose working convulsively. Molly watched with that expression mothers use when you examine their infants.

"She likes you," she said. "She usually bites Effie."

"Does she ever get out?" I asked, mesmerized by the soft little paws that alternately squeezed and released my finger.

"I take her out every day but I think she feels safer inside."

I nodded. Safe in a cage with lots of love and all your food brought in. The scene struck me as distressingly familiar. "I don't blame her," I said.

Carsey and Toddy started up a tune on the horn. The rhythm sounded fairly indecent.

"I have to go," I said reluctantly. "I'm being paged."

Molly followed me to the door. I wanted desperately to give her a big hug. After an awkward pause I cleared my throat and said, "Merry Christmas, Molly."

She leaned forward suddenly and gave me a quick awkward peck on the cheek. Then, with head down, she said, "Drive safely."

I nodded and backed out the door, then with a quick smile and a wave turned away toward the elevator.

I got into the elevator, my heart wanting me to go back in the worst way. *Molly,* I could imagine myself saying, *I want to spend Christmas with you.*

Well, I wouldn't be doing that. I knew what else I wouldn't be doing. I wouldn't be with my family this year. After weeks of constant nagging Mom had persuaded Dad to leave the farm in the care of the hired man for a few days. Everyone was going to visit my younger sister in Fredericton. I knew what that would be like—wall-to-wall kids (my nephews), sticky candy canes and mountains of discarded wrapping paper. Part of me wanted it. Another part didn't. The part that wanted it was standing in line at Pearson International Airport. The part of me that didn't was headed for Kingston. Still another part of me clung morosely to the gloomy hallway outside the door of Molly Gavison's apartment, holding the memory of that fleeting brush of her lips against my skin, the expression in her eyes as Sam gave me her seal of approval.

But the warning bells were gonging in my head. She's not good for you, Alison. Stay clear of her. Keep it professional. She's crazy. God knows what else. She's spent the last couple of years strung out on drugs. That's what they say, isn't it? Even Dale Yalden says that and he's a fan. She dyes her hair purple. She has a tattoo of two women "doing it" on her butt. She shuts herself off from the world and talks to a hamster. Of course she's crazy. I'm in love with her. Pause. It must be physical attraction. Lust. Pause. She tears my heart out.

"Hey, Alison, this is our exit."

I darted across three lanes and made the exit. Pat said, "Yikes!" Toddy said, "Way to drive, Coach."

The trip to Kingston turned into a nightmare. Shortly after we left McDonald's we ran into an unexpected blizzard that followed us through to Belleville. The center line of the 401 East was obliterated. I hunched over the steering wheel, peering into the whiteout, depending on the tail lights of the car ahead to guide me.

Pat had brought a ton of packages for her mother-in-law and the kids. As the snow deepened she clutched them tighter and tighter.

I pulled off the highway near Trenton at the Chicken Villa and treated everyone to coffee and donuts. Ten minutes later Ingrid pulled in. Together, we waited for the remainder of the storm to pass.

I dropped off Toddy and Pat and went home to Landlady and Mandy. Mandy met me at the door. I gave her a hug and handed her my bag of gifts.

"I'm sorry I didn't get the one you asked for," I said, referring to the first place in the standings she had hoped for. "We did our best."

"It's OK," she said.

I knew she didn't entirely mean it.

"I'm glad you're going to be here, Alison," said Landlady. "With my sister away it would be, otherwise, a sparse Christmas." She used the word "sparse" with indifference as if she meant "boring". She really meant "lonely". She said it, also, looking at me as if she knew I had an empty space in my heart that wasn't going to be filled. Not this Christmas.

I went into Landlady's kitchen and had hot chocolate and cinnamon toast and shook the chill from my bones. We made shortbread. We decorated the tree. We cracked walnuts. We did all the things you're supposed to do Christmas Eve and at eleven we went down to city hall and sang Christmas carols with Landlady's feminist glee club. "God Rest Ye Merry Gentlewomen" worked quite well. "We Three Queens" didn't have quite the same ring to it but did earn a smattering of applause from a group of passing leatherboys.

As the songs tumbled out through the swirling snow, I felt my heart torn in all directions.

I saw a grudging Nomi at midnight mass, wedged in firmly between dour older brother and wide-eyed younger brother. I saw Julia with her big family in East Lansing. I saw Pat hanging stockings for the kids, taking a break with her mother-in-law over some coffee and Christmas cake. I saw Joy slouching in front of the fireplace at her grandparents' beautiful country home, her mind a million miles away in some wonderful snow-filled lane, buried deep in Sosnoski's big overcoat. I saw Molly, red-cheeked and graceful, under the amber lighting of the ritziest of the ritzy downtown hotels, eating caviar, speaking French, talking about music, her green eyes sparkling, her lips curved, the light washing her face and neck in a rosy tan, picking up the fine soft hairs along her forehead and neck. I sighed, a creaky sigh of longing and covered it hastily with a cough. Mandy squeezed near me and took my hand in both of hers.

CHAPTER 11

When I got back to Toronto, I found out that Nomi Pereira had been traded to the Detroit Dynamos for their first-string goalie. The letter bearing the news was on my desk when I arrived at the Mussyford.

I phoned Phil immediately. He was in a meeting, and according to Mrs. Toop, refused to be disturbed. I asked if she knew about the trade.

"Of course," she said, unconcerned.

I asked if she knew anything else. Why, for example.

"Players get traded all the time," she said. "The girl was properly notified. Mr. Tweddell sent her a letter by courier first thing this morning."

I felt like slamming the receiver down in her ear. If she had been in the same room with me, I would have wrung her scrawny old neck.

The dressing room was like a tomb. Most of the players were in the weight room, honoring the old baseball adage: nobody wants to watch another player clean out her locker. Sosnoski sat on a bench, going through the pretense of lacing a skate, trying to hide her tear-stained cheeks. Dorsey sat very still, holding a stick across her knees, a strange frozen smile on her face. I noticed her eyes glistened. I went into the weight room. The other players looked at me and shook their heads.

"Why?" asked Ingrid.

"I don't know," I said, ashamed.

There were no other questions. They looked at me expectantly. Clearly they thought I should do something.

"Excuse me," I said.

I marched back to my office and called Phil.

Mrs Toop greeted me icily. "I'm sorry, Alison—as I've told you, he can't be disturbed."

"Disturb him," I said through clenched teeth. "Or I'll do it for you."

Phil was on the line within seconds. "I'm into it with the accountant," he said in a low, aggrieved voice.

"I don't care. I want to know what in hell is going on with Nomi Pereira."

He turned angry. "Forget Pereira. She's gone."

"I want to know why."

"Don't argue with me. Do as I say. I want her in Detroit today. She's got until two to report." He slammed the receiver down hard.

I hung up, stunned and sat for several minutes, staring at the ink blotter on my desk. Finally, I forced myself to stand up, and on rather wobbly legs, made my way to the dressing room.

Nomi had just finished packing her gear. I took her by the shoulders and shook her. "Don't you have a no-trade clause in your contract?" I was close to tears.

"Nope."

"Why in hell not? I told you all to insist upon it in camp." I dug my fingers into her arms so hard she flinched.

"Didn't know if I was going to like everybody. I thought I'd wait and see."

"Nomi!" I broke down completely. I tried to hug her. She wouldn't give. She held herself away, rigid as a board.

I bundled her into my car and pulled away from the Mussyford, choking with tears. She sat beside me, tight-lipped and sullen.

When we arrived at the Aero, I tried to help her with her gear. I tried again to hug her. She took the bag from me at the entrance, said, "So long," and walked away from me toward the locker room. I drove back to Toronto feeling as empty as a milkweed pod in November. It was after six when I got back to the Mussyford. Sharon was still in the dressing room when I arrived. "She can't read," she said.

"You mean, she's illiterate!"

Sharon nodded. "When they handed her the contract, she signed where she saw the *X*. There wasn't any *X* beside the no-trade clause and they didn't bother pointing it out to her."

"I thought her brother was going with her for the negotiations."

Sharon shrugged. "Yeah, he was supposed to but they had a big fight the day before, so she went alone."

I didn't sleep a wink that night.

Phil called the apartment before nine the next morning. "The trade's off," he said. "Pereira's been notified."

My heart leapt with joy. "Phil, I don't know what to say. How did you do it?"

"Look," he said, "don't thank me too much." He sounded uncomfortable. I imagined him sitting at his desk, plucking peevishly at the ends of his mustache. "The trade was arranged through Dad. The majority owner of the Dynamos is an old pal of his. It seems the old bugger made an ass of himself at the Christmas party and put the moves on the Dynamos' goalie. The wife found out and threw a fit, demanded he get rid of the goalie. Now, the wife's changed her mind. She's embarrassed at all the fuss. Figures she made too big a thing of it. Maybe she just wants things where she can keep an eye on them. I don't know. Anyway, the trade's off."

If I had been in the same room with Phil at that moment, I would have choked him with his own "Made-in-Canada" paisley tie.

"You put us through this grief because your Dad's pal can't keep his zipper fastened?" I said with controlled fury.

There was a long pause. "Welcome to show biz, Alison," Phil said quietly. He waited for a few seconds, then hung up.

I called Pierre Deschamps and made arrangements to pick Nomi up. Then I drove like hell to Detroit.

Nomi was waiting for me at the door to the arena, champing hard on a wad of gum. I offered to take her equipment bag but she jerked it away from me. She carried it to the car and stuffed it into the trunk.

When we were in the car, I turned to her and said, "Nice to have you back, stranger."

She threw herself into my arms, sobbing as if her heart would break.

Three minutes later she tore herself from me, wiped her nose on her sleeve and said, "Don't tell nobody nothing."

We arrived at the Mussyford just as the afternoon workout finished. The players stormed into the dressing room to celebrate our return. Nomi accepted this display of emotion with grumpy stoicism.

Dorsey had hung off to the side while all the hugging and kissing was going on, staring at Nomi in the strangest way. When the crowd had dispersed she sidled up to her and said in a low growl, "So, what'd you pick up in Detroit?"

"Nothing," said Nomi. She gave Dorsey a hard stare. "Not even a good case of the crabs."

CHAPTER 12

After the trade debacle I thought I deserved a long period of tranquillity. It was not to be.

Two weeks later we played the O'Brien's at the Civic Center. The following Monday I got a call from Phil. He sounded as if he had just swallowed a very bitter pill.

"Alison," he said, "we've got trouble. Big trouble."

"Either you can't make the payroll or the Zamboni at Varsity has broken down."

"I wish it was that simple," he said, unmoved by my attempt at humor. "I've canceled an appointment for you. I'll see you in half an hour."

"Phil, I've got practice in half an hour."

"Be here," he said. He hung up before I could object further.

Phil was sitting at his desk, twitching the ends of his mustache and looking extremely hard-done-by. He motioned me to sit down.

"I've just spent an hour with Alice Todd's mother," he said by way of opening the conversation. "She was camped out on my doorstep when I arrived at the office this morning."

I looked at him blankly. "Alice's mother?"

"Yes, he said very precisely. He paused, coughed dryly and said, "It seems Alice didn't come home until Sunday."

"I know," I said. I felt suddenly on the defensive and didn't know why. "She stayed over in Ottawa with her cousin. She's done that before."

"She arrived home Sunday afternoon," Phil said as if he hadn't heard me. "Just in time to have dinner and catch her ride to Toronto."

"She came with me," I said, bewildered. "She always does."

Phil paused, pressing his lips tightly together as if he found my interruptions unfortunate and painful. "Anyway," he said, "she was in such a hurry, she didn't have time for dessert. So, while she was brushing her teeth or whatever, Mrs. Todd decided to bundle up a little care package of goodies and hide them in her bag as a surprise."

"Yes?" Phil was drawing his story out deliberately, trying to drive me to distraction. For some reason he seemed to feel I deserved punishment.

"Know what she found?" He looked at me, sudden and hurt.

"Why, no," I said, caught off guard by his sneak attack. My God, I thought, the kid's smoking pot.

"This." He reached into his desk drawer and took out a crumpled envelope. He slammed it down on the desk in front of me. "And this." He took a small book from the same drawer and tossed it toward me.

I stared at the title, agape.

He settled back in his chair, plucking peevishly at his ink blotter. "Is it yours?"

"No!" I picked the book up as if it were burning at the edges. "I've never owned a copy of *Lesbian Love Sonnets* in my life."

"Alice's mother thinks you or one of your girls has been playing house with her daughter. She wants to create a big stink, Alison. Damn it," he said, "I know this stuff goes on on girls' teams. But a seventeen-year-old? Jesus Christ!"

"I don't—"

"It's not *just* the book," he said. "I mean, there are all kinds of excuses for having a book. But there's the letter to account for—a very suggestive love note I am told."

"You mean you haven't read it?" I said, proud of my ability to show disgust in spite of the numb feeling in my brain.

"Of course not," he said. He paused, then said with annoyance, "Oh, I tried to figure out the signature. But it looks like some kind of pet name."

"Pet name?"

"Honey or something," he muttered. "The point is, I can't identify who the letter is from."

"Well, why in hell didn't Alice's mother just speak to Alice."

"She tried. Alice won't tell her anything. She's refused her calls." He shifted uncomfortably. "Alice's mother is afraid to go near the apartment building. She feels it might be ...er...a hostile environment."

"She's afraid some big dyke will jump out and break her nose?"

"Well, she didn't say that."

So Toddy's a baby dyke, I thought. I checked a smile. "So what do you want me to do about this, Phil? It seems to me this is Toddy's private business."

"She's only seventeen," he said glumly. "Her mother had to co-sign her contract. We have a special responsibility for her. You agreed to that. That's why she's bunking with Pat Carsey. That's why we keep a solicitous eye on her."

"Whoever she's involved with, Phil," I said, "I can assure you it's not one of her teammates. The players dote on her. They're very protective. They..."

Phil interrupted. "Her cousin says it was a player. She won't say which one but she confirms Alice spent the weekend with a hockey player. A *female* hockey player."

"What do you want me to do? Poll the team?"

He looked at me, exasperated. Apparently, I wasn't approaching this situation in the right spirit. "Mrs. Todd wants us to get to the bottom of this," he said. "She's threatening to cause a lot of trouble. She's threatening to take Alice home if we don't come up with some answers. Hell, Alison, if there's any fuss, we'll have to let her go. We can't have this kind of scandal."

"Phil this is just a mother's reaction to finding out her daughter is a lesbian."

He shrugged. "Probably."

"Then we should let them work it out between them. Why involve the whole organization?"

"Because that's the way Mrs. Todd wants it. As far as she's concerned, some big bull dyke on our team jumped her daughter and made her a lesbian. That's the mind-set you've got to respond to." He slumped in his chair, looking helpless and defeated. "Alison, you've got to handle this."

I stared at him across the desk. He looked like a craven rodent— a mouse in suspenders. I succumbed.

"Oh, all right. I'll do it for Toddy's sake. But I'm not conducting an inquisition."

"Damn," he said, totally deflated, "what a mess."

I didn't respond.

"I don't care if Alice Todd is a lesbian," he said. "You know I've never made a big issue about that sort of thing, though"—he shrugged—"she sure fooled me. She certainly doesn't look like a lesbian."

"What do you mean by that, Phil?"

He measured me uneasily. "Well, you know...she's really pretty. Kind of feminine. She gets her hair done."

"Where does that leave me?"

"Well you're...oh, come on, Alison," he said, annoyed. He got up from his chair and went to stand at the window, giving me his hard-working tycoon, boy-wonder-surveying-the-city-he's-conquered look. "You know how many seats there are at the Mussyford?"

"Sure. Eight thousand plus."

"Nine thousand one hundred and fifty-three. Next year—if we're still around—we'll have the Mussyford and we'll fill every seat."

"Of course..."

He interrupted hastily. "You have to remember, though, we're selling a product. We're after a certain market. Our product's got to be suitable for that market." He took a turn around the office, hands stuffed in pockets. "Do you remember that article *The Star* did on Alice?"

"Yes."

"Well, it got a big response. All sorts of letters. Do you know who most of them were from?"

I shook my head.

"Teen-age boys," he said with triumph. "That's a market we haven't even begun to exploit. I asked my nephews. They think Alice Todd is cute, really sexy. Teen-age boys. That's the group she appeals to."

"Teen-age boys and middle-age men with bizarre power fantasies," I murmured.

There was a pregnant pause. Clearly I was to understand I had tried his patience to the limit.

"The point I want to make," he said, "is that this business with Alice has to be resolved quickly. I want Mrs. Todd to go home happy. I want Alice on our team. I want everybody happy. I don't care what Alice Todd does in bed as long as her appearance and behavior leaves some teensy margin for doubt."

Before I could protest he said, "This is your problem, Alison. Deal with it. Mrs. Todd's staying at the Chelsea. She expects an answer tomorrow."

"I see."

"And she wants to see her daughter."

"Great."

"Well." He sat down in his chair, slapping his palms down on his desk, obviously relieved to have this unappetizing morsel off his plate. "I guess you'd better get to work, Alison."

By the time I reached the Mussyford, the players had finished practice and were in bathing suits for the morning swim. I sidled up to Toddy as inconspicuously as possible.

"I need to talk to you after the swim."

"What about?" she mumbled.

"Personal stuff," I said.

She turned and ran off after her teammates. "Hey, Ingrid, wait for me."

Fight or flight—the typical response of the teen-ager under duress. I'm not cut out to be a mother. I looked at Pat Carsey, looming invitingly large and mother-like in the corner. No, this was a coach's job. On second thought—it was a big sister's job.

Toddy was waiting for me by the water fountain in the foyer, pretending to be examining the swim-club trophies in the cabinet opposite.

"Come on," I said as cheerfully as possible, "let's get something to eat."

I led her to the car, making nervous small talk. I drove to the nearest Tim Horton's, went in and loaded up on sandwiches, donuts and coffee.

I was trying to decide the best way to broach the delicate subject when Toddy said, "I guess Mom's been talking to you."

"She talked to Phil." I said. "He talked to me." I handed her the book and the letter.

She groaned. "Why did she have to bring Phil into this?"

"I don't know."

She slumped down in the seat, folding her arms sullenly.

"It's nobody's business. I didn't do anything wrong."

"That's not how your mother sees it."

For a moment she looked very defiant. Then her posture relaxed and she said, with surprising calm, "Alison, it has nothing to do with anybody on the team. I've told her that."

"She doesn't believe you."

"It's none of her business. Why is she doing this to me?"

"Because she's your mother. Because she's afraid you'll get hurt. Because she had dreams about white dresses and big church weddings."

Toddy flushed and looked away. "I've told her before there won't be any weddings," she said. "And, she doesn't have to worry about me getting hurt. What more does she want?"

I shook my head. "She wants a name, I guess, a face she can relate to."

"Well, I can't tell her. She'd cause too much trouble for..." She paused and looked at me pleadingly. "Alison, I'll tell you if you promise not to tell. Then you'll know it's all right."

"OK."

"It's Willie deGroot," she said with pride.

"Willie." I started to smile. Willie deGroot played for the O'Brien's. At nineteen, she was the second youngest player in the league.

"I met her when we did that interview for *The Citizen*."

"I see."

"You can't tell anyone. Connie Siebart would have Willie thrown off the team."

"I won't."

"We're in love," she said.

I called Toddy's mother after dinner that night. She agreed tersely to meet with me early the next morning. She insisted on meeting at the Chelsea—on her turf. I took Toddy with me, also by agreement.

Mrs. Todd opened the door on the first knock. She barely looked at me. Toddy barely looked at her. She had ordered coffee and had arranged chairs around an occasional table which she had moved to the window. The curtains, unfortunately, were tightly drawn. Never had I so longed for a view of Yonge Street.

"How are you Alice?" she asked. Her tone was terribly formal.

Toddy looked down. "I'm all right," she mumbled.

I gave her a short, pleading look then forged ahead."Mrs. Todd," I said, "I've talked to Toddy...er...Alice and I can assure you none of this...business...involves any member of our team."

She swallowed as though she had a sore throat.

"Then who, does it involve?"

I gave her my best Pollyanna smile and said, "The young woman in question is just that. Not much older than Alice and very respectable."

There was a lengthy silence.

"Miss Gutherie," she said finally, "I have no doubt the girl is respectable from the view of a particular lifestyle. That doesn't mean I want my daughter exposed to that lifestyle. It's clear to me now, whether any of the women on your team are involved or not, they have set an unhealthy example."

I swallowed my considerable irritation. "Mrs. Todd," I said, "this is a once-in-a-lifetime opportunity for Alice. She's making history. She's a pioneer—the youngest woman in the WPHL. She has a good chance to be on the first championship team."

"Then there's her education to consider," Mrs. Todd said as if she hadn't heard. "I've never been comfortable with Alice's decision to postpone her education."

"Mom, we agreed!"

I shot Toddy a warning glance.

"Mrs. Todd, playing for the Teddies is no barrier to her education. There's an..." I stopped.

Mrs. Todd was staring at the floor, jaw set. She wasn't paying the slightest attention to me. "I've come to a decision," she said.

I had a feeling she'd come to her decision before we arrived. "Yes?"

"Alice will continue to play with the team but she will move in with a friend of mine—Betty Glossner."

"Mom!" Toddy started to complain.

I put my hand on her wrist to silence her. "Shh. Wait until your mother has had her say."

Mrs. Todd gave me a curt, prim nod. "Thank you," she said. "Alice will report for practices and games," she continued. "Otherwise, she'll spend her time with the Glossners. I will have to depend on you to chaperone her on road trips. I'll speak to Mr. Tweddell to ensure that's understood."

Toddy was rolling her eyes. I knew this arrangement was not going to work.

"The Glossners have a fine family," said Mrs.Todd, her voice now firm with confidence. "They have three boys, two of them in their late teens. I think the male influence will be good for Alice. Perhaps it will arrest this aberration."

The red flag that Mrs. Todd had been fluttering coyly at the corner of my eye dropped like a theatrical curtain.

"Toddy," I said, clearing my throat, "would you wait for me in the coffee shop?"

Mrs. Todd started to protest but Toddy was up and out of the door in a flash. I waited until I heard the elevator door shut before speaking.

"Mrs. Todd," I said, "I could sympathize with you if Alice had been seduced by an unscrupulous woman, an opportunist, whatever her age. But that's not the case. What we have here are two young kids involved in what is in all likelihood their first affair."

"Why, I don't see..."

"This isn't about Alice being hurt or in danger or in any way emotionally or psychologically compromised," I said. "This is about you not being able to accept the fact your daughter's a lesbian. I can understand that, given your upbringing, but Alice's sexuality has nothing to do with her surroundings. You can put her alone in the middle of the Gobi desert and she'll still be a lesbian. She'll just be a lot less happy. Taking her away from the team isn't going to solve anything."

"But I want her to be with men!" Mrs. Todd stared at me wide-eyed and bewildered. "Why, if when she's thirty or some such responsible age she decides she wants to live that way, I can't do very much about it. But I want her to at least give men a try—a good try, a fair try—to make sure she's making the correct decision."

I struggled to keep my voice even. "You'd prefer her to learn about her sexuality through casual alliances with men than through an affectionate relationship with a woman?"

"This woman..."

"This woman, Mrs. Todd, is an innocent child—just like your daughter."

"Still..."

"You'd rather have Alice learn about her sexuality in the back seat of a car with some asshole teen-age male stabbing wildly in the dark," I said.

"Please!" Mrs. Todd recoiled, cheeks flaming.

"Than with a young woman who buys her gifts and writes her love letters."

"But it's not normal."

I lowered my voice, moving in for the kill. "Than with a young woman who loves her, who won't get her pregnant, and who is unlikely to expose her to any one of several wonderful sexually-transmitted diseases."

"What..."

"Gonorrhea, syphilis, chlamydia."

"But..."

"You're willing to expose your teen-age daughter to all these good things because you can't handle her sexuality."

"The Glossner boys—"

"Oh, are you going to have the Glossner boys and their friends checked out or do you assume that nice, middle-class boys don't get girls pregnant and give them clap?"

"I have no intention of altering my plan." She sprung forward in her seat. "You just don't see, do you? You people...how can a young woman possibly arrive at an understanding of her sexuality without knowing the other side."

I was by now totally out of control. I knew that because I was starting to talk like Landlady. "So, you think female sexuality is defined by men."

She sat back, agape.

"And how many men did it take to define your sexuality? One, two, seventy, several hundred? How many did it take, Mrs. Todd? And did you try a woman just to make sure?"

"I will have you know, Mr. Todd..." She was babbling incomprehensibly and looking at me in abject horror.

I knew I had gone too far. I had blown it. I mumbled some sort of farewell and bolted.

Toddy was waiting anxiously in the coffee shop. "How did it go?" she asked as I dropped into the chair across from her.

I took a deep breath. "Well, I think you'll be allowed to stay with the team," I said, "but I might have to go."

"I guess I'd better go see her," said Toddy. She got up and trudged off to the elevator.

I sat for what seemed forever, chewing on cold toast and staring over the ugly sludge-filled street.

Finally—about an hour later—Toddy reappeared. She slid into the chair opposite me and ordered fresh coffee from the perplexed waitress.

"It's OK," she said. "There won't be any more trouble."

"Thank God," I said. "I'm sorry I was so rough on her but—"

Toddy shook her head. "That's not what settled the issue. I just told her I wouldn't come home anymore and she'd never see me again."

"Blackmail?"

She nodded.

"And she gave in?"

"Yeah." Toddy moistened her lips. "She said it was OK. I could do what I wanted. She said as far as she's concerned, it's OK if I never come home."

"Oh."

Toddy started to cry. I reached across the table and took her hand. She cried. I cried. We held hands. The rest of the patrons looked on in sympathy. After a tearful ten minutes, I said, "Do you want to give her another try?"

Toddy shook her head.

We left the restaurant together, forlorn.

CHAPTER 13

I felt very fragile after that, after almost losing Nomi and Toddy, even more protective and emotionally involved with my team. Life seemed dangerous outside the game, ready to interfere with us, waylay us, cut us loose from our moorings.

Only the bus felt safe. Nothing outside seemed as real or as pure. Once on board time stood still. We were encapsulated, cut off and protected from the rest of the world. I wished the vehicle could sprout wings, take off, soar and never come back.

We were chugging out of Buffalo, bruised but victorious. The carburetor was acting up and Harriett handled the bus with kid gloves to avoid stalling it at every intersection.

"Get me out of here," she muttered at one point.

I didn't feel like talking. I snuggled down in my seat, closed my eyes and absorbed the life around me.

Julia and Pat were deep in conversation. They were discussing art and philosophy and international events. Pat didn't understand half of what Julia was saying but she was interested. She stayed with her, listening diligently.

Sharon and Joy sat behind me, talking oh so quietly. They'd been very discreet about their relationship but they couldn't deny their passion. It seeped through the seat cushions like a hot wind. From time to time their conversation drifted into a profound silence. I knew, under the cover of darkness, they were kissing.

Molly lay on the back bench seat as usual, stretched out, arms flung over her head, close enough for me to touch. The gulf that separated me from Molly was far wider than any aisle or any bank of seats.

Effie was telling her story. It was one of those small vignettes of life that helped us keep our bearings in this somewhat topsy-turvy world.

"I dropped my broccoli on my way home from the A&P. I guess my cart was too full and it fell out. Do you suppose anyone said anything? Did anyone say: 'Hey, you, you dropped your broccoli'? Not a soul! When I got home and found it missing, naturally I retraced my steps. It was lying on the grass beside the exit ramp. I had to pick it up with hundreds of people looking on. I expected someone to yell: 'Hey, you, do you always find your groceries on sidewalks?'"

Effie's voice rose higher and higher as the story progressed, ending with a squeak on the punch line. Everyone laughed except Lou.

"Hey," she said, "is that the broccoli you fed me for dinner the other night?"

The voices rose and fell, snippets of conversation and feeling. I was riddled by the emotions around me—Ingrid's easy, earthy sexuality, Sosnoski's slow burn, the intense, savage denial and blunt sensuality between Dorsey and Nomi, my own impotent, confused feelings for Molly Gavison.

After the New Year, the season seemed to take wings and escape from me. I tried to slow it down. I wanted to savor the good stuff—every minute of it—but it kept getting away from me, buried under a mountain of trivia.

We blew London out at home. The next day after practice I wandered into Willard's. Dale was behind the bar. He plunked down a Blue Light without asking.

I handed him the envelope. "Dale, thanks. It was well-written."

He acknowledged my compliment with a curt nod and stuck the envelope on a shelf under the bar.

I watched him for a moment, then said, "You know, one thing I don't understand. I have trouble reconciling the excitement, the charisma with—" I tried to sound noncommittal but my sentence ended in a nervous laugh. "This Molly seems so different—subdued, reclusive, almost—"

"Well…" Dale sighed and paused to slide a whisky and soda to a regular patron halfway down the bar. "What you've got to understand is what you've got is a shell. The old Molly Gavison was as open as a book, wore her heart on her sleeve. She left herself open for all kinds of hurt and she got it. I don't blame her for shutting the door."

"But it's a shame after what she's been."

I'd obviously struck a raw nerve. "Don't try to be a shrink," he said. "Just let her play hockey. She's had enough people messing around with her life, wanting a piece of her. Give her a break."

"OK," I said, taken aback by his vehemence. "Sure, that's fair."

"Yeah, just let her be," he mumbled. "It's better that way." He bent over the counter, his face reddening with annoyance, rubbing the wood with his towel. Finally, he looked up at me, his anger dissipated. "So that's a great line you've got there with Dorsey Thorne and Molly. I'm looking forward to using those tickets you left for me."

CHAPTER 14

It was a rare three-game week. We played the Hurricanes at the Copps Coliseum, entertained the Lambs at Varsity, picked up an automatic two points, then headed down to Buffalo.

It was Friday night and the Buffalo players were restless, as eager as we were to get away for the weekend.

The noise of the crowd hovered over us like a swarm of angry bees. Mauler Mason had succeeded in creating an illusion of "bad blood" here. The game was only five minutes old and already sticks were flying. By the ten-minute mark it was clear the referee had lost control of the game. Dorsey took an elbow in the head. She retaliated by hooking the skates out from under the Buffalo defender. The crowd roared. The referee ignored the infractions but moments later sent Nomi to the penalty box when an enterprising Belle took a dive in front of her. Nomi slapped the ice with her stick and earned a ten-minute misconduct. I glanced at Joy in the net and prayed she wouldn't get injured for the next few minutes. I hadn't played goal since I was a kid on the pond.

The Belles were after Molly from the opening face-off. Mason egged them on. He yelled at her. He called the players to the bench for a time out and pointed at her. He held her in his imaginary gun sights.

Molly streaked up ice with Dorsey back. She cut toward the net, drew the goalie, then flipped the puck to Dorsey who whipped it past the Buffalo netminder in one fluid motion. The Belles were on Molly at once, driving her into the boards. The referee's attention was directed to the net, confirming the goal.

Molly lay in the corner, writhing and gasping. She tried to get up, then fell back to the ice, clutching her midsection.

Harriett grabbed her bag and ran out onto the ice. The players crowded around, forming a curtain of privacy.

I had my foot on the bench, ready to vault over the boards. I think I was about to make a fool of myself. Maybe it had something to do with what I yelled at the referee but Sharon stood up suddenly, blocking my exit with her left arm.

"She's probably winded," she said.

Nomi had left the penalty box.

Molly began to stir in the corner. Through the screen of the players I saw Harriett help her to one knee.

Nomi and the Belle defender had been chewing each other out behind the net. Suddenly the sticks and gloves went down and they were up against the boards, pushing and shoving.

Ingrid was engaged in a heated discussion with the referee. "You didn't see it!" I heard her say. "They're doing it all the time. Boarding, charging, cross-checking. You know that."

The referee turned and skated away. Ingrid followed. "You've lost control. Call the period. Send the players to the dressing room before someone gets hurt."

The fight in the corner continued, much to the delight of the crowd. The linesmen stood back and watched. The Buffalo player knocked Nomi to the ice and fell on top of her. She then grabbed her by the jersey and proceeded to shake her like a cat with a mouse. All the time Nomi uttered a string of epitaphs that could be heard clearly throughout the arena.

On the bench Sharon quivered with indecision. She had made the decision to go, had one leg over the boards when the linesman intervened. They pulled the Belle defender off Nomi and shoved her toward the corner.

Molly was finally on her feet. Julia and Pat ushered her to the bench. She collapsed there between her linemates.

I grabbed Harriett. "Is she OK?"

Harriett nodded. "She's winded. Lost her pre-game meal. Otherwise she's OK."

Dorsey draped a towel around Molly's neck and handed her the water bottle.

"Are you OK?" she asked in her funny, adolescent-boy's voice.

I was struck by her expression of concern. She glanced around quickly to make sure no one had noticed.

I leaned over Molly. "Are you all right?"

She turned slightly, even managed a feeble smile. "Sure, I'm fine."

Nomi was still on the ice. Her helmet was off. Her sweater was off. Her shoulder pads were off. She had nothing on the upper part of her body but her underwear. The crowd whistled and stamped its feet as she circled the ice making rude gestures. The Belle player stood by rubbing a welt over her eye.

Nomi got a game misconduct. The Belle player got two minutes for fighting and a ten-minute misconduct. The referee cleared the ice and asked the timekeeper to tack the remaining three minutes on to the start of the second period.

Nomi left the ice to a chorus of boos. We retrieved her equipment and made our escape.

For a few minutes the dressing room was like a tomb. Molly leaned against the wall, eyes closed, white as a sheet. Even Ingrid couldn't come up with an appropriate quip.

Suddenly Nomi's voice rose above the noise of the shower, belting out something raucous and raunchy.

"Oh, shit," said Ingrid with a laugh. "And we have to go out there again."

Dateline: Toronto

Subject: *Playing by the Rules* by Faye Surgenor

Alison Gutherie prides herself on "playing by the rules". Last night was no exception. She allowed Molly Gavison, a talented player, to go out and be brutalized once again by a player emulating some macho model of sportsworld. Intimidation. Taking the 'good' penalty. She then sent out Captain Ingrid Eklund to complain to the referee. The referee wasn't about to call a penalty. He'd been told a little violence sells tickets, pays his salary. The fans were enjoying it. Besides, what good would a two-minute penalty do? Gutherie's failure of leadership shifted the burden of seeing justice done to the small, pugnacious shoulders of Nomi Pereira. Retaliation is an honorable word in the lexicon of the sportsworld. What Alison Gutherie should have done was remove her players from the field of play the minute the rules were so severely abrogated. To do so, of course, would have brought on her the wrath of the owners, the fans, perhaps even some of her own players. There were risks to be sure. But she might have changed the sportsworld. Then, maybe that's what she's afraid of."

Dateline: Toronto
Subject: *Rebuttal* by Mary-Beth Jones-McAlpine
Alison Gutherie played by the rules. She did nothing to contribute to the ugly mood that gripped Memorial Auditorium in Buffalo last night. The two game suspension handed down to Nomi Pereira was certainly inadequate, though, given her conduct last evening.

Dateline: Toronto
Subject: *Don't be a Wimp, Alison Gutherie* by Jim Gough.
Nomi Pereira received a two-game suspension for her part in a stick-swinging duel with Belle defender Brenda Hughes last evening. Pereira went after Hughes in retaliation for some punishment meted out by the Belles to speedster Molly Gavison. While the two-game suspension was, in my opinion, adequate punishment, the burning question is: Where were you, Alison Gutherie, when Molly Gavison was being savaged? Where have you been all season while your right-winger has been taking the punishment? Ingrid Eklund can complain to the referee until the cows come home and it won't change a thing. Instead of complaining why not send out large Julia Martin to push and shove or let silent but sturdy Sharon Sosnoski show her stuff. For that matter, why didn't Gavison fight back? She's no puny, ninety-pound weakling. Is she afraid to defend herself or simply exceedingly sensitive to Alison Gutherie's aversion to fighting?—an aversion Nomi Pereira, hockey's only five-foot-five enforcer, chooses to ignore.

I posted the articles on the bulletin board. The players drew pictures on them. One drew a mustache. Two days later they disappeared.

CHAPTER 15

January bonded us, chilled us with its inklings of the fragility of human relationships, told us that in the sportsworld friends were interchangeable—they could be traded, suspended, replaced.

Men like to talk about a trade as a chemical experiment, as a business transaction. Trades are seen as inevitable, even desirable. They're part of the wheeling and dealing mentality of sports entrepreneurs where the object of the exercise is not so much to improve a team but to show who has the balls. I guess I should have understood this but in the back of my mind I held this naive belief when we started out that we would play together until some of us chose not to.

In February we hit the doldrums—a collective biorhythmic collapse brought on by the emotional strain of January. We couldn't buy a goal during that period. Goalposts grew into tree trunks, goaltenders into towering Goliaths. To alleviate the general frustration I stopped discussing offense. We talked defense.

Great offense is startling and beautiful but good defense is pure and sacred. It's about defending ourselves, defending our persons. Men love to mix the metaphors of sex with sport, of sport with sex, of sport and sex with war and battle. Our game is purer, less psychologically extreme. A goal represents skill, a celebration of our strength and abilities. We surrender only to ourselves.

Defense is key. By the third week in February we were back on track.

I didn't feel the full impact of the February blahs until later—not until the Friday night of the last weekend of the month. I had contemplated spending the weekend in Toronto but the depression hit me like a ton of bricks.

Everyone but Molly had left. I stood by her door for the longest time, then fled, Sibelius and Sam's squeaky wheel echoing in my head. I drove home alone.

Landlady wasn't at home when I arrived. I trundled upstairs, made a cup of tea and dragged out my well-worn tape of Molly. Mandy came up and watched with me. She didn't ask the usual questions and she didn't eat much of the popcorn she'd made. She sat beside me very quietly. Every now and then I caught her glancing at me anxiously.

CHAPTER 16

The Hurricanes came to town the following Monday. Their shiny new charter rolled up to Varsity Arena on the coldest February 29th in forty years.

"If we want to win this game," I told the players, "we've got to contain Lauren MacDonald." I drew a rangy stick-person on the blackboard. "We all know Lauren—three times MVP at the Nationals, all-star team for so many years its a given. She can skate; she can stickhandle; she can score from any point on the ice. She throws so many head and shoulder fakes, if you followed them all, you'd end up at center ice in a different city. Remember your fundamentals. Focus on the chest. The legs go where the chest goes. Step into her with a nice, solid, respectful shoulder check. Get your shoulder into her chest and straighten her up. Lauren's played the game a long time. She's not going to role over and play dead because she gets dumped a few times. But we can give her a little something extra to think about."

"And while you're helping her up, ask her if she's going out with anybody," Henny called out.

I tossed the chalk back onto the board as the room erupted in laughter.

Win or lose, I knew the Teds would play a good game. My team loved playing the 'Canes.

I was not disappointed.

Joy played a superb game in goal. The defense was rock solid in front of her. The offense forechecked tenaciously, creating a number of excellent scoring opportunities, negated only by the brilliant play of Hamilton goaltender, Ives. In spite of a great team effort—the best performance of the year, in my opinion—with a minute remaining in the game we trailed two to one.

I sent out my big scoring line—Young, Thorne and Gavison.

"One minute left to play in the final period," the public address announced intoned.

In a tight game that announcement is enough to send a chill down your spine. For the team with the lead, it's an invitation to go into a tough defensive shell, to focus on clearing the puck, shut down the attacking team, frustrate its efforts to organize an attack in the neutral zone. For the team trailing, it's go for broke.

The 'Canes won the face-off and came in with a quick shot on goal. Joy smothered and held. Time to add some extra scoring punch. I tapped Ingrid on the shoulder. Ingrid went over the boards and Carol came off the ice. Val stood pat.

I glanced at the net. Joy nodded. As soon as we had control of the puck, she would scramble for the boards in favor of an extra attacker.

I looked down the bench. I had Henny, Effie, Toddy, Nomi and Lou to choose from. Nomi sat, mumbling to herself.

"Get ready," I said.

She nodded curtly.

The puck was deflected over the boards off the face-off. The face-off came back to the right of our goal.

Dorsey won the face-off. The puck went back to Ingrid. As Ingrid headed out with Sharon back, Joy raced for the bench. I held onto the back of Nomi's jersey until Joy was within the required ten feet, then released her.

The play was stopped at the blue line as the Hamilton defender poke-checked Dorsey off-side.

The face-off came to the neutral zone.

I glanced toward our empty net, surely the loneliest sight in the world. Joy squirted water over her face and blotted it off with her towel.

The 'Canes won the face-off and shot the puck down the ice. It slid into the corner. Ingrid scampered back, circled the net and passed to the player she saw breaking into the clear. Nomi took the puck and cruised to center. Dorsey had eluded her check and was in the clear looking for the pass. Nomi faked the pass, then deftly decked the Hamilton defender. The player got a piece of her but Nomi drove around her, lifting a hard shot from the backhand.

As any goalie would tell you, you cover the angles; you give the shooter the five hole. If she's good enough to hit it, you have no regrets. That's life.

The net bulged.

Ives shook her head in disbelief.

Twenty seconds left on the clock. Time to settle the players down, make sure we didn't squander our hard-earned tie.

Joy went back into the net. I sent out Effie, Henny and Toddy with Pat and Julia. Val sent out her top-scoring line. Val wanted the win. So did I but I was prepared to take my chances on getting a break on a changeover.

Lauren MacDonald won the face-off and led the charge up ice. She managed to get a good shot away but Joy got her skate out and kicked the puck away. Julia lifted the rebound down the ice.

Nomi was named first star, an honor traditionally reserved for the player who gets the dramatic winning or tying goal.

I waited for Nomi as she came off the ice.

"Good going, chum."

You can teach a player a lot of things—skills, basic strategy—but you can't teach a player tenacity or the courage to stand in against an opponent who is four inches taller and thirty pounds heavier. Nomi wasn't the best forward on the team, but in this circumstance, she was the right player.

After the game Val invited me for a drink. She had an interview with Global and had elected to stay over. She had driven down in a car loaned to her by the daughter of the team owner—something big, a Cadillac or Lincoln Continental. Whatever it was it compared favorably to my car. I left the bucket of bolts in the parking lot for Nomi to drive home.

I took Val to the Pink Carnation. Most of my players were there, shooting pool and rattling the pinball machine. They watched us like hawks, whispering and tittering among themselves.

When we finished our drinks Val said, "It's quaint but let me take you somewhere more private."

We went to a fashionable liqueur bistro in Cabbagetown. Val ordered a delicate chocolate dessert, orange liqueur and coffee. Our dessert arrived on real Limoges. The silver was real. So were the leather and mahogany chairs. It was a setting made for Val.

Val seemed rather pensive.

"Anne and I are considering a trial separation," she said, prompted by my concerned frown. She said the words easily and without emotion.

"I'm sorry," I said.

"Perhaps we're too involved with our work," she mused. "Perhaps it's been too intense. Perhaps we've had to work too hard." She frowned and fingered the stem of her liqueur glass. "It shouldn't be that way, should it? Love should always be easy and fun." She laughed as she said this. There was a tiny catch in her laugh, a crystal tinkling in her throat.

I had worked desperately hard in my relationship with Gail, thwarting my desire to be nurtured, giving in to satisfy a capricious woman-child. Where did the effort get me?

"I don't think relationships should be hard," I said. "They should be easy and natural."

She nodded and smiled. "Me too."

She spent the remainder of our dessert being flirtatious in her light, mischievous way. I liked that side of her much better. Val frightened me when she was too serious.

Afterwards, she drove me home, walked me to the door, kissed my hand. "Someday, Gutherie," she said, releasing me with an enigmatic smile. "Someday."

I went inside, poured myself a double scotch and pulled out the tapes of Molly.

The next day after practice I went to the Royal Ontario Museum, a popular spot for late-afternoon rendezvous of the romantic sort and an oasis of civility in a wasteland of hype for a dispirited country kid— a perfect place to blank the mind when the desire to forget is overwhelmed by the ferocity of memory. Over the past few weeks, I had come often.

I spent an hour wandering through the Paleozoic fossils, visited the Egyptian mummies and dawdled over the insect collection. It did me good to know that everything around me was older than I was, although on that particular day I felt as old as Methuselah and as dead as megadoptera.

Afterwards I went down to the coffee shop, had a donut and coffee and watched the multi-colored dinosaurs prance across the pale-peach walls. By the time I had finished my snack, it was almost six. Time to go home.

But my faithful Datsun betrayed me. Instead of taking me to the Gerrard Street Roach Motel, it delivered me to the doorstep of Willard's.

Dale picked up a Blue the minute I walked in.

I shook my head. "Double scotch."

Dale poured the scotch. There was no one else in the bar. He stood politely, staring at the far wall as I downed half the scotch in one gulp.

Emboldened by drink, I approached the subject head-on. "Tell me about Molly's family," I said. "Have they disowned her? No one ever comes to visit her. Her roommate says she never gets letters or phone calls."

Dale stared at me for a moment, then turned away with a soft snort. "Yeah," he said, "great family. Her father beat her twice—badly. The first time was when he found out she was gay. The second time was when he found out she was doing drugs. I hear he broke half her ribs."

I looked at him, dazed. "Pour me another," I said.

Dale cleared his throat, reached for the bottle of scotch and set it on the bar in front of me.

"Molly wasn't always a zombie, an emotional cripple, you know," he said with controlled evenness. "She used to be a normal kid—well a little flaky, but a terrific kid."

I topped up my glass. "Go on."

Dale examined his hands for a few moments, then leaned toward me and said in a low voice, "The story is this. Molly fell in love with one of her teammates. It was a real mess. I don't know if Molly misread the signals or if the other girl led her on, then panicked when the moment of truth arrived. Anyway, she rejected Molly. That in itself would have been enough of a kick in the gut but the other girl—the silly bitch—told her coach, her teammates, Molly's parents, several of the officials. Everybody was let in on it. Molly was devastated. She was dragged up in front of a bunch of adults—some sort of kangaroo court—to answer a charge she'd molested a teammate." He said the words into his mustache, glancing about as he spoke.

"Molested?"

"Yeah. You can imagine how you'd feel at that age. You're grown up but not grown up. Molly was shattered. Her coach was shattered. Her parents—well—they were apoplectic. Her father tried to choke her right there in the hotel room. They had to drag him off her. It was a bad scene."

He paused, looking for my reaction. I stared at the floor.

"Oh yeah," he said grimly, "her coach had a thing for her too. He was a weird guy, an old bachelor. He'd coached her since she was eight—in some ways he was more of a father to her than her own father. He wanted her, apparently. He'd just been waiting around for her to grow up. Anyway, after the big blowup, he started giving her extra attention. Her parents encouraged it." He paused at the sudden rush of color to my cheeks. "He started to get very physical with her, touching, kissing, hands all over her at every opportunity. I always thought he did enough of that before." His face tightened with anger. "Anyway, he tried to force her one night. Ripped her clothes off, had his hands all over her. She managed to fight him off but she really freaked out."

"Was he charged?"

Dale shook his head. "No, he was fired and the whole thing was swept under the rug. Her father called her a slut. Told her it was her fault."

"What about her mother?"

"She denied anything happened."

"Who was there for her?"

"Nobody." Dale looked away, ashamed. "Everybody just walked away from her. Some of her friends were afraid. Some of them saw it as a chance to get an edge. You wouldn't believe how cut-throat some of these people are until you've been around them for a while. Molly had rocked the boat. She was a pariah. She was left to do a high-wire act without a net. All of a sudden, the familiar territory was a mine-field. She didn't know where to turn. She started drinking, doing soft drugs. Her performance started slipping. Her father hired a sports psychologist to get her motivated. The psychologist was a nice young woman—warm, supportive. Molly fell in love with her. The psychologist couldn't handle that. She bowed out. Molly's performance slipped some more. More booze. More drugs. One day she's an Olympic medallist. Then one day she doesn't qualify for the team. The word is she flunked a drug test at the trials."

"Are you sure?"

"Yeah, I used to date a girl who worked for one of the committees."

"Then what?"

"She disappeared. It was all very hush-hush. The word is she went to Switzerland. There was a rumor she'd been busted. I don't know about that one. I was as surprised as anyone when she showed up with the Teddies."

"Why didn't you do something?" I said bitterly.

He hung his head. "I don't know. I ask myself that question frequently. I wasn't just another newsman after all. I was her biographer. But Molly was in pretty rough shape at the time. How was I to know if she was reliable? I didn't know if she would stand by her story when things got rough. I didn't know if all the stories were true. It was very delicate. I didn't want to compromise my girlfriend. Some of the stuff she told me was confidential. I saw law suits all over the place." He shrugged. "What can I say, Alison. I can come up with any number of good reasons for not being a hero."

"Have you ever thought of finishing the book?" I asked after a long silence.

"Sure, I've thought about it. I'd like to vindicate Molly. Most people see her as a privileged kid who couldn't handle the pressure, a kid who had all the chances and still messed up. And that just isn't so."

I stared into my beer.

"Some people never recover," he said. "They're always a little guarded, self-protective. I know. I see them in here all the time. It's a shame if that's what's happened to Molly. She was always so open, so alive. Well—" He shook his head. "This is confidential," he said, suddenly curt. "Don't let it go any further."

"I won't."

"Good."

He turned from the bar and walked away.

CHAPTER 17

The following Monday Phil summoned me to his office.

"We're going to do a calendar," he said.

"We've already done a calendar," I said. I was referring to the five-by-eight on heavy cardboard with a thermometer and smiling team picture.

"This one's a little different," Phil said carefully. "We're going to use it as a promo for next season's ticket drive."

He had captured my interest. "Phil, this is the first time you've talked about next season without adding several qualifiers."

Phil waved the remark aside abruptly. "Alison, I've got a meeting in five minutes. I just wanted to let you know about the calendar and confirm I have your cooperation."

"Tell me about it," I said.

"It's a group effort," he said. He looked at me as if he expected trouble. "The league's putting it out under its logo. If there's a profit, we split it."

I said nothing so he went on. "Each team will get two months. The league office will select the pictures. We're looking for something informal—not the usual action stuff. Maybe some casual stuff, locker-room candids. Something that shows off the girls' personalities."

"Just what kind of pictures are we talking about?"

He glared at me, then hauled out his pocket watch and gave it a look of exasperation. "How in hell should I know, Alison. You'll have to talk to the photographer. He's been given the guidelines. All I want to confirm is that you and your players will cooperate."

"When?"

"You're scheduled for next Monday." Phil stood up and picked up his jacket and briefcase. He had one leg out the door.

"I'll talk to the players and let you know," I said.

He was gone before I could finish my sentence. I heard him yell "OK" from the elevator.

The photographer arrived the following Monday immediately after the morning skate. He was a hairy, stubby-fingered guy who looked as if he made his living photographing mud wrestling and soft porn. I asked him what he had in mind.

He slid his cigar out of his mouth and said, "Whirlpool, massage-table stuff. You know the scene." He paused, then said earnestly. "The Lambs did some cute stuff with the weights. The O'Brien's did some pool shots. Bathing suits. Nice. Maybe a little—"

"You mean like the *Sports Illustrated* swimsuit issue?" I proceeded to lay down the law. He could have legitimate weight-room shots, action shots, pictures of players taping sticks, sharpening skates and the like. "I don't want my players posing for any pictures they couldn't show their very conservative grandparents."

He looked at me as if he thought I was quite strange. "Lady," he said, "I was told the photographs should present the girls in a feminine, attractive manner and also provide some appeal to the imagination. I can get tape in a hardware store."

I phoned Phil and laid it on the line.

"OK, Alison," he said with a sigh. "No cheesecake. Let me talk to the photographer. We'll see if he can do anything with action shots."

To my surprise the action shots were superb. I was even more surprised that the league took a serious look at them. The governors selected a shot of Sosnoski circling the net for November and one of Dorsey unloading from the slot for December. I phoned the photographer to give him my compliments.

"Look, lady," he said, "I may be a pig but I'm a pro with the camera."

Phil was pleased too.

"The pictures are good, Alison," he said. "They make the Teddies look like a class act." He paused to let this sink in, then got up from his chair. "But they're not going to sell the calendar," he said triumphantly. He flipped through the pile of pictures on his desk, selected one and thrust it toward me.

I held the picture on my lap, staring at it with a rueful grimace.

The Lamb forward lay in the crease on her stomach, spread-eagled, wearing a tutu and peeping coyly over her shoulder at the photographer.

"This is the picture that's going on the cover," Phil said. "This is what sells women's sports."

I pitched the photograph back onto his desk. "Only because that's what you've decreed will sell them."

He sighed and said, "Alison, this is the way of the world. You can rant and rave all you want but you'll never win. You know why? Because there will always be women who'll do this sort of thing—for a buck, to be good sports, to please the men in their lives, whatever." He paused, avoiding my gaze, and said peevishly, "I suppose you're not going to like the next promo either."

I merely stared at him.

"We're sponsoring a 'Win a Date with a Teddy' contest," he said.

"Very interesting."

"It's in conjunction with Mr. Smoothie Shocks and the Pizza Theater," he said. "You buy x number of dollars of whatever and your name goes into a barrel. The lucky winner gets to select the player of his choice for a date."

"I assume she has to agree."

"Oh, I don't think so. That sort of thing would come under promotional obligations in the contracts, I would imagine."

"We'll see about that." I got up and walked out of the office before I hit Phil in the mouth. Mrs. Toop smiled at me as I left.

The following week the calendar prototype went out to the media for review.

Dateline: Toronto

Subject: *Calendar Girls! Give me a Break!* by Faye Surgenor.

Alison Gutherie was tested twice this week. Each time she failed. Take the hockey calendar: Alison was very firm in insisting that her players be represented in a dignified fashion. She was, however, quite willing to participate in the degradation of women by permitting her players to be included in a calendar that, in fact, debases all women and makes a mockery of the woman athlete as a role model. Also remarkable was her easy acquiescence to the "Win a Date With a Teddy" contest. Does she really think it's acceptable to permit women athletes to be disposed of as trinkets, given away as prizes? Her attitude to the contest seems to be to wait and see. Presumably, if the woman selected isn't offended, Alison won't be either.

Dateline: Toronto
    Subject: *Calendar Girls. Right On!* by Jim Gough.
    So what's wrong with calendar girls, Faye Surgenor? Even men do calendars now. Besides, accept the facts, sex sells. Women's sports relies on that fact for their survival. The number of people who support women's sports as real sport can be counted on the fingers of a very few hands. Women's sports survive because women allow themselves to be sold as sexual accessories. End of story. Period. Wake up and smell the coffee.

The players were a little uneasy about the calendar. They were less concerned about the "Date" contest.

"There's nothing in the rules that says you can't take your friends along," said Ingrid.

I sent a copy of the calendar to Mandy. I knew she couldn't wait for the weekend. She phoned to thank me, delighted to be the first kid on the block with an authentic autographed WPHL calendar. Landlady took over the phone after a few minutes.

"Mandy and I had a long talk about the calendar," she said. "I wanted to brief her on the politics. I'm thankful the only pictures she expressed any interest in were those of Sosnoski and Thorne."

She paused.

"Sportsworld," I said.

"Told you so," she said.

The next day I found a fax of some feminist literature in my mailbox. Landlady couldn't wait for the weekend.

Molly had a new toy for Sam—an ivory tower complete with spiral staircase. Effie told me about it. She described how Molly's face lit up when Sam crawled into it and settled in.

I said nothing. Effie took my silence for indifference.

"I thought it was kind of cute," she said with a shrug.

I went home that weekend and spent most of Saturday, going over old boys junior hockey league films with Mandy. She told me, dead serious, if she hoped to make the team she would need an edge. She watched me anxiously, wanting my approval. I tried to hide my disappointment.

Mandy seemed to sense the emotional gap. She snuggled closer to me and tugged at my elbow. I put my arm around her shoulder and pulled her close to me.

By the time Landlady arrived home, we had watched the films at least four times. Mandy was half-asleep, her cheeks smeared with caramel and little stray bits of popcorn.

I asked Landlady how her evening had turned out. She had gone to see a feminist play with her friend Helen.

"Very fine," she said thoughtfully. "Very uplifting."

Landlady did everything with Helen except sleep with her. Helen did nothing with her husband except sleep with him. She did everything else with Landlady.

Landlady was remarkable. She had entrusted a vital part of her daughter's education to a lesbian. Teaching a girl to sweat was a highly personal task. I had done my best to be appropriate and neutral in the right places. But it was getting tricky. This afternoon while we were playing some street hockey she asked, "Did you like boys when you were my age?"

I smiled bravely and lied. "Sure," I said.

She looked at me and frowned. "I'm not sure if I do," she said.

It was getting tricky.

CHAPTER 18

By March 4th we knew our chances to finish first were slim to none. We entered the final week of the regular season three points behind the Hurricanes. The Hurricanes were scheduled to conclude the season with two games against the Lambs, games they would win handily. We finished our season with a home-and-home series against the Belles. The Lambs were well out of it but the Belles and O'Brien's continued to struggle for the final play-off spot. The fact that the Belles remained in the hunt was bad news for us. With the season on the line, we expected them to be more punishing than ever.

The Belles were determined to make the play-offs and no one was more determined than Mauler Mason. Rumor had it he would be fired if the team was eliminated. Mauler had never had such a good job. He had no intention of losing it. From the opening face-off, it was obvious he had told his team to "stick it to us".

The Belles always left us sore and scared. This time they left us injured as well. We lost Effie McGovern to a badly bruised leg the first night in Buffalo, hammered across the thigh with the heel of a stick.

We lost Henny at home on Friday, her shoulder dislocated from a collision on the boards.

We won both games but the Hurricanes had already clinched first place the previous night. The O'Brien's lost twice to the Dynamos, thus the 'Canes gained their play-off spot by default. We felt blessed. We hadn't finished first, but we were finished with the Belles for the season.

Now I had some decisions to make. League rules allowed the addition of two named players for the play-offs. Sue Germaine from the Yellowjackets and Britt Blakey from the Red Barons would join us in the morning. I was also allowed to call up substitutes for our injured players. But that option meant Effie and Henny would be ineligible for the play-offs and that was no option at all.

With that decision out of the way, I wrestled for a while about how I would adjust the lines. Henny would be out until the middle of the final series. Effie needed another three or four days. Two-thirds of my checking line had vanished. I considered playing Toddy on the line with Dorsey and Molly and asking Chris to steady the line with Britt and Sue. But, in the end, I decided to leave Toddy where she was, anchoring the checking line. Playing with two unfamiliar linemates was a lot to ask of a youngster but I had the feeling she was up to the challenge.

The semifinals opened in Toronto, March 14th. We spent the weekend doing an exhausting series of radio promos and shopping-center appearances. By Sunday people who hadn't known a Teddy from a hole in the ground were stopping to wish us well.

Even so I was surprised to see the crowd on hand at the Gardens that night. Phil flashed us the A-OK sign from Big Frank's private box as the arena filled beyond my wildest expectations.

"You should see the crowd out there," Henny ducked into the dressing room, her excitement unabated by the sling that strapped her left arm against her chest. "This place is almost full—and noisy. Real people. Not that bunch of stuffed shirts who showed up for the opener."

"I hope nobody bothered to cut anybody's laces into tiny little bits," Harriett said. "Because I left the spares back at the Mussyford."

Chris Young was waiting to have her ankles taped.

"The bigger the game, the more tape," Harriett said. "What are we going to do if she ever develops an allergy to the stuff?"

I made the rounds, checking to make sure everyone was OK, stopping to go over a few plays with Sue and Britt. Around me the excitement continued to build. I was glad when the signal came to take the ice.

The O'Brien's came at us like a lion unleashed, throwing our forward lines into disarray, turning our defense to stone. Joy promptly let in two goals.

I tapped Toddy on the shoulder. "Go out there and make like Effie. Slow them down."

I watched as she circled the net and started slowly up ice, ragging the puck, taking the forward checking her on a merry wild-goose chase before finally passing off to Britt. Britt passed back to Toddy who turned and circled lazily back to the neutral zone. Finally, the O'Brien forward got impatient and went after the puck with a sloppy sweep check. The check missed and Toddy was home free.

Our bench went wild as the red light over the goal flashed. My number one line was over the boards, flying.

I spread my arms to encompass the goal-scoring line as the players settled onto the bench.

"Great puck control. You played that just right."

As they say in sports, there's a turning point, a critical juncture of emotion or performance, often from an unheralded individual, that taps into or alters the vital energy of the game. As I watched Dorsey win the face-off, I knew Toddy had provided that catalyst. Under the pressure of a big game, she had gone out with a pair of unfamiliar line-mates and taken control of the game. The goal, I felt, marked not only the turning point for our team, but a turning point for Toddy. I turned to Henny and Effie who were behind the bench in street clothes.

"You taught her well."

We went on to win the game and took the second game with apparent ease. Our number-one line turned in its best performance in a season of memorable performances. Dorsey got the hat trick on goals set up by Molly's speed and Chris' determination. Nomi got the shut-out and was named the game's first star. Somehow, Dorsey managed to trip her as she stepped out onto the ice to acknowledge her selection. Nomi slid across the ice on her belly as the crowd laughed and applauded.

"Did you trip her?" I asked Dorsey in the dressing room.

Dorsey shrugged. "She fell over my stick," she said, unconcerned. "Clumsy, I guess."

We lost the first game in Ottawa but won the second and returned to Toronto with a comfortable three to one lead and home-ice advantage.

The Hurricanes in the, meantime, swept the Dynamos. Val's team was gearing up.

Before a home crowd of fifteen-thousand we won the final game four to one. The noise at ice level was deafening throughout the game. A quick glance told me that every woman hockey player and every dyke in Ontario was in the stands.

Although Henny couldn't play, Effie was back in the line-up. I rotated her at center with Britt Blakey.

The game was auspicious for several reasons: We were headed for the finals; all three lines had contributed to the scoring—the kind of balance that does a coach's heart good; and Julia Martin got her first goal as a Teddy on a long, low shot from the point. Naturally, she had to put up with a lot of good-natured ribbing.

"I suppose you're going to want to score goals all the time now," Dorsey said. "Next thing I know, you'll be after my job."

"Can we expect to see you parked in the slot, waiting for a pass?" Ingrid asked.

"No and no," Julia said. "That goal was an accident. I was attempting to set up Lou."

I noticed, however, that she asked the referee for the puck and tucked it carefully into her bag.

The players were pleased with their performance as a team and pleased with their individual efforts. The series had ended on a note that put us in the perfect frame of mind for the work ahead. I gave the team the next day off. We needed time to heal the wounds, time to rest, time to reflect and dream.

"Athletes are like artists and other creative people," I told Harriett as we watched the players celebrate. "They need time for mental rehearsal, visualization."

Harriett thought about this for a moment. "Yeah, I'll bet Chris dreams she's Bobby Baun, scoring the Stanley Cup winner on a broken leg."

I nodded. I realized Chris cherished her reputation as a "gamer", while for Dorsey nothing short of perfect domination would suffice.

"What do you dream about?" I asked Harriett as she flung a wet towel into the laundry basket.

"Of a bus with a working carburetor, of a week where everyone's skates are perfect, where Chris' ankles don't need taping, and where no one puts shaving cream into Dorsey's helmet."

"I think your dream is attainable—all except the part about the shaving cream."

"What about you?"

I shrugged. "I visualize a game where nothing but pearls of wisdom fall from my lips, where the team is holding up the Cup and

I'm standing to one side, looking as if I knew it was going to happen all along. I know when it does happen, I'll be out on the ice, screaming and throwing my loafers into the crowd."

Harriett laughed.

The players filed out. I would join them shortly. But for now...I stood in the middle of the deserted locker room...if life could be one long game, an endless stream of locker-room banter, locker-room antics, surrounded by affection and companionship without the necessity to make hard choices or take personal risks...feelings carefully limited by the confines of the game.

I wandered over and sank down onto the bench where Molly had been sitting just a few minutes ago. What did Molly dream about? Probably an endless stretch of frost-covered ice. A red and white lycra suit with a maple leaf emblazoned on the chest. To be able to skate free without the confines of the boards, without the need to share the ice with eleven other individuals. To be able to focus on the moment, the perfect stride, the perfect position of head and hands. To skate free without worrying about the need to keep her head up to avoid being leveled by an enterprising defender who had built a career around the rush of meeting a fleet-footed forward with her head down.

I glanced at the big sweater with the number eight to my right. Sharon Sosnoski probably dreamed about doing this forever, of lacing on those skates every year when the mornings had that special nip, not taking them off again until the last chunk of ice melted and dribbled down the grate in front of the Memorial Center.

A defender comes into her own late. With luck, Sharon could play in this league until she's forty. Longer if she wanted to. Usually the heart goes before the legs. For Sharon, the desire would not abate. Hockey was a way of life.

The only thing that could alter Sharon's desire was what the future held for Nomi Pereira. Playing goal wears a player down—even a player with Nomi's physical and mental courage. The reflexes go; the gloved hand comes up empty on shots that once seemed so easy. Some athletes retire gracefully, bowing out when it's time to go. Nomi would stay until the bitter end, lashing out in frustration, blaming the goal posts for deserting her, cursing her equipment, wondering silently and sullenly about the fickleness of her defense. I was sure of one thing: Nomi wouldn't go until Sharon did and Sharon, sensing Nomi's deterioration, might decide to retire earlier than planned. Why would they do it any other way? They'd done it together all along.

I sighed. I wished they could be young forever, always in their prime, playing their best with a little left to strive for. I wished they could always play in innocence, needing nothing more than a bus with a faulty carburetor to get them where they're going, keeping their wide-eyed excitement about being on television, playing before a big crowd and having the kids line up to get autographs.

In my wildest dreams, I saw myself leaving the bench and joining them "out there". But even creative visualization would not make that dream come true. My time had come and gone. Too slow. Too fragile. After the Belle game I'd been so sore I'd winced at the thought of anyone as much as brushing against me. I no longer had the guts for the fight.

Harriett came out of the training room, flicked the lights off without looking around and left. I sat in the darkness for a few minutes, listening to the echo of Harriett's shoes along the corridor. Then I got up and walked away.

The first game of the finals was set for Hamilton that Saturday.

On Thursday Phil summoned me to his office. Mrs. Toop offered me coffee as I waited in the outer office. That meant the news was good. After a ten-minute wait I was ushered into the office. Phil sat at his desk, beaming. Pop loomed in the background.

"We made money," Phil told me gleefully. He looked to big Frank for reinforcement.

Big Frank smiled his unpleasant smile and grunted. Then he shook my hand abruptly and left. The expression on Phil's face told me I was supposed to be flattered.

Phil took a moment to rearrange the items on his desk blotter, then said in a deliberately offhand manner, "The other news is, we've got a TV contract."

I knew CSN was toying with the idea of showing the deciding game at a later date—in place of a CIAU college basketball rerun. I merely nodded.

Phil looked at me for a long moment, then said, "Hey, Alison, you don't understand. CSN wants to carry the series live—in its entirety." He settled back in his chair, pleased he'd secured my attention, and said, "The network was really impressed with the crowds we drew for the semis. The figures were impressive in all four venues, in fact." He paused, then shrugged. "Besides, the big boys had a hole in their schedule. That big fight card from Halifax had to be canceled and rescheduled. The fire in the Met Center caused more damage than they realized at first. The network had hoped to milk the fights for a few hours of reruns. We're getting a flat fee for each game televised. We tried to get a package but the network wanted to hold off in case the fights got rescheduled."

"There's nothing like being called upon to replace the reruns of an amateur fight card," I said.

Phil raised his eyebrows beseechingly, the way he does when he feels good about something and wants me to go along. "The important news, Alison," he said, "is we're in."

The players were ecstatic.

CHAPTER 19

Two days before the final, winter lost its grip on Metro. The air turned spring-like and whenever I inhaled deeply, I smelled and tasted sap. A warm wind blew unerringly from the southwest, as if it were following an invisible tunnel directly from the Copps Coliseum.

I felt totally connected to Val during those final days of preparation. I saw her going through the same routines, feeling the same anticipation, felt the pride in her team and, at the same time, a growing, bittersweet separation from the team. In the early days, I saw the strengths and weaknesses of the players. As the season progressed, I saw the improved performance, took personal pride in seeing the results of my tutelage. At this stage, the hard work had been done. Play-offs were the icing on the cake, a theater where the players could show off their talents. Like the music teacher who has guided her student to the big recital, or the parent who has turned a child loose in the world, the result is larger than the parts you have contributed. The team was more and more theirs.

If the players felt the same bittersweet sentiments, they showed no signs. The team was antsy and cheerfully bellicose. The players laughed a lot, wrestled on the ice between scrimmages and hugged each other for no reason other than unabashed affection. Even Harriett was a bit giggly.

Around town interest in the team grew as fans continued to jump onto our bandwagon. Two-foot-high cardboard cutouts of Ingrid, offered to shopkeepers as promos, popped up in store windows all over town. One radio station ran hourly Teddy contests giving away Teddy T-shirts as prizes. The questions were simple but managed to mystify listeners nonetheless. One caller thought our coach was Carl Brewer.

Our first game was Saturday at the Copps Coliseum. We had

arranged to leave Toronto at noon in order to get settled into our hotel—yes, Phil had actually sprung for a hotel—and enjoy a leisurely pre-game meal.

I went down to the Gardens early in the morning to help Harriett with the equipment. After we had loaded everything into the bus we went across to Stages for breakfast.

A member of the Gardens crew was taking a coffee break at the counter. When he spotted us he hopped off his stool and sauntered over to our table, holding the sports section of *The Star* folded open in front of our eyes.

"It's in the bag, Alison," he said.

My eyes were forced to the item under his tapping finger.

Late last evening, a station wagon carrying six members of the Hamilton Hurricane hockey club was broadsided by a tractor-trailer while returning from a rally in downtown Hamilton. Goaltender Karen Ives, a passenger in the front seat, sustained fractures to the collarbone and right arm. Goaltender Bernice Laughlin, also a passenger in the front seat, broke her right tibia. Defenseman Jane Woodly received a broken jaw and multiple lacerations to the face and head. All three players are lost for the season. Forwards Michele Landry, Thea Blinder and Jackie Mulholland received scrapes and bruises. They were treated in the emergency room at St. Joseph's and released. They are expected to be in the line-up when the 'Canes open the final series against the Teddies at the Copps tonight.

Coach Val Warnica has called up goalies Jenny Kitchen and Connie Order and defenseman Hailey Jacques from the Senior Flyers.

"You're a shoo-in, Alison," he said with a wink.

As soon as we got to Hamilton and were settled in our hotel, I called Val.

"They kept Bernice overnight for observation and released her this morning," she said. She sounded tired and worried. "Jane and Karen are still in. Karen's going to the OR today to have her arm pinned.

Jane's got a head injury. She's been drifting in and out since the accident. The doctors say the variation in consciousness is no reason for concern but it scares the hell out of me, nonetheless."

I surmised she had spent the entire night at the hospital.

We spent the next few minutes chatting about inconsequential things. She seemed glad to hear my voice and unwilling to let it go.

Finally we said good bye.

"Good luck, Val," I said.

"Thanks," she said. "We'll see you at the game."

The Hurricanes drew a standing-room-only crowd at the Copps. In the dressing room, ten minutes before the game, I waited until the players had settled, then delivered what I hoped would be my last inspirational speech.

"Folks, we're playing our favorite opponents tonight, the people we like and respect the most. What happened last night has given us a lot to think about. We're distracted; most of us don't feel much like playing hockey tonight—some of us may question whether we *should* be playing hockey tonight. We're worried about the injured players, about what the injuries might mean to their careers; we're worried about Jane Woodly. That's the way it should be." I paused, waiting for the murmurs to die down. "The fact remains there's a full house out there, waiting to see a hockey game. Thousands more are watching on television. We owe it to our fans to give our best performance. We owe it to women's hockey. This is our best chance to show the fans our skills, the excitement we can bring to the game. Indeed, the future of women's hockey may hinge on how well we play tonight. You know what I'd like to hear when this series is over?" I paused, glancing from face to face. The players waited expectantly. "I'd like to hear the Hamilton team say: 'The Teddies beat us because they were the better team. Even if we had had our big guns out there, we couldn't have beaten them. They were that good'."

"Hear, hear," said Ingrid.

The rest of the players thumped their sticks on the floor in assent.

"Good going," Harriett whispered. "This place was beginning to feel like a tomb."

The buzzer sounded. It was time. Nomi led us onto the ice.

Val's players were pumped. They took the ice to a dramatic burst of organ music and thunderous applause. As the novice netminder, Connie Order took her place between the pipes, the players skated by, gave her a tap on the pads and circled the net in a protective ring.

Lauren MacDonald won the opening face-off and dashed up ice. Dorsey missed the check. Lauren stepped neatly between Carol and Sharon and snapped the puck low on the stick side. Nomi took a swipe at the ice as the Hamilton crowd went wild.

The public address announcer had barely finished announcing the goal when Lauren was in again. Sharon caught a piece of her but she was still able to get off a shot. The puck clanged off the crossbar, hit Carol in the backside and bounced crazily in the crease. Nomi fell on it as the Hamilton winger bore down on her.

"Lauren has made up her mind to win this one all by herself," Harriett observed.

Both teams changed lines. I sent out my checking line—Toddy, Effie and Sue.

"Change the tempo," I said as I eased them over the boards. "Put a brake on that runaway train."

Val was doing the unexpected. Faced with a situation—two novice goalies and a weakened defense—that cried out for a close-checking style, using all her players in a defensive mode, she had stayed with her game plan, but in spades. She had given the reserves a vote of confidence and unleashed her finest forward line to do what it did best—overwhelm us with its awesome rushing attack. She had set us back on our heels and served notice that: "banged up or not we're still the Hurricanes, those marvelous black and silver-clad women who won this league. It was a plan not unlike Val herself—daring and a bit cheeky.

We are what we are. When our backs are against the wall, we go with what feels natural. As a stodgy old defensive specialist, I continued to play my familiar tune—check like crazy and look for a break. True to the philosophy of Anatoli Tarasov, my plan was to turn their offense into my offense.

Some people think the defensive game is boring. True, there's nothing more boring than watching a game where the team with the big lead goes into a shell. On the other hand, there's nothing more exciting than watching a center with great mobility shadow and poke check, break and come in on goal alone.

Effie's shot was blocked but Sue Germaine was there to grab the rebound and drive it home.

"Looks like we've got ourselves a game," Harriett said.

The period ended in a one to one tie.

It was a different dressing room at the first intermission, filled with lots of chatter and sighs of satisfaction. Molly alone seemed wound up. She sat, staring at the floor, the lower part of her face masked by a towel. Ingrid who was making her rounds as always, grabbing a drink, giving everyone a pat on the shoulder, said, "Good play, Molly."

Molly glanced up, smiled, then returned her gaze to the floor.

The 'Canes came out gunning in the second period, mounting an offensive flurry with such intensity that the puck always seemed to be in possession of the silver and black. Nomi turned away shot after shot before, finally, being beaten on the high stick.

I sent out my checking line to slow the play down, then countered with my scoring line. Dorsey won the face-off in the neutral zone, got the puck back to Chris. The puck hopped over Chris's stick to the boards. She went in with the Hamilton player draped all over her but managed to scoop the puck ahead. Dorsey gave her check one of her patented herky-jerky stutter steps, flipped the puck over the defender's stick and recovered it for a shot on goal. The puck rose, then dove like a dying quail under the glove of the Hamilton goalie and into the net.

With the score tied, Val sent out Lauren MacDonald.

Our number-two line played very effectively during the second period, forechecking tenaciously, not letting Val's big line get into full flight in the neutral zone. Nomi continued to be solid in goal.

The period ended, two to two.

The players downed the soda, hair soaked with sweat and plastered against their foreheads and necks. Nomi soaked a sponge in cold water and squeezed it over her face.

"You're doing a good job containing the attack," I said. "Val's plan is to grab as many goals as quickly as she can because she knows they're weak on the right side defensively and they're not as strong in goal as they're used to being. Connie Order is a good goalie but she can't dominate a game like Ives and Jane Woodly is awfully hard to replace on defense. Hailey Jacques is a good defender—Val wouldn't have called her up otherwise. But she's used up the adrenaline rush; she's getting tired. She's not used to playing in a game situation where the level of play is as intense and as good for so long.

"The next goal is critical. I want us to have it. We know the 'Canes are great first-goal scorers. And we know they're great front-runners. But the stats will show that nobody is better at protecting a one-goal lead than the Teds. So, keep doing what you're doing and work on Jacques. Make sure she gets to handle the puck a lot."

Good thing Faye Surgenor wasn't in the room. She would have jumped all over me for suggesting we key on a disadvantaged player. But I knew Hailey Jacques would understand. As a player called up to replace an All-Star defender, playing in front of a goalie replacing someone of Karen Ives's stature, she knew she had been called upon to do the impossible.

The fact was, Val's "disadvantaged" team was putting up a hell of a fight. We needed the next goal and the sooner the better. The last thing I wanted to do was to go late into the third period of a tied game with Lauren MacDonald lurking in the weeds.

At five-forty-five of the third period I sent out my number-one line. Val countered with MacDonald's line. The 'Canes had stacked their offense on the face-off, looking for the quick shot on goal. Nomi slashed her pads an extra time and dug in. MacDonald got off a shot from the face-off. Nomi caught the puck, but instead of holding it, rifled a pass to Chris. Chris took a look for Dorsey, saw that Dorsey and Lauren had fallen together and sent a rink-wide pass to Molly who was speeding up the right wing. The Hamilton goalie took a look, saw no one near Molly, came out to cut down the angle and committed the cardinal sin of trying to poke-check without a defender in the area. Chris who was chugging up the opposite wing with the Hamilton winger furiously backchecking was able to get her stick down and slide the puck into the open net.

As soon as the red light went on, Nomi whacked the ice, congratulating herself on the assist. I knew that behind the mask she was smirking at Dorsey who still lay in the face-off circle with her skates locked with the Hamilton center. I gave Nomi a smile and a shake of the head for her daring but rather reckless play.

The next minutes were filled with hectic, nail-biting hockey. The 'Canes came out, all guns blazing. I played three players back. Nomi played with abandon, taking every opportunity to clear the puck down ice.

I cringed as Nomi caught a booming shot and almost fell back into the net with it. Several times she was called upon to stop what she couldn't see as the 'Canes worked to set up the screen.

"She's got horseshoes up her ass," Harriett said.

One minute to go in the period. Val called a time-out and brought her players to the bench. The face-off would be in our end. Val gave her goalie a pat on the head as she slid onto the bench.

The 'Canes would play the final minute with an empty net.

Who did I want on the ice? My best face-off person, of course. I sent out Dorsey with Chris and Molly and replaced a dead-tired Sharon and Carol with Pat and Julia. Although I gave something up in terms of experience with this maneuver, I reasoned that having a pair of big defenders with long reaches was not a disadvantage in setting up the zone defense.

Dorsey lost the face-off but effectively tied up MacDonald. The puck went to the wing then back to the right point. Right point to left point. The left point took a shot on goal. The puck hit Nomi in the chest and bounced right to the Hamilton player in the slot. Julia went down to block the shot. Molly recovered the puck and fired it down ice. The 'Cane defender circled the net and the play began again. MacDonald unleashed a wicked shot from the blue line. The puck screamed off the crossbar, directly to the right winger. She turned bewildered. The puck had got caught up in her equipment and the play was whistled dead.

Some games end exactly as they should with a mad scramble in front of the net, the goalie down, the puck knocked out of the air by an alert defender and fired down ice for an empty-net goal.

Molly corralled the puck, took a quick look at the clock, then lofted the puck down the ice. The puck slid wide of the net as the siren sounded to end the game.

"Hey, you could have had yourself an easy goal," Dorsey said to Molly as the players filed past me.

Molly shrugged.

"What the hell. Those easy goals make up for the tough chances," Dorsey added.

Nomi was named first star. I waited for her in the alleyway.

"Hey, you outdid yourself, partner."

Nomi answered with a self-conscious twist of the shoulders and clumped off into the dressing room. Dorsey congratulated her by throwing a wet towel over her head.

I paused at the sink in the dressing room to brush my teeth and splash some cold water over my face. Out of the corner of my eye, I saw Molly hurriedly pull her clothes on. She picked up her equipment bag and left.

What in hell was she doing? Trying to escape the post-game frivolity? I made a bold decision. I grabbed a comb and ran it through my hair. I wasn't going to let her get away this time. Tonight—the night of our most important victory—Molly's place was with her teammates, to enjoy their sociability and receive their accolades. I knew there would be many. I wanted to tell her how well she had played and what a classy move she had made in sending the puck deep, deliberately missing the net.

I picked up my bag and stepped casually out into the hall.

Molly was standing near the side exit, staring out the door, hands stuffed deep into her pockets. I was about to approach her when, suddenly, the young man who had been using the pay phone in the corner slammed down the receiver and trotted toward the exit. He said something to Molly, then with a hand on her shoulder steered her rather abruptly out onto the sidewalk. They disappeared into the street.

I stepped back toward the dressing room, stunned. I'd seen this guy talking to Molly before, the same guy, a student wearing a University of New Brunswick black and red jacket. Where? Here in Hamilton, I suppose. Probably right out here in the same corridor. So, she had it both ways. I clenched my jaw in helpless rage. I felt angry, then sick.

Val grabbed me as I paused, one hand on the dressing room door. "Alison." She steered me quickly around the corner. "Alison, I'd love to take you home but I'm knee-deep in relatives. Jane's family is staying with me. I've got mothers and sisters all over the place. Lovers too." She paused, then said casually, "I suppose you're sharing."

I nodded.

She looked at me, searching my face, trying to decipher my expression. I was struggling valiantly to hide my pain and bewilderment. I was glad she was there, solid and close to me. I wanted her to take me in her arms and let me sob out my frustration and need.

I think she understood. She leaned forward and kissed me lightly on the lips. "Come with me," she whispered. Her lips lingered dangerously near my left ear lobe.

I nodded and said, "Yes," in a low voice.

I've never taken a hotel room before. Not this way. I felt as nervous as a schoolgirl watching her lover sign the registry Ms. and Ms. Jane Smith.

The desk clerk handed Val the key and said, "I'm sorry about the game, Val. Maybe tomorrow will be better."

"Maybe." Val smiled, then asked the clerk to have some white wine sent to our room.

The room was warm and peaceful. Val helped me out of my parka. Then she removed her own all-wool navy topcoat. She took off her jacket and loosened her tie. She was wearing black pants and vest and a ruffled white shirt. I glanced anxiously at my rumpled sweater and baggy tweeds and felt relieved to find no gum, saliva or stray jelly beans stuck to my person.

Val held out her hand to me. "Come, lie beside me," she said. "Talk to me."

We talked for at least an hour. During that time room service brought the wine together with a complimentary tray of cheese and grapes. We nibbled at the cheese, sipped wine and talked. We talked about the NBA play-offs, about downhill skiing. We didn't talk about hockey at all. We never do.

We were lying very close, leaning on our elbows, about six inches apart. The conversation trailed, then stopped. Val was looking straight at me, looking straight into my eyes. Suddenly she was kissing me, her lips scarcely grazing mine, testing the corners of my mouth with the tip of her tongue. The touch was light but terribly insistent.

I froze. She pulled back a few inches and said very gently, "Anne and I have broken up. I want you to know that because I want to make very hot love to you and I don't want your conscience pushing me away." She was smiling but she couldn't disguise the pain in her eyes.

"I'm sorry," I said awkwardly. "About Anne."

"Me too." She bowed her head for a moment, then looked me straight in the eye and said. "And you?"

I shook my head and said very bravely, "No, it's gone. There's nothing."

She took me into her arms. I resisted at first, going through the motions, still unwilling to let go, refusing to concentrate on the beautiful things her tongue was doing inside my mouth. Finally, I was able to relax. We necked until I was practically delirious.

After what seemed hours she eased herself from me. She ran a finger along the bridge of my nose and said mischievously, "Don't go away. I'll be right back."

She went into the bathroom. A few minutes later the bathroom door opened. I turned my head on the pillow. She was standing beside the bed, naked except for the vest and ruffled blouse, both unbuttoned. She wasn't wearing a bra.

"I wanted to leave you a little something," she said.

She held out her hand to me. I stood up, watching her hands as she reached to ease the sweater over my head.

"Landlady's cooking," I muttered as her hands caressed the soft pockets around my middle. "Butter tarts. I can't seem to get rid of that."

She smiled.

"You're a beautiful woman, Alison," she murmured. "Women are always more beautiful after thirty." As she said this she slipped off my shirt and slid my bra from my shoulders with fascinating slight of hand.

We made love once, twice, three times. She was everything I had imagined she would be—accomplished, funny, considerate, teasing and awfully sexy—and some things I had not expected yielding, nurturing, totally unmacho. I went at her a little too vigorously, I think, when it was my turn to orchestrate the lovemaking. I was terrified I couldn't meet her expectations. Twice she gasped and squeezed my arm very tightly. I knew she was trying very hard for me. I was stunned, almost paralyzed by her vulnerability. I know in some circles the importance of orgasm is pooh-poohed but, believe me, I experienced major relief when she climaxed against me.

I pulled myself to her chest and collapsed there with a little sigh, my face pressed against her left breast. Her great athletic heart pounded in my ear with a triumphant, joyous tribal beat. After a time she lifted my face to her and said drowsily, "See we didn't need to put it off so long. It wasn't so bad."

We rose very late the next morning, held each other and mumbled some morning things. Then Val dressed and drove me to my hotel. She kissed my hand as she released me at the side door.

"*Bravissimo*," she whispered.

I went straight to my room and fell asleep. I didn't stir until Joy woke me for the pre-game meal.

The players piled into the locker room that evening, confident and enthusiastic having exorcised the demons of playing against an injured opponent.

I spoke briefly to the team.

"Folks, you played a great game last night. You contained an explosive offense. You created scoring opportunities with heads-up defense. Go out there and play your game. Don't take any unnecessary risks and you'll come out on top."

I didn't look at Molly as I spoke. I had resolved to avoid her during the pre-game meal, sitting on the opposite side of the table, several seats away. I longed to ask Effie what time Molly had come in last night, but I wasn't sure if I wanted to know. The image of Molly in bed, surrendering to the dark-haired student drove me mad.

In spite of my good intentions, I found myself stealing long glances down the table. A couple of times, I caught her watching me. What was she thinking? What did she want me to know? Coach, I know I was out until 3:30 a.m. I can explain?

I shook my head. With the biggest game of the season on the line, I was obsessing about the bedtime of my right winger. This is what happens, Alison, I told myself with chagrin, when a foolish old coach steps over the line and develops an infatuation with a player young enough to be her daughter. Val Warnica would never have allowed herself to get into such a predicament.

Question: Val, have you ever developed an infatuation for one of your players?

Answer(shocked): Of course not, Alison. My players are strictly *verboten*. I *do* have a code of ethics (wink), *you* have some players who could turn my head. Ingrid's involved, you say? Pity.

I watched Molly as she filed past me. She seemed even more subdued than usual, the whimsical smile conspicuous by its absence.

The game itself was anticlimactic. Dorsey scored at 6:48 of the opening period. Ingrid scored with nineteen seconds remaining in the period. Joy was solid in goal; Nomi played the wing with relentless tenacity. Hamilton scored early in the second period but the Teds lived up to their reputation as the best team in the league at protecting a one-goal lead.

We were scheduled to return to Toronto immediately after the game. I lingered in the alleyway to say good bye to Val. She gave me a nice soft kiss and said, "Thanks for last night."

I climbed onto the bus, trying very hard to look suitably preoccupied and coach-like. Fourteen pairs of eyes watched me gravely as I took my seat.

Molly was stretched across the rear seat, one arm flung over her eyes. I sank into my seat with a sigh.

I had just left Val, had scarcely departed her bed, but all I could think about was Molly.

Everything about Val was so right; everything about Molly so wrong. I knew I could have a wonderful relationship with Val—warm and loving and hassle-free. What kind of life could I have with Molly? I began to wonder if I was a masochist; if I held a mirror up to Molly would I find Gail reflected back to me?

No. Molly wasn't Val. But she wasn't Gail either.

I stole a glance at her, trying to fathom the hold she had on me.

Maybe it was that impish grin—rare but hinting at some irrepressible optimism that neither time nor circumstance had been able to snuff out, that confused and confusing look in her eyes when I caught her watching me. Maybe I couldn't believe the old Molly, the Molly in the films, the Molly in Dale Yalden's memory, the Molly I was hopelessly in love with, was dead.

I knew one thing for certain, whatever the nature of the attraction, my desire to know who she was and what she was all about had become an obsession.

I rested my head against the bus window, hoping the coolness of the pane would seep into my brain, damp out this dangerous fire.

There were hundreds of nice women with whom I could have a full and rewarding relationship. Landlady was forever saying: "Alison, there's someone I should introduce you to. She's very nice. I'm sure you'd hit it off."

Out of the corner of my eye I saw Sharon climb onto the bus. Carol beckoned her to the seat beside her. Joy smiled and took the seat beside Lou. Joy and Sharon could be miles apart and still be together.

I longed for that feeling, felt the yearning grow stronger and stronger, fueled by Joy and Sharon, set on fire by the night before. It felt so good to be held and stroked again. My body hadn't been so well-cared for in years—perhaps forever. I spent seven and a half years with a woman who barely touched me the last three and sparingly before that.

All of my lovers had left me. As I sat, entombed, on that rough-idling bus the realization hit me like a sledgehammer. I wasn't good at leaving; I was weary of good byes. At this stage in my life, I wanted the sure thing.

Then for God Sakes, why Molly?

I must have looked distressed because just as the bus started Ingrid slid in beside me and asked, "Are you all right, Alison?"

I smiled and said, "Yes."

She gave me a firm, quick hug and went back to the seat she was sharing with Henny.

Nomi and Dorsey were sitting ahead of me, across the aisle from each other, conducting a conversation in intense, low voices.

"If we weren't in the bus, I'd punch you out," Nomi growled. She got up abruptly and walked to the front of the bus. She dropped into the seat beside Chris without a word.

"Prostitute," muttered Dorsey. She harrumphed about for a while, then finally stretched out on the seat and turned her back to the world.

We were going home to our own arena, two games away from the championship.

CHAPTER 20

We had four days off before the next game. I told the players the Monday practice was optional. Nevertheless, at ten, everyone showed up except Molly and Effie. I assumed they'd accepted my invitation to skip. Halfway through the skate, however, Effie arrived, frazzled, distracted and breathless.

"Alison," she said, "can I talk to you?"

I took her aside at the bench.

"I don't know where Molly is," she blurted out. "When we got home last night, she went straight to her bedroom to see Sam. There was the poor little thing, wedged into one of the spirals of her staircase, as dead as a doornail. Molly grabbed her and ran out. I haven't seen her since."

I handed the skate over to Harriett as inconspicuously as possible. I drove to the apartment, parked my car and began to wander the streets, searching for Molly Gavison.

My search was fruitless. I knew it would be from the beginning. I had no idea of her haunts, and with the exception of her teammates, knew nothing about her friends. Finally, reluctantly, I gave up and went home. I didn't sleep a wink that night.

Molly showed up for practice the next morning, one hour late. I took her aside and asked her if she was OK. She nodded, barely looking at me. She reeked of booze. I was appalled at how hard she looked and how distant she seemed.

"Have you been drinking?"

"A little... I'm sorry."

"Effie told me about Sam," I said. "I'm awfully sorry."

She shrugged.

I couldn't think of anything else to say. She hesitated a moment as if waiting to be excused, then skated away.

I tried to concentrate on practice but I felt depressed and distracted, a condition not alleviated by watching Molly plough listlessly around the rink. The last thing I needed was a call from Mrs. Toop, asking me to report to Phil's office at one.

"What's this about?" I asked.

"Mr. Tweddell didn't tell me," she said in that haughty tone that always set my teeth on edge. "I was told to have you at the office at one sharp. That's all I know."

I went home and changed from my blue jeans into a respectable pair of slacks and shirt. Phil kept me waiting in the outer office for ten minutes, but when I was finally ushered into his presence he was all smiles.

We chatted about the first two games. Phil sat back in his chair, his necktie loosened, relaxed, as if he felt no urgency whatsoever, as if I'd dropped in casually to pass the time of day on a slow Monday afternoon.

"I hear one of Warnica's reserves—that Jacques girl—is on the limp," he said. He began to talk more generally, rambling on about the season as a whole, making vague comments about finances. "The season seems to be hurtling toward a conclusion," he said, suddenly abrupt. "After all the build-up, after all the hopes and dreams, we're down to this. You've got a two-game advantage, Alison. That's great. You've worked hard. Maybe it's time to give some of the regulars a rest. Give the reserves some ice time."

"Effie's one-hundred-per cent now, Phil. Henny's ready to come back. I'll probably ask Sue to spell Henny for a few shifts. Britt's here for insurance. The reserves have already logged quite a bit of ice time."

He studied me carefully, all the time rearranging items on his blotter. "I was thinking more of Thorne, maybe Eklund. Hell, they've played a lot of minutes, haven't they?"

I looked at him, incredulous. "Are you crazy, Phil?"

He cleared his throat, twisting his chair a quarter of a turn away from me. "I'm not at all crazy, Alison," he said. "What's at stake? You lose a game or two. I simply feel... I mean, as a good general manager, from a management point of view, it wouldn't hurt to have the season go the distance."

"And you want me to mess the lines up to produce that result?"

154

"I don't mean to suggest you shouldn't be aiming to win in the end."

I gave him a shaky laugh. "Oh, that's a lot better. You're merely asking me to throw a couple games, not the whole series. Apart from the ethics involved, there's the little problem of trying to win once you've given up a two-game advantage. No way. On both counts—no way." I set my jaw firmly, tried to clear my throat, then added, "The players have worked too hard to be cheated like this. No way, Phil."

He stood up, his brow wrinkling in dismay. "For God's sake, Alison," he whimpered—he tried to sound tough but he whimpered— "for God's sake, winning doesn't matter at this stage. It's the money. Who cares if a bunch of women win or not—at least at this juncture? Who cares? We're trying to sell the sport—as a package. We're all in this together. We're only as strong as our weakest link. We're laying a foundation for the future. Hockey is a product. We're selling a product. In the long run, it's good for your girls. It'll mean job security, more money, more opportunities, expansion, more for more players." His voice dropped to a desperate whisper. "There's big money at stake here. We can't afford to pass up a chance like this."

I gripped the arms of my chair to contain my anger. "Did Val agree to this?"

"There's no need to bring Val into this." He fingered his mustache uneasily. "There's no reason to bring anybody in but you and me. Your players don't need to know anything. Make a few errors in judgment, use your reserves. You've called up two players, taken them away from their work, put the kibosh on their vacations. You'll want to give them some ice time. That's the kind of person you are. Your players will accept that, even if it does mean messing the lines up a bit. Hell, if Brophy could look like a jackass and have half the country successfully second-guessing him, why not you? It might not work anyway," he said, giving me a pleading look. "The Hurricanes may have too many weak spots to take advantage of our miscues. But even if we give them one game—every game is worth a cool twenty-thousand."

I looked him right in the eye and said with the righteous confidence available only to those who are one hundred per cent sure of their infallibility, "I'll take your proposal right to the president of the league, Phil, and if I don't hear what I want to hear from him, I'm going to the press."

"No you won't," he said. He looked at me, his mustache quivering as if he expected to be hit. "If you go near the president's office or the press, Molly Gavison will be in the Don Jail before you can blink an eye." He didn't look triumphant when he said this. Instead, his face registered that look of quiet relief, common to all gamblers who have gone for the big one against the odds and have won. He could see his victory all over my face. "Gavison's a druggie," he said quickly.

"She drinks a little." My voice was as weak and thin as a badly tuned E-string.

"She drinks a lot," he corrected. "She's an alcoholic, a weekend binger. She's also into cocaine." He raised his brows then said with a sigh, "Before she joined the team she was in a very ritzy, very private psychiatric facility, getting dried out. Booze mainly. A little cocaine. It was the cocaine that got her committed. Oh yeah," he said, staring into space, "she was not a voluntary admission. It was a compromise with a soft-hearted Crown. A year in a psychiatric facility in lieu of a criminal record and all the adverse publicity that goes with it. It was not a first offense. Her parents are friends of Dad's," he said ruefully. "I know the story well."

"You're guessing about the cocaine."

He shook his head. "Her pusher is a college student. We call him Flash Gordon. He's working his way through med school, dealing very selectively in drugs. He hangs around the smaller centers, the university jock scene. I know Flash's habits very well. We had trouble with him when we had the soccer team. Molly's been seen with him two or three times." He paused, measuring my reaction. "She's not in too far yet but she's getting there. I'm willing to bet she has some coke on her person at this very minute. I can tip off the police and get her busted anytime I want. And the Crown won't go so easy on her this time."

My heart sagged. "I don't believe you."

He turned quickly and picked up his phone. "Dad," he said brightly, "are you alone?"

"What's the problem?" I could hear Big Frank's rasping voice across the desk.

"I've got Alison Gutherie here, Dad," he said, his voice unnaturally light and high-pitched. "She doesn't believe what I'm telling her about Molly Gavison."

Big Frank's voice snatched the phone from Phil's hand and thrust it toward me. His words scraped my ear drums. "We got Gavison out of the gutter and we can put her back in. Hell, when she was busted, she was downtown turning tricks for a joint."

Before I could as much as gasp, he slammed the phone down.

Phil, very generously, paused to let me catch my breath, then said, "If you cross me, Alison, I'll hurt you. I'll hurt your players. Gavison's not the only one. Alice Todd is also vulnerable. I'm sure there are others. Drinkwater—she walks a pretty thin line. All these people are on one-year contracts. We don't have to renew anyone's contract. There's plenty more players where they come from. Nomi Pereira's a tough little bastard. Who needs that? Carol Gee's a slob. Hell, if I wanted to, I could dump the whole goddamned team."

I was numb with anger, helplessness and grief. Disgust.

He took my silence for assent. "You're in then?"

"No, Phil, I'm not in."

He looked at me sorrowfully. "Then, you're fired, Alison," he said. "You can make up some story for the press. Say we had a fight about strategy. Say I wanted to waive helmets for the play-offs to give the guys a good look at the girls. Yeah, say that. That'd be good, consistent with what's gone before. But if there's as much as a sniff of a fix, I'll see to it your players pay."

I took a deep breath. I was close to tears.

"Damn you," I said bitterly, "you'd sell your own mother to make a buck, to impress Big Frank. Damn it, Phil, this may be the one chance in a lifetime for some of these women to be winners."

He looked away. I'd like to think he was ashamed.

"I'm going," I mumbled. "If this meeting's over... I've got to tell the players."

He looked at me, fear in his eyes. "No, you won't," he said abruptly. "I'll tell them...tomorrow, after the practice. I'll arrange a press conference right after that. In the meantime, not a word to anyone. I want you off our property by noon tomorrow. Out of your apartment too. We'll forward your stuff."

"Am I that dangerous?"

He shrugged. "You're a loose cannon. Loose cannons cause trouble."

I stood up to leave. Phil stopped me with a question.

"Can we shake hands?"

I glared at him and left.

I wandered around the streets most of the afternoon. Around four I found myself on the steps of the ROM. I used the pay phone near the Ticketron to phone home. I told Joy I had decided to do some shopping and probably wouldn't be home until very late.

"Don't wait up for me," I said.

She asked about my meeting with Phil.

"Oh, it was nothing," I said. "He had some goofy idea about getting rid of our helmets."

"Oh goody," said Joy. "Face masks too?"

I used my second quarter to call Debbie Grunewald. Debbie was a compatriot of mine in Introductory Psychology. She was now a clinical psychologist with a solid private practice.

My third call was to Molly Gavison.

Effie answered the phone.

"Hi, Alison," she said. "I was just on my way out."

I asked to speak to Molly.

"Sure," she said. "Just a minute."

She was back in a few seconds. "She's coming, Alison," she said. "I think I woke her up. She sounded tired. I'm going downtown. Do you want me to pick up anything for you?"

"Oh, no thanks," I said, trying to sound casual.

Molly didn't come to the telephone for some time, not until Effie had left the apartment. I heard the door close as part of the background noise before Molly picked up the receiver.

"Hello," she said. She sounded groggy.

I told her tersely what had happened. "I want you to get help," I said, my voice suddenly husky. "I've arranged for you to see Debbie Grunewald. She's a psychologist—an old friend of mine. She can help you. She'll be discreet, and if anything does come out, it will make a difference if you've accepted treatment."

She hung up on me.

I went to the washroom behind the coffee shop with its dinosaur wall and cried. What had I expected? Thanks, Alison, for saving me from the thing I love most in life, the thing I squandered my career for? Thanks, Alison, I'd love to dry out, then follow you happily into the sunset. Say, how old are you anyway?

I continued to wander the streets. I had dinner at three different restaurants. I went to the Cineplex. The movie was a comedy. I don't remember the title and I didn't laugh once.

It was after one when I got home. Joy was asleep. I quietly packed my things in a couple of boxes and a duffel bag and stashed the evidence in my closet.

I slept late the next morning. I doubted my ability to fool Joy for any extended period of time. When I did get up I told her I had the flu. I gave her the keys to my office at the Mussyford and asked her to have Harriett conduct the practice. I think Joy assumed I had been out drinking and wenching all night. She made sympathetic noises and felt my forehead.

The minute Joy walked out the door, I called Molly.

"Have you thought about what I said?" I asked.

"No," she said, "I don't want that." Her voice was low, almost a whisper.

"I'm coming over to talk to you," I said.

"I'm leaving for practice," she said. She hung up on me again.

Phil was supposed to give the players the news at the end of the morning skate. I waited until I knew the practice would be well under way, then drove to the Mussyford. I sneaked into the arena by a side door and positioned myself in the shadows of the alleyway behind the north end net. I waited until Molly skated toward me, then moved directly into her line of vision.

"Come with me," I mouthed. I gestured toward the side door in an exaggerated fashion.

She paused for a moment, startled, the surprise in her eyes mitigated by the smoky visor. Then she turned abruptly and skated away. I watched as she swept toward the opposite net, made a big sweeping turn then circled the net, gathering speed for her dash up ice.

Near the center line she slowed inexplicably and began to skate around in frantic, confused circles, her arms dropping to her sides like the wings of a spent eagle. Finally, she turned, and with her stick dragging inertly, skated toward the bench and disappeared into the alleyway that led to the dressing room.

I wobbled out to my car, got in and proceeded to wait for Molly.

The minutes dragged by. Why wasn't she coming? I felt short of breath and rolled down the window. After a few minutes I was shivering with cold and had to roll the window up again. I had nothing to read. I had given up cigarettes years ago. I watched for Phil's car, feeling totally exposed, the only car in the back parking lot in the glaring sunlight, feeling as if I were involved in a heinous conspiracy, fearful this was my last chance with Molly, the last chance for Molly. Phil was the wicked witch of the west come to turn Molly into a pumpkin, the wicked witch of Hansel and Gretel, fattening her for the kill. I laughed at myself for mixing my fairy tales, chided myself for my irrational fears and practically jumped out of my skin when I saw Phil's car pull off the boulevard and swing around the circular driveway.

The car disappeared. I supposed Phil had pulled up at the main entrance.

But where was Molly?

Two minutes later—two minutes and three seconds to be exact—the side door opened and Molly emerged. She came toward the car, head down. I met her halfway and relieved her of her equipment bag.

She whispered thank you without looking at me. I loaded her bag into the trunk and swung the side door open. She got in.

"We're going to your place," I said once we were in the car. "We're going to get rid of every shred of dope you have." If my statement had been any longer I would have cried. As it was, the last couple of words barely escaped a badly constricted larynx.

Molly stared hard at the windshield, barely blinking all the way home.

Once at the apartment she went into a shell, sitting on the bed, head bowed while I disposed of the dope. There wasn't much. I helped her pack her bags. We drove to Debbie's office in tears.

Debbie was with Molly for what seemed hours. When she finally emerged she looked glum. "I think we've arrived at the best arrangement," she said, "given the circumstances. Since she refuses institutionalization, I've arranged for her to board with some associates who help me out occasionally with cases like this."

I must have looked every bit as desolate as I felt because she smiled and gave me a sympathetic hug.

"You've done everything, you can, Alison," she said. "Most people in your position would have tried to sweep the problem under the rug."

The worst of it was, I didn't get to say good bye to Molly.

I left Debbie's office, feeling as empty as a beer bottle at a Queen's homecoming. I wanted to say to Debbie, "I'm sorry, you can't have her. She's coming home with me." I imagined walking into Debbie's office, taking Molly by the hand and walking away with her, away to my car, away from Toronto. "I'm taking you away from all this," I would say, "away from all the fuss and turmoil. I'm taking you somewhere you'll be safe and no one will ever bother you again."

There was nothing left for me to do in Toronto. I had no reason to remain in the city. I left my Kingston phone number with Debbie in case she needed to get in touch with me. Perhaps it was my imagination but it seemed she accepted it reluctantly.

I had no reason to return to the apartment. I'd already left a note for Joy and a check to cover my portion of the bills.

I felt completely numb as my car made its way to the 401. Kennedy. Warden. Morningside—the exits flashed by. I passed Oshawa, Cortice Avenue, the church placed so unfortunately near the highway.

Near Port Hope the traffic thinned. I was alone in a metal box on a slab of concrete five hundred miles below the treeline, far enough from Toronto to feel the desolation of the separation, not close enough to home to draw from its comfort. I had been fighting tears all morning. Now, I broke down and cried without restraint. I cried so hard I was forced to pull over to the side of the road.

I climbed out of my car in Landlady's driveway to find a dozen reporters clustered around the step. A police car stood out front. The officer was wedged between the partially open screen door and the door jamb, talking to Landlady.

The reporters turned on me like a herd of Holsteins.

"Alison, is it true? Did Phil Tweddell fire you over helmets?"

"Are the players going to play without them?"

"Come on, Alison, there's got to be more to it than that."

"What's the story about the personal differences. Phil Tweddell is quoted as saying:'Gutherie isn't a team player'. Give us the story."

I made my way to the door, bouncing off them with muttered apologies.

Landlady plucked me up by the arm and said, "Thank goodness you're here." Before I had a chance to say a word, she added, "I fully support what you've done, Alison. So will Mandy when she stops crying. The phone hasn't stopped ringing. Ingrid Eklund called. Joy Drinkwater called. All sorts of media people. I've taken dozens of messages. Your mother, your brother, the president of the OWHA. I had no idea so many people were interested in women's hockey. Hockey is the key I'm sure. None of the callers seemed particularly interested in the feminist issues involved. Some of them seemed frankly anti-feminist, not the least of whom was your brother Michael."

Out of the corner of my eye, I saw the policeman take a long deep sigh. He was staring into space, his gaze fixed morosely on an imaginary point between me and Landlady.

"Is it all right. ma'am?" he said. "Do you still want to press charges?"

"No, just get rid of them," she said briskly. She took my arm and steered me inside.

As soon as I felt settled and had had my tea, I called Ingrid. We hemmed and hawed and talked past each other. When it was time to go, she said, "I'm not supposed to tell you this but they all cried when they heard the news, even Nomi... We love you, Alison," and she hung up.

The story of my firing made the evening news. Val phoned immediately thereafter.

"What they said is true," I said bravely.

"I think there's more to it than the helmets," she said. "Something more fundamental. You're quite a rabble-rouser." She paused, then said, "I'm going to miss you, Alison. I'm going to miss watching you coach. I'm going to miss flirting with you across the ice with my eyes."

She didn't add, fucking you between silk sheets at the Montclair. She didn't have to.

"I'll be thinking about you," she said just before she hung up. "I'll be in touch with you soon."

I stretched out in the chair beside the phone, propping my feet up on the footstool. Why couldn't it be Val? I stopped and stared out the window, beyond the maple tree and the rim of the street light. Val was like Christmas—wonderful, magical, overwhelming. But as daily fare? Molly was a gentle spring day. There could never be enough of them.

I thought of Molly in a strange place, her life disrupted, virtually friendless. I remembered the expression on her face when she looked at Sam. Obviously she had been everything to her. Now that too was gone.

I woke at one, dry-mouthed and drained and feeling very much alone. My heart ached for Molly Gavison.

CHAPTER 21

Dateline: Toronto

Subject: *Unbearable! Top Teddy Leaves the Picnic* by Jim Gough

Alison Gutherie did the right thing. She had a fight with her boss over an issue of player safety and was fired for her objections. Eschewing helmets in order to bare their faces for the TV cameras was a dumb idea on Phil Tweddell's part. Hockey is, after all, a contact sport. The irony of the situation is the players have refused to play without helmets and their owner has, apparently, declined to press the issue further.

The bottom line, though, is this: With Alison Gutherie gone can the Teddies pull together and get on with the business of winning the championship? Phil Tweddell plans to coach the team for the remainder of the season. Phil, you must realize, wouldn't know a hockey stick from a jock strap. We're not even sure if he likes the sport. As a lad he played soccer—never hockey—and it is here, we suspect, his sporting affections lie. Phil's ineptitude will hurt the team. But Molly Gavison's absence will hurt even more. Gavison is, at last report, in Switzerland with her family, recovering from a bout of mononucleosis and a badly sprained knee. How is Phil going to complete the speedy line of Dorsey-Young in Gavison's absence? The smart thing to do would be to slot in Sue Germaine who filled in for Henny Buskers. Buskers is one hundred per-cent fit now and ready to rejoin her regular line with Alice

Todd and Effie McGovern. Phil, however, seems eager to try his hand at line-juggling. He's already talking about switching Effie McGovern to fill Gavison's spot on right wing beside Dorsey Thorne. The fact that McGovern hasn't played right wing in over a decade doesn't phase Phil a bit. And by removing McGovern from the center position on the line with Buskers and Todd, Phil has effectively dismantled the Teddies best checking line. Phil, go back to your tabletop game and leave real hockey to the big boys...er...big girls.

Mandy was still teary-eyed next morning when she agreed at last to talk to me. I tried to apologize but how do you apologize to a kid you'd promised could stand beside you at the bench of the home play-off games?

"I'm awfully sorry, Hon," I said for the tenth time.

"Mom says it's the principle of the thing," she said. She looked absolutely desolate.

"Yeah."

"Is Molly going to be able to play?"

I took a deep breath. "Molly's very sick," I said. "She won't be better for a long time."

"She *is* going to get better, isn't she?" Mandy looked at me, shocked.

"Of course she'll get better." I gave Mandy a hug, holding her close so she couldn't see the expression on my face. What if she didn't get better? What if—

The telephone continued to ring off the wall. I got an answering machine. The messages piled up. Frustrated with the machine—and my failure to return the messages, no doubt—people began to phone Landlady again. At first Landlady gave me the messages. Finally, she announced she would deal with my calls personally. She removed the answering machine to her telephone and unplugged mine.

My zest took a vacation. I was sure I had leukemia. I stopped eating and sat on the couch in my living room, wrapped in a comforter, and watched the ALL WEATHER CHANNEL. That morning a severe storm that had paralyzed Quebec and the Maritimes moved into Ontario. The mounting snowbanks and swirling winds made being a recluse more socially acceptable.

Mandy was sent home from school at noon.

The next day—the day of the first home game—was more of the same. At Landlady's urging, I crawled out of my comforter, bathed, washed my hair and went in search of Mandy. We spent the whole day making brownies, Rice Krispie squares and chocolate fudge. Landlady made apple pies for the freezer and answered the telephone.Canadians were like squirrels. Bad weather turned us into hoarders.

At eight that night, Mandy and I gathered up our booty and settled in front of the television for the third play-off game.

My firing was a big story. The commentators shook their heads over the idiocy of firing a coach in the middle of the play-offs and railed at Phil for unnecessary, poorly plotted line changes. The hockey men put it down—albeit in nicer words—to the fumbling of a dumb, non-jock front-office man tinkering with a well-oiled machine for no reason other than a desire to be seen as an active, hands-on coach.

The Teddies took the ice to thunderous applause. The players seemed irritated, skating around like a swarm of angry bees, slapping the ice with their sticks. Nomi slashed the goal posts with her stick and spat unceremoniously into the crease as the camera swept over her.

Val looked directly into the camera as it turned toward her, hesitated for a moment, then winked.

The Teddies looked totally uncoordinated. I watched as they worked to make the adjustments necessary to accommodate the line changes. Effie was ineffective on the wing. Val's team took advantage of her disorientation to concentrate on Dorsey, double-covering her whenever she had the puck. Dorsey's frustration mounted as she was either sandwiched between two Hamilton defenders or had to watch helplessly as her quick passes, perfectly timed for a speedy Molly Gavison, sailed off the tip of Effie's outstretched stick.

While the offense fumbled, Nomi was brilliant.

As the final seconds ticked away, the crowd was on its feet. With the Hamilton defense clearing the puck with four seconds remaining, it was apparent we were headed for overtime.

Dorsey stole the puck at the blue line. Her long shot ricocheted off the stick and bounced over the shoulder of the Hamilton goalie. The goalie stared behind her in forlorn disbelief.

Mandy squealed and jumped up off the couch, spraying stray Rice Krispies and potato chips in all directions. I sat back, curiously subdued.

Nomi, Dorsey and Hamilton goalie Kitchen were selected the stars of the game. The TV commentator chose to make a goat of the Hamilton defender who had coughed up the puck at the blue line. Dorsey for once didn't try to trip Nomi as she stepped out onto the ice to acknowledge the crowd.

Phil stood at the bench as the players filed past, clearly bemused. Afterwards he told the press that, while Pereira was brilliant, it was the line changes, the "chemistry" of the checking lines he had put together that made the victory possible. I don't think the hockey men swallowed this line of reasoning for a minute.

The next morning Phil announced he would start Joy in goal. "We've been alternating goalies all season," he said innocently. "Why stop now?"

True. I would have started Joy in goal automatically. Phil's motives, though, had nothing to do with fairness. The last thing he wanted was a hot goalie in the nets that night.

The shock came at game time when Phil announced he had decided to switch the defensive pairings.

"Get a load of this guy," said Pip Blackburn who was providing the color commentary. "He gets away by the skin of his teeth with messing up the forward lines. Pereira saved his bacon there. Now he thinks he's some kind of Houdini and he's going to swap defensemen. Now Big Julie and Pat Carsey are a super defensive unit. They complement each other perfectly. Gee and Sosnoski have played together in the sticks since Caesar was a pup. That kind of continuity takes a pretty good defenseman like Gee and makes her a great defenseman. Now they're going to be confused. They can make the adjustment eventually but they don't have eventually. They've got a few games. Phil Tweddell should take the cup and run like hell with it because Val Warnica, even with a crippled team, was able to coach circles around him and his messed up lines all night. If it hadn't been for outstanding goaltending and a lucky break, the Hurricanes would have won that game because that's the way things were headed. Hamilton got fifty-four shots on goal. Count them—fifty-four."

Mandy and I resurrected some stale popcorn balls and the Rice Krispie squares—now gooey. I sprung for a new plate of fudge and put a bottle of Canada Dry on ice. Mandy tried to be optimistic about Phil's latest juggling act.

"They're all good enough," she said. "Maybe it'll be OK."

I was as nervous as a cat.

The Teddies took the ice with a look of grim determination. They took a brief skate, then clustered around Ingrid, talking earnestly.

When the starting line-up took the ice for the national anthem, I thought Phil had changed his mind. Sharon went out beside Carol as usual. Sue Germaine went out on the line with Chris and Dorsey.

"He's put the lines back together," Mandy crowed.

The camera panned the bench. Phil was leaning over Ingrid's shoulder, whispering intensely into her ear. Ingrid turned her head slightly and shrugged. Then she turned back to the game. Phil dropped his arms to his sides, completely befuddled.

The players had elected to ignore him. Ingrid and Harriett were coaching the team.

By the middle of the second period, the Teddies led five to one. I watched Val, wondering what she was feeling. She seemed as calm and unruffled as always, speaking quietly to her players, squeezing shoulders, giving encouraging taps on helmets. No grandstanding, no ranting, no throwing pennies onto the ice, no intimidation. I watched her make love to her team, whispering, teasing, trying to woo her battered team into making a fight of it.

I was afraid for the Teddies as Val's team pulled to within two by the end of the second period. But Ingrid scored with only thirty seconds elapsed in the third. They knew then it was theirs. They knew they were going to win. They soared. Their passes got sharper, their checking more intense and skillful. They were their own team now, not Phil's and not mine. Their talents grew in my eyes as I watched them relax and savor their victory, a victory which for many of them had been a long time coming.

The fans were on their feet, cheering and whistling. Phil stood up on the bench, trying to bask in the reflected glory. No one paid any attention to him. Harriett stood to one side, smiling darkly.

The siren blew to bring down the curtain on the inaugural year of the WPHL. The players embraced and threw their gloves into the air. Harriett dashed about with her 35mm camera, snapping photos like mad. Val gave Phil a perfunctory handshake, then went directly to Ingrid and gave her a big hug. It was all dreadfully unprofessional and I loved it.

The trophy presentation was simple and brief. There were no losers with heads down, no winners rubbing salt into the wounds, no locker room shots of naked players pouring champagne over fully dressed coaches and managers.

Pip interviewed Phil.

Phil was a little poorer than he had wished to be but managed to be a pretty good sport about it. He gushed about the team's performance, said there would be an extra bonus for everyone. Finally he said very earnestly, "You know, Alison Gutherie did a great job. In spite of our personal differences, I have to give her high marks as a coach. I'll make sure her name goes on the Cup. She deserves it."

Mandy cheered at that announcement. I smiled and gave her a little hug. Having my name on the Cup didn't matter that much. Phil was playing by his own rules, accepting defeat graciously. It's one of his better qualities—"You won fair and square. No hard feelings". For a moment I felt the teensiest bit of warmth for him. Then I remembered what he had done to Molly Gavison and felt sick and angry.

Val was the first to call. The warmth and sweetness in her voice brought tears to my eyes.

"I wish you were here," she said. "It was lonely without you tonight. To be in Toronto and not to see you is obscene."

We agreed to meet for dinner in one month.

Ingrid called next. The players were dressed and about to head out to the postgame dinner. Everyone took a turn on the phone. They tried to share their excitement with me but it was impossible. I was no longer part of the team. I was a stranger.

"We'll get together when I get home," Ingrid said.

CHAPTER 22

I was desperate to make contact with Molly. The morning after the final I went downtown and searched for a card that seemed remotely suitable.

I went to the coffee shop next door, ordered a coffee and donut, opened the card and tried to write a note.

Dear Molly,

Leaving the team and leaving you are the most painful things I've done in a life that's included its share of tender spots. Leaving the team hurts but it ended well. We accomplished so much, much more than we dared hope for.

I don't know if you end well. I get a little frantic thinking about it. It's a double whammy too, that one. Will it end well for you and me? Being together—hell, that's too rich even to contemplate. That would be the icing on the cake. But, as I've said, I don't know if you end well. I'm not at all sure I've done the right thing. I feel as if I've deserted you when every impulse told me to take you and run. I'll bet you need my caring more than you need therapy.

It's not too late. I could still ride up on my white charger—in this case, my grey Datsun—and take you away. Leave a light on in the window. We'll tie some sheets together ...

I wrote a second note *Best wishes, Alison Gutherie.*—I never actually wrote the first letter—put it in the envelope and trudged off to the mailbox.

I died a thousand deaths on the way home.

Landlady came to the door at the sound of my key in the lock.

"Alison," she said, "you look awful."

I mumbled, "Thanks." I looked at her rather dazed for a moment, then said, chagrined, "Damn it, I forgot Mandy's hockey game!"

"It's all right," Landlady said calmly. "When I didn't hear you moving around this morning, I assumed you'd slept in. I told Mandy not to wake you. She was disappointed but she felt important knowing she was helping you get the rest you so obviously need."

"I've done nothing but rest for days," I said with bitter resignation, "and I've never felt so tired."

"You look like hell," she repeated. "I want you to join me for lunch. I've homemade soup on the stove and a loaf of bread fresh from the oven."

"Oh, I couldn't—"

She ignored my protests. "I have a few things to discuss with you, Alison." She took my arm and steered me gently toward the kitchen.

I thought she looked troubled. I had a sinking feeling that at least one of those "few things" involved Mandy. Perhaps Mandy had started to ask questions. I sat down at the kitchen table, feeling uneasy. Landlady ladled the soup into bowls and placed several thick slices of brown bread in front of me. She poured a cup of tea for each of us from the familiar brown teapot with its yellow-flowered cozy. She then took a notebook from her hip pocket, sat down at the table and said very seriously, "We have to discuss your future. Have you made any plans?"

I shook my head. Apart from drowning myself in a vat of mulled wine, I hadn't thought of a thing. "I thought I'd phone Don Hamilton and see if I could get my old job back," I said without much commitment, "or some facsimile thereof. I'm sure the board's got something for me."

Landlady looked at me in that long-suffering way of hers and said, "I've had quite a few inquiries, Alison."

"Inquiries?"

"I let it be known you would be taking a few days off before considering any offers."

"What offers?"

"The owner of the local OHA franchise called. He wants to talk to you about a job with the organization. He refused to give specifics."

My heart skipped a beat. The OHA, the AHL, the NHL. I saw myself behind the bench at the Forum with Bob Gainey, Larry Robinson et al crowded around me, hanging on my every word.

Landlady must have seen the glimmer in my eye. She frowned.

"You've also received a number of requests for interviews and lectures. Brian Butler called. I think he has a book in mind. I'm sure he's not the one we want, though. We'll hold out for Stephanie Scott or Laura Pederson. We want a feminist perspective on sportsworld."

"Does any of this involve money?"

Landlady looked at me as if I'd physically injured her. "Of course, Alison. I wouldn't permit you to be exploited. There are several commercial opportunities—promotional work—which I'll get to later."

"How will I be able to work all this around my teaching job?"

She looked at me a trifle impatiently and said, "Alison, you won't need your teaching job. I'm sure there'll be enough money available to provide you with a reasonable income. You're a *cause célèbra* right now. Haven't you been reading the newspapers? There are scores of people wanting interviews. I've taken phone numbers and details. You can contact them yourself when you're ready—by the end of the week, I hope. I've divided the requests into three categories—newspaper, magazine and book possibilities," she said in a business-like manner. "I've also hired an answering service." She paused, shaking her head. "You need an agent, Alison."

I stared at her, completely befuddled. She was nodding, not so subtly prompting my response.

"Will you be my agent?" I asked.

"Do you want me to be?" she asked coyly.

"Yes," I said.

"Then I'd be very happy to be," she said.

The next afternoon I went down to the M Center where Pete Gradowicz was putting the Junior A team through its paces. Pete stood behind the bench, leaning against the glass with a look of friendly disinterest. The rumor was Pete had been short-listed for a job as assistant coach with the Leafs. I could tell from his expression it was in the bag.

"Hello, Alison," he said without turning.

"Gord's looking for me," I said. "Do you know what it's about?"

The skin around his eyes crinkled into a smile. "Just between you and me? I think he wants you for the Frontenacs. Gord thinks you're a pretty good coach."

"What do you think?"

He shrugged. "You're a good coach, Alison, but this isn't the league for you."

"Or for you?"

"It's a stepping stone for me." He swept an arm toward the ice. "Look at them. Most of them are assholes. A few of them will go on to be professional hockey players. The rest of them—"

"Professional assholes?"

"You've got it," he said.

We stood together for a few minutes, watching the practice in silence. The players were big and fast and powerful. I saw very little of the delicate touch, the finesse I had become accustomed to over the past year.

"What do you think?" Pete asked after a while.

"I'll wait to see what Gord has to say."

But even before I left the M Center, I knew there would be no Montreal Forum, no red, white and blue jerseys clustered around me, hanging on my every word. This was not for me.

By the end of the week Landlady had my future settled.

"I've drawn up a tentative schedule," she said briskly. "Conditional upon your approval of course."

I looked at the timetable she handed me.

"This looks like grade-nine remedial," I protested. "Reading? Writing skills?"

She ignored my disdain. "It never hurts to brush up," she said. She took my silence as assent. "The first week actually is quite light. Paul Nokes is local. It's a radio phone-in show. No one asks hard questions. The *Global* interview will be conducted by Kathy Shelly. You don't like her but you know her and know what to expect. John McCabe is very sweet and easy-going. His interview will be only pseudo-controversial. There's no money involved in any of this but the exposure will be valuable promotion for the paying events. Queen's has approached us to do a special Ban Reigh lecture in September. U of T is interested in featuring you in a seminar series. There are many opportunities of this sort available. But we need to firm up our ideology," she said severely. "The next couple of months will give us ample opportunity for that." Noticing my bewilderment she said, "It's penciled in under *Education* on your schedule."

"What about softball?"

She ignored me.

"We need to establish your credibility as a bona fide feminist—a credible representative of the women's movement. Your impulses are correct," she said soothingly. "You need coaching, though, to form your philosophical foundation." She looked at me, her expression painfully serious. "I'm not doing this for the money, Alison. It's the cause."

"I have no job," I reminded her. "What if we don't make money on the lecture circuit?"

She dismissed my objections airily. "I won't throw you out if you can't pay the rent," she said.

CHAPTER 23

March was luxury. I read some wonderful, inspiring books, books that made me want to leap up and swat Phil on the head (if he'd been handy) and run amok through the streets of Kingston, waving banners and screaming: "Male-dominated Sportsworld sucks!" April was a little more hectic with more demands on my free time. May leapt at me like a lion, claws unsheathed.

"Time to get down to business," Landlady said.

I was everywhere, seeing everyone. Under Landlady's tutelage, I learned the language of feminist politics, refined my rhetoric, squeezed my gut feelings into an acceptable ideological framework.

"And don't forget to get a haircut," said Landlady, "and eat a properly balanced diet. Health shows."

I appeared on *Front Page Challenge, The Journal, The News at Noon.* I was tapped to do an ad for CCM hockey helmets: "These helmets are so good, I'd stake my job on it. Right?"

I tried to be honest, at least as honest as I could be given the circumstances. But sometimes I found myself saying things I wasn't sure I believed in, parroting things I'd heard Landlady say, things I'd recently read. Sometimes I said things I believed but knew would make the athletic sorority cringe. There were times I wasn't entirely sure what I believed in or if I was telling the truth or not.

Question: Why did you leave the game?

Answer: Because I found it impossible to conduct the game of hockey within a feminist framework.

Real Answer: Because I was asked to cheat.

False Question: Why didn't you blow the whistle?

Real Answer: Because I was trying to protect a drug addict, an insane woman, the woman I'm in love with, the woman whose body I crave.

False Question: Would you have protected her if you hadn't been in love with her?

Real Answer: Of course. Yes. Sure. I don't know. Why do you ask such hard questions? (subdued) No, I would have made her come clean.

False Question: For her own good?

Real Answer: Sure. Yes. For the good of the team.

It's enough to make a radical feminist cringe.

In May the winner of the "Win a Date With a Teddy" contest was announced. Henny said she was a very nice woman.

I saw the players as often as I could. I saw Ingrid more than anyone. She had taken a job for the summer with a graphic-design firm. We had lunch together often.

"There's a rumor the Teddies are being sold," she said one day. "Inside the family."

"With any luck the buyer won't be Big Frank," I said.

Ingrid grimaced. "Who knows? The story is that Phil is selling his interest to raise the money to buy a franchise in the new arena-soccer league."

"Well, he's made his point with Big Frank," I said. "He's proved he too can be a success. Now he can return to the macho sportsworld his mild exterior so obviously craves."

"With Phil gone, maybe you could get your old job back." Ingrid paused, stunned by the beautiful simplicity of the idea. "Alison, that would be great. We'd all be together again...just like old times."

I was caught off balance. "Ingrid, I don't know. I never thought—"

She grabbed me by both shoulders, gave me a gentle shake. "Then think about it. We could have it all—the same magic, the fun...everything."

I gave her a hug. "I'll think about it."

I managed to get together with Julia in June. I had been invited to speak to the Association of Women for Amateur Sport in Detroit. We met for lunch. She described with enthusiasm her job supervising the basketball program at the downtown Y.

"I'd forgotten that occasionally it's fun down here," she said.

"Maybe you'll be tempted to hang up your skates," I said.

She laughed and said, "No way. Not as long as these old legs hold together."

Joy called me religiously every week. She was on the road for the summer, doing promotional work for the league—giving speeches, attending Girl Scout dinners, holding clinics. The trip would take her from St. John's to Vancouver south to Chicago and through Michigan and upper New York State. The league was thinking expansion.

"Everywhere we go people ask questions about you," she said dryly. "I like to check in every now and then to make sure I'm giving the right answers."

Joy enjoyed the job but she missed Sharon.

"Being separated for the summer is bad and it's good," she said. "If you know what I mean."

I knew exactly what she meant.

Sharon was working for her uncle, doing industrial and commercial plumbing around town and pitching for Number nine Legion evenings and weekends.

Dorsey was in town too, taking courses at Queen's, doing her best imitation of Joe College, hanging out watching "chicks" at the Student Union. When she wasn't thus occupied, she played a nifty shortstop for Number nine.

Nomi had a job with Parks and Recreation, looking after the flowers in the city parks. She apparently had talents and sensibilities I had never imagined.

I asked Ingrid very tactfully how Nomi and Dorsey were getting along. "Now that they're playing softball for the same team," I added.

"They're the same," she said. "Still fucking each other's minds." She laughed, then after a pause, frowned and said, "Nomi and Dorsey—I don't like that setup, you know. Someone's going to get hurt. The weaker one."

"Which one is weaker?"

"I don't know," she said.

I didn't know either. I liked to think of Dorsey and Nomi as a pair of burrs, prickly and mean on the outside, soft and giving on the inside. Or maybe they were both marbles. In that case there would be neither a winner nor a loser in the game they were playing, just a lot of noise and static. I hoped I wasn't looking at a marble and a burr.

I cherished my time with the players. As my schedule grew more hectic, I fought for the few hours together. I had never made an effort for friendship like this before. This is where I draw the line, I thought.

I'm tired of people getting away from me.

I got to know the players in a way that seemed impossible before. We were all on an equal footing now. We were friends. Being their coach had separated me from them more than I had imagined.

Occasionally, the talk would turn to Molly. "She was a really nice person," they would say. "I wish we'd gotten to know her better." They spoke as if they didn't expect to see her again.

I would shrug and look away as if Molly Gavison was the last thing on my mind.

Mandy started to grow breasts that summer. It wasn't a traumatic event for her and Landlady handled it very well. It was traumatic for me, however. Mandy was growing up and I had no idea what she would become. What if she turned into one of those boy-crazy airheads I saw hanging around the hamburger joints? Landlady warned me over coffee one morning that sort of thing might happen.

"We should be prepared for the worst," she said matter of factly. "She may reject our values for a time. She may even reject us. Eventually, she'll come back to them and to us. As an adult."

I groaned. Ten years divorced from Mandy.

Val came to visit, warm and vibrant and teasing me about a tumble. When I demurred she laughed and said, "Just lie down, then, and let me give you a back rub."

I loved the touch of Val's hands and I loved Val's voice. It was comforting to feel her presence, her hands stroking my back, her warm breath against my cheek and neck.

Finally she lay down beside me. I rolled over to face her. She put her arms around me and gave me a long, lingering hug. She released me at last, pulling back from me slightly, tracing my face with her eyes.

"Is there someone else?"

I nodded.

"Has anything happened?"

"No."

"Tell me about her. Tell me what she's like."

"I can't."

"I mean, generally." She looked at me, her eyes now mischievous. "Come on, tell me."

I shook my head.

"Is she attractive?"

"I think so."

"Is she dark like me?"

"No."

"Oh. Is she old, young, in between?"

"Young."

"Hm. Under thirty?"

"Younger."

"Under twenty-five!"

"Yes."

"Alison!"

"I can't help her age."

"It's all right," she said. "Young is good. Sometimes overrated. Sometimes unfairly maligned. Like old." She paused, then tracing a finger along my lower lip said, "Why's nothing happening?"

"Problems," I said.

"Oh," she said. "Can't you fix them?"

"I don't know," I said. "I'm not even sure she would want me."

She smiled, then said in a low voice. "Then let me be your lover while she thinks about it."

She made love to me with her voice and with her eyes, told me how she was going to make love to me until I was uncomfortably swollen and blushing like crazy. "I think you should go back to Anne," I said as soon as I was able to utter a coherent sentence.

"Why?"

"Because you're in love with her."

"Yes, I love her very much." She looked away, then said sheepishly, "There's something I should tell you."

"Yes?"

"She won't take me back—not on my terms." She averted her eyes, ashamed. "Amazing, isn't it? She's the first."

"I'm sorry."

"She couldn't handle my roving eye," she said with a small laugh, "my deep down sweaty jockdom, my affection for Steeltown. But mostly it was my roving eye. She wants stability, a country house, children—three of them. Alison, she already has the donors lined up. The best string men in Canada, she tells me. She's thirty. She's not getting any younger, she says." She looked at me, horrified. "Can you imagine me with children?"

"Yes," I said with conviction, "I can. It doesn't seem a strange idea at all."

"I don't know," she said, now restless. "What if I screw up? It's one thing to walk away from a lover. It's quite another to desert a pregnant woman."

I had moved into a semi-sitting position by this time. She curled up beside me, head in my lap, her face pressing against my abdomen. I reached down to smooth the hair from her forehead. She raised her head to my touch, looking surprisingly young and vulnerable.

"Yes it is," I said.

"Being a couple isn't all it's cracked up to be," she said with a frown. "I've never had a monogamous relationship. I've never had a live-in. Marriage isn't all it's cracked up to be. I've watched my friends fail. I've seen what happened to you."

"Marriage isn't all it's cracked up to be. Neither is being single."

She was subdued for a moment, then looked at me with that hint of an imp in her eye and said, "But damned it, Alison, I'm so good at it."

Later that month I learned Molly had left Toronto without leaving a forwarding address.

I sat on the floor beside the telephone until well after dark, tears streaming down my face.

Molly was gone and wherever she was, she didn't want me to follow.

August was hectic. I was busy all the time and actually making money. In the middle of the month, a sports reporter brought me a rumor.

I was having coffee at Wimpy's when Neil Hopper came in. He ordered a burger at the counter, grabbed the greasy concoction in one hand, a beer in the other and lumbered over to my table.

"Hi, Alison, how goes the battle?"

"Not bad. How about you?"

He waved my question aside with a greasy paw and sat down. "Same shit. Trying to write something intelligent about the Blue Jays from the boons. Pretending to give a damn about the CFL, put together a hockey pool. Who knows? Maybe next year, I'll catch a break. I'd like to attend spring training without paying my own way, for example."

"No budget?"

"Budget sucks." He took a bite of hamburger and chewed it noisily. "I've got a hot rumor for you, though. Impeccable source."

"Oh?"

"Phil Tweddell's aunt Lulu Morgan has bought the Teddies."

"You're kidding."

"Nope. Lulu's been south the past couple of years, pouring wads of money and attention into a couple of tennis phenoms. The kids have joined the satellite tour and Lulu's ready to come home."

"That's all the Teddies need," I said bitterly. "Another dabbler."

Neil chugged his beer, mopped up the droplets that drizzled down his chin. "*Au contraire*. From what I hear, Lulu actually likes the game. In fact, she used to coach in house-league."

I left Wimpy's with my head spinning. I had assumed the Teddies would be picked up as a sideline by one of Big Frank's sons—probably Frank Jr. who was busy building his own empire. I had no desire to go that route again. But, Lulu…

There was only one easy way to find Lulu Morgan. I swallowed my pride and called Mrs. Toop.

"Alison," she said, "how nice to hear from you."

I ignored her sarcasm and stated my business.

"Well, I do have Ms. Morgan's private number. Of course, I can't give it out without authorization. I will tell her you called."

I hung up not expecting to hear another word.

In spite of the trauma of the past few months, the idea of being back with my team drove me mad with desire. It was August, after all. Soon September would be here, the first nip of autumn heralding the siren call of the ice, the milk-like glaze minutes after the Zamboni has passed over, the scrape and glide of skates, the clickity-clack of the puck against hockey sticks. I saw myself standing behind the bench, caught the noise of the crowd, the shouts of the players, the sight of sweat dripping off the ends of fourteen noses.

My team.

The phone rang an hour later. I answered it casually and froze at the sound of the deep, old voice. "Lulu Morgan here. Mrs. Toop gave me your message." When I hesitated she added. "I assume you've heard the rumor I'm buying the Teddies."

"Yes."

"It's true, although, if you repeat it, I'll call you a liar. The sale won't be official until tomorrow."

"I understand."

"I assume you're calling for a number of reasons. First, let me assure you that I'll treat your players well. You have my word. I like the team you put together. It's got style and spunk. I like that."

"Thank you."

"I guess the next thing you want to know is whether I've hired a coach. I have."

My face dropped a foot.

She waited a respectful few seconds, then said. "Don't think I didn't consider you. I did. I liked what you did with the team. The truth is, when I decided to buy the Teddies, I already had a candidate in mind. If she had declined, you would have been on my short list.

"Even then," she continued, "You might have called it an honorary inclusion. I would have had serious reservations. You're not the same person you were last fall, Alison. You've removed yourself from the fray. You've become a critic. I don't know the whole story about your falling out with Phil. Not that it would matter if I did. I don't like the way he does business. And it's not that I don't respect your opinions. I do. I think a lot of what you're saying is dead on. But, you've assumed a different relationship to the game."

"I don't know what to say."

"Say you're disappointed. I would be disappointed if I were you. The game gets in your blood."

"It does."

"But before you get mired down in what might have been, think about this. The team won't be the same. Oh, the players will be the same. But the team will change. It will get better but it won't be the same. You'll never find the same excitement again...not with this team." She hesitated. "Do you know what I'm saying?"

"I think I do."

"OK." I heard a ponderous sigh. "Alison, I wish you the best. I'm looking forward to hearing what you have to say this season."

We said good bye and hung up. I sat by the telephone for several minutes, chin resting on drawn-up knees.

I was reassured to know if I wasn't the first choice, I wasn't the second choice either. I could handle the fact I wasn't in the running. I couldn't have handled the fact that I might have lost my team on a coin toss.

I got up, finally, and made a cup of coffee. Lulu was right. I realized when I thought of coaching the team again what I saw in my dreams was pure illusion. I saw myself as a rookie coach, starting out on the greatest adventure of my life. I saw my players getting ready for the season in their kiosk-stenciled T-shirts, with a lot of excitement and a great deal of uncertainty. I saw fifteen people setting out together on a journey, destination unknown. The Teddies would experience other exciting moments, times of great satisfaction, but nothing would ever compare with our first year.

I took my coffee over to the window and sat down. A lot had changed since our inaugural year. The league had entered into a contract with the sports network for a game of the week. Julia Martin would no longer be a roller derby queen recruited for entertainment value, but a bone fide defensive specialist with years of hockey crammed into her head in one short season. Alice Todd would no longer be the youngest woman in professional hockey. The rosters had been expanded to eighteen players and the Hamilton Hurricanes had snapped up the next teen-age sensation. Lauren MacDonald and Dorsey Thorne were on the threshold of becoming big stars. And players like Lou Frampton, Effie McGovern and Henny Buskers would finally earn a bit of recognition for their less flamboyant but entirely essential roles. Sue Germaine would add a gritty veteran presence to the Young-Thorne line. Britt Blakey would gain recognition as a role player. And there would be no Molly Gavison slipping up the wing, graceful as a jaguar, silent as a ghost.

I took a long look out the front window where Mandy was playing a game of street hockey by herself. She had a net, guarded by a goalie with the prime scoring spots cut out. I watched with pleasure as she hit each one in turn. She finished her performance with a nifty backhand to the high glove that brought a grin to her face and mine too.

Had I really expected to go back and find Molly Gavison waiting for me in the dressing room?

Two days later Phil Tweddell held a press conference to announce he had sold the Toronto team to Lulu Morgan. Lulu would be the sole owner. Camille "Cam" Roberts, Aunt Lulu's goddaughter would coach the team.

Aunt Lulu, wearing a floppy hat and enough costume jewelry to stock Sears, took the microphone to announce she had signed a long-term contract with the Mussyford. No more shuttling players and equipment across town. No more preppy camp.

"How are the ticket sales going?" A reporter asked.

"Just lovely," Aunt Lulu said.

The season got underway October 15th as the Teddies took to the ice against the Detroit Dynamos.

The woman behind the bench was Cam Roberts, a beautiful little jock with a soft, chivalrous, baby-butch manner and excellent hockey credentials. Her Dad had put her on skates as soon as she could walk. She played collegiate hockey at the University of Toronto and coached women's hockey at Rhode Island and Northeastern. She got the job coaching the Teddies, though, because she was Aunt Lulu's god-daughter. Nepotism never worked so well.

I was in the stands, thanks to Aunt Lulu who had sent seasons tickets. I took Mandy who was delighted but couldn't understand why we hadn't been invited to sit in Aunt Lulu's box seats.

"There aren't any box seats at the Mussyford." I pointed to a seat just behind the bench where Aunt Lulu sat, munching a hot dog.

At the first intermission I was invited to the press box for a chat.

Question: What do you think of the hockey you've seen so far tonight?

Answer: Excellent. I'm enjoying it.

Question: The new coach, Cam Roberts, seems to have swallowed your play book.

Answer: Cam spent her playing career as a defender. It shows.

Question: Is there any truth to the rumor that Aunt Lulu offered you the job and you turned it down?

Answer: None at all.

Question: You've said some tough things about the governors. Three coaching positions fell vacant during the off-season. Bill Mason was fired in Buffalo. Perry Hartschorn stepped down in London. You weren't offered anything. Is this a vendetta on the part of the owners?

Answer: The Lambs aren't my kind of team. And I think Buffalo got a good coach in Jose Lalonde who coached the women's team at McGill for years. Buffalo will be a better team because of her. I don't think there's a vendetta. The teams got what they wanted.

Question: Would you consider coaching again?

Answer: I am coaching. I've got a team of bantam girls. We start play next week.

Question: Do you miss the big time?

The arena erupted in a burst of applause as the Teddies took the ice to start the second period.

Answer: Sure but life goes on.

Real Answer: For a few brief shining moments I shared the lives of the best women hockey players in the world. I miss it like hell. I miss them like hell.

I was in Toronto last week to give a lecture to the Toronto chapter of the NFA. I had a few hours to kill before my train at six. The Teddies had left at noon for a game in Detroit so I had nowhere to hang out. I wandered about, ending up—drawn by some subtle but powerful radar—to Willard's. Dale and I chatted for a couple of hours, reminiscing about the "old days".

"Who got the over-time winner the other night?" he asked at one point.

"Sue Germaine," I said, naming the player who had replaced Molly at right wing.

"Oh, yeah," he said.

There was a long silence during which we stared at the counter. I couldn't hear a thing but the sound of Dale breathing and the clock ticking behind the bar. Finally Dale cleared his throat and said, "I haven't heard a thing either."

I was away from home a lot that winter. I had a one-night stand with a woman in Montreal and another with a woman in Halifax. Both times I left town feeling as empty as a wineskin after a Gaels football game.

The hockey year came and went. The Teddies made the finals once again but this time they lost to the Hurricanes in seven games. The Teddies were a better team in many ways than the team that won the Cup but the Hurricanes, injury-free, were still a little better. The rivalry between them was developing the way I had hoped it would— fierce competition softened by growing affection.

The caliber of hockey throughout the league had improved over the previous year. Even the Lambs were learning to play.

"It's good stuff," said Farrell of *The Star*. "Reminds you of the way they played hockey in the '40s and '50s—carrying the puck in, making the plays. None of this dump-and-chase routine so common in the NHL today."

Oh, yes, in October Val gave up her bachelorhood and moved with Anne into a comfortable restored townhouse with a deep back yard and garden. Anne became pregnant in January. Val told me, somewhat ruefully, that after the news came out several of her old girl-friends had called to congratulate her and say, "We knew you could do it."

My life was becoming comfortable again. Landlady had learned to schedule my commitments to give me ample time at home between engagements and to divide my travel time into manageable little chunks. I always was a homebody.

I gave Laura Pedersen permission to write my story. Laura had plenty of enthusiasm for the project, but she was taking her time. "There's more to this story than meets the eye," she said. "I want to let it simmer."

Laura was too smart for her own good.

I wished I could say Molly Gavison had become a sweet but faded memory. That was not the case. I had a picture of her in my wallet that I looked at often. It was one Joy took with a Pocket Instamatic at a party just before the play-offs. Molly was smiling for the camera but her eyes looked sad. She looked like someone who has tried hard but is on the verge of losing it. Why hadn't I seen that? Because I was too wound up in my own fantasies, too busy figuring out ways to cut my loses to see what was really going on with Molly Gavison.

The prospects of seeing Molly again looked pretty bleak. Phil didn't know where she was. My letter, written in care of her parents, was returned with a curt dismissal: *Our daughter is not at this address.*

And now, Debbie had lost track of her.

"She dropped a note to say she was moving again," Debbie said "but she didn't give a new forwarding address. That's not uncommon. Often people who have been in therapy want to make a clean break with the past. They want to put their old lives behind them. It's a dec-laration of independence."

I spoke to Debbie in April. A year had passed since I last saw Molly Gavison.

CHAPTER 24

The phone call came one hot June afternoon.

"Alison?" The tone was light and fresh like a spring breeze. She said my name tentatively, the way people say names they're not used to using familiarly.

"Yes?"

"This is Molly Gavison," she said. "I'm in town. I'd like to see you."

My heart did a quick flip in my chest and began to bang wildly against my rib cage.

"I want to see you too. Do you want to come here?"

"Yes," she said.

So far, so good. I took a deep breath. "When can you come?"

"Anytime."

"Now? Can you come now?"

"Yes."

"Where are you? Can I come to get you?"

"I'll walk," she said. She sounded terribly cheerful.

"Are you sure?"

"It isn't far."

"I'll put on the kettle."

I hung up the receiver. I'd been out in the garden all morning, helping Landlady weed and cultivate. I needed to touch up a bit—cut my hair, remove ten pounds from my body. I ran a comb through my hair and reached into my closet for a clean shirt.

I stood by the window, standing on tiptoe to see the street over the gable, rehearsing my greeting, going insane.

In spite of these preparations I managed to miss her. The doorbell rang without warning. Mandy got to the door first. Under the cover of her excited chatter, I managed to back up the stairs, slip into my apartment and close the door. A few seconds later Mandy barged through my door unannounced, dragging an apologetic Molly by the hand.

"Guess who's here?" she cried.

Molly smiled at me over the top of Mandy's head. She was wearing a pure white shirt, an oversized black jacket, blue jeans and patent-leather oxfords—still the polite punker, Molly Gavison. She looked tanned and healthy—sunburnt around the ears and nose—and had a bit of a dimple in her cheek. She wasn't wearing the dark glasses. I noticed that right away. Her hair was cut very short, except for a patch over the right eye, and stuck up at the crown in a frisky, unheeded cowlick.

My heart melted and ran all over the rug.

"How are you?" I asked. I was shaking like a leaf. My eyes said, "I love you. Where have you been?"

"I'm fine," she said.

"Are you going to play again?" Mandy demanded. "Is your knee OK? Is your mono gone?"

"My knee's OK and my mono's gone," Molly said "but I'm not going to play again. Not professionally."

"Are you going to stay long? Are you going to stay here?"

"Yes, I'm going to stay quite a long time. I've moved here. I've already got an apartment." She was speaking to Mandy but I was sure her words were meant for me.

"You've got an apartment?"

"Yes, it's on the opposite side of the park, near the skating oval." She paused, then said quietly as if there were just the two of us in the room, "I've got a job too."

"Here?"

She nodded. "It's with the regional speed skating association. I'll be doing some coaching and some administrative work—setting up clinics, fund-raising, looking after correspondence and so forth."

"How?" I was sounding more cerebral by the minute.

I think she interpreted the question to mean, "Who got the job for you?".

"I got it myself," she said with defensive pride. "I saw the ad in *The Canadian Coach*." She smiled ruefully, then added, "I had to practically get down on my knees and beg but I convinced them to hire me."

"Why didn't you tell me? I know people here. Maybe I could have..."

"I wanted to *do* it first," she said.

At that point I handed Mandy a bill and sent her to the store for a package of cookies. She rolled her eyes but at least she didn't volunteer her mother's cookies.

"I couldn't stay in Toronto," Molly said when Mandy had left. She walked over to the window, stuffing her hands into her pockets. "There were too many memories—good and bad. It would have been difficult being near the team and not part of it. And I think you can be lonelier in a big city than in a small one." She paused. "You know, when I heard Lulu had bought the team, I almost phoned her to ask for my job back. I'm egotistical enough to believe I'm a better player than Sue Germaine. But, it wouldn't have been the same. Do you know what I mean?"

I nodded. "So, where have you been?"

"After I left Debbie I went north," she said. "I worked in a fast-food restaurant in Thunder Bay. I thought I'd work my way back south until I knew what I wanted to do. I worked handing out fliers, washing dishes. I worked in Sudbury, North Bay, The Sault. Then I saw an ad for strawberry pickers in Prince Edward County. It seemed like fate. This is where—" She stopped abruptly.

I waited.

"I'd like to play hockey again," she said. "Just for fun. Someone suggested I check with the Martellos."

"Good team," I said fervently.

"I've got to keep busy. I've got to make an effort to spend time with people." She said the words almost to herself as if she was repeating a hard-learned lesson. " It's so easy to shut yourself up." She paused, then said happily, "I've got a dog—a little spaniel about a year old."

I was looking at her and smiling with unrestrained pleasure. I had never seen her so animated.

"Her name is Violet," she said.

I wanted to turn the conversation to more weighty matters but I didn't know how. We talked about my work and about her work. Mandy returned too soon. She had Landlady in tow.

"Here she is, Mom," she said as if she had personally produced Molly from dust. "Can we have her for dinner?"

"I'd love to have her for dinner, dear," said Landlady, "but tonight's not good. I have to go out at seven. How about Wednesday? That way we can do it properly. Is Wednesday all right with you Molly?"

"Yes, Wednesday is fine."

I wanted to take Mandy in my arms and hug her to death.

Molly glanced at her watch. "I have to be home in half an hour to let the telephone installer in," she said. "Wednesday then. That's great."

She said something nice to Mandy and Landlady and me too but I was too distracted to hear what she said. I just grinned and continued to parrot inanities.

Everyone went to the door to see her off. I lingered surreptitiously by the window to watch her walk away. She looked strong and confident and totally comfortable with herself.

Molly had made it. I had helped. I felt proud.

Then an uneasy thought crossed my mind. Now that Molly was strong, what would she want with an old war-horse like me? She had come to say hello and perhaps good bye.

CHAPTER 25

Dinner on Wednesday went by me like one of the more confusing chapters in Alice in Wonderland. Landlady monopolized the conversation. I was tongue-tied. I sat throughout the meal, grinning like a fool, agreeing with everything that was said. Landlady and Molly talked politics. I discovered Molly had a degree in political science from Carleton and had been something of a campus radical. I learned that she spoke several languages and played the piano. Landlady revealed that she spoke French and German and played the pump organ. They told jokes in German and laughed. Mandy rolled her eyes. They laughed and told more jokes—several of them in Latin. One or the other would translate periodically. The jokes seemed to lose something in the translation. I laughed anyway, happy to see Molly so alive and getting on so well with Landlady.

"Alison," Landlady said as she passed me later on her way to bed. "I approve."

"What do you mean?"

"You know perfectly well what I mean," she said with pleasant annoyance. "We'll have her for dinner again—soon."

We did have her for dinner again—quite soon. The next week we had a barbecue, roasted corn and soyburgers, sat out on the back porch, played scrabble and crokinole, drank lemonade, laughed and carried on until we had the Olsen's dog barking and Violet yipping in unison.

Sitting there under the maple tree at the edge of the little splash of light from the door, looking at the fireflies and inhaling the deep scent of lilacs, I felt transported back to our front porch on the farm with Grandma just before she died, and Aunt Maude dropping in for a cup of coffee, drinking it with lots of sugar and cream and a piece of homemade apple cake. A thick mixture of coffee and lilacs and fresh-cut hay. I sighed so deeply I caught myself out of my reverie. I was then aware Molly had been watching me intently. Her eyes held mine for a moment. Then she smiled.

"You've been on a long trip," she said.

I nodded. "Very long."

"Look at that firefly," Mandy chimed in. "That's the biggest I've ever seen."

Grandma and Aunt Maude were both dead now. The people I loved most in the world were gathered around me in Landlady's back yard.

Mandy had pulled Molly away to wrestle a June bug from Violet. Molly was wearing a T-shirt and cutoffs. I engaged in some unabashed leg-watching. I couldn't help myself. Her legs were pow-erful, powerful enough to propel her across the lawn and allow her to capture Violet with amazing ease. Violet had the last laugh though. She swallowed the June bug. Mandy groaned and flung herself on top of Molly. Molly lay on her back with Mandy collapsed against her side and Violet washing her face vigorously.

Landlady looked at me and shook her head. I felt as if Molly and I were an old married couple.

Shortly after that we went inside, into the bright light, and the spell was broken.

CHAPTER 26

I saw Molly at least once a week after that. Only in the presence of Landlady and Mandy, though, was I able to relax and enjoy her. When we were alone, I felt tense and unsettled. Every time I saw her I feared it would be the last.

"I thought she might be interested," I told Landlady over a pot of tea. "I thought I was getting signals from her but I must be getting rusty. She tells me she's been to three dances. Wouldn't she have invited me if she were interested?"

"I'm certain she cares for you," said Landlady.

"As a friend."

"Can you relate to her that way?"

I nodded. "Sure," I said with a conviction I didn't feel. "It's not as if we were involved."

Later in my room I sat immobile, staring into the gloom. Putting away my romantic feelings for Molly Gavison was going to be incredibly painful. I decided to put off the exercise as long as possible.

Fall came, then winter.

Molly often accompanied me to Mandy's hockey games. Mandy and I attended all the Martello home games. Molly brought crowds to the M Center such as have not been seen since Orvil Tessier and the demise of the EPHL.

After the games we invariably ended up at Tim Horton's for hot chocolate and donuts. The Tim Horton sessions were full of warmth and laughter and serious, serious sports talk. I felt, though, we did a lot of our talking through Mandy.

Molly was very much on her own, finding her own way, making new friends, leading a life quite separate from mine. Our lives were circles touching only tangentially.

The second last week in February we went to a movie together. Molly seemed pensive and restless. There was an unpleasant tension in the air, the kind that surrounds a couple on the verge of a breakup. And we hadn't even had the pleasure of a relationship. I wondered if she was on drugs again. The very thought chilled my heart.

"How's work?" I asked.

She looked very serious for a moment, then gave me a quick smile. "I'm sorry, Alison," she said. "I've been preoccupied tonight. Work's fine. The office is running like a top. My students are doing very well. I think Barb is going to do something at the Provincials. The kids are ahead of schedule. I couldn't ask for anything more. It would be nice if Barb won her age group of course but I'm not counting on that."

We walked to her house after the movies. It was too late to go in for coffee. I waited on the steps while she got Violet. It was her custom to walk me home when we had been out late.

"Be careful," I said as she was taking her leave. "Don't walk too near the park."

She smiled. "I'm always very careful," she said. "Better still I'm also very strong." She smiled again. "I'll meet you at the skating oval at lunch time, Friday."

"OK," I said.

She started to say something, then changed her mind. "See you then," she said. She turned and walked away, Violet padding happily at her side.

Molly and I had agreed to meet at the skating oval at twelve sharp, Friday. She was already there when I arrived, circling the oval with her long, easy strides. Sometimes she wore hockey skates. Today she was wearing her speed skates. I sat down on the bench beside the oval, took off my boots and began to lace on my skates.

Molly waved to me from across the ice. A moment later she whizzed past me, circled the oval once again, then coasted to a stop in front of me, dropping a rose into my lap.

I stared at the rose.

"This is my way of inviting you to have dinner with me," she said.

"Oh," I said, bemused. "What would you like me to bring?"

She smiled and shook her head. "I'm not inviting you to my place," she said. "I'm taking you to a fancy restaurant. I've already made reservations. Wear something great. It's a date."

"A date?" I stammered.

"If I'd waited for you to ask…" she said with gentle exasperation. She dropped to her knees on the ice in front of me and began to lace up my skate.

For some inexplicable reason I felt like crying. "It's been very hard the last few months," I said hoarsely. "Not bad…I mean, difficult…but it's been a very sweet time too…I…"

She understood. She hesitated for a moment over my left skate, then looked square into my eyes. "Why didn't you ever touch me?"

"Why…"

She wasn't about to let me off the hook. "You touched the other players. A pat on the back, an arm around the shoulder. Sometimes a hug. Just anything…"

I looked away, my jaw slack. "I was afraid I'd show too much."

"Would that have been so bad?" She must have thought I was cold because she pulled my booted foot into her lap and cuddled it against her knees.

"Yes, it would have. I was your coach. I thought…"

She grimaced and said, "Maybe you were right." Then she laughed and finished lacing my skate, tying the bow with a flourish. "But now?"

"No," I whispered, "not now."

She jumped up and sprinted away. I tried to follow but my knees were wobbly. I sank back down onto the bench. She laughed and skated back to pull me to my feet. She dropped my hands and skated away quickly.

"Tonight," she called over her left shoulder. "Seven o'clock. I'll pick you up."

Her voice rang out on the air, young and strong and healthy.

I was as nervous as a teen-ager on a first date.

"What'll I wear?" I asked Landlady who had come to find out why I was in such a dither.

She went to my closet and leafed through it briefly.

"God, Alison," she said, "you need some new clothes. Your grey suit," she decided after a moment. "Gentle butch. Makes you look sophisticated. White shirt. Red ascot for color."

"Should I wear the vest?"

She studied it for a moment. "Yes. Wear your filigreed ring and small link chain to soften the effect," she said. She paused, then added, "You don't want to attract the *whole* baseball team."

Molly arrived at seven sharp. She was wearing a navy blue pinstripe, soft white shirt open at the neck, a pale yellow tie, loosely knotted, a heavy box-link bracelet and wide gold ring.

Landlady watched us leave solemnly.

Dinner was wonderful, unbelievably tense in the nicest way. We talked in shorthand, blurting out our feelings for each other in embarrassed, eye-avoiding oblique snatches.

"I was so lost when you left me at Debbie's," she said at one point. "I felt so deserted, mad at you for leaving me, mad at myself for fucking up. I'd wanted so much to impress you when I joined the team. You were my childhood hero after all. I had a picture of you over my bed—that one they took after you played in the CIAU game."

I remembered the picture. I was twenty years old—kind of good-looking and butchy.

Finally, after we had drunk more coffee than anyone needed, she slid her hand across the table, touched my fingertips with hers and said with a helpless smile, "Your place or mine?"

I wasn't ready to explain to Mandy. "Yours."

We held hands all the way home. Once there she took Violet for a quick stroll while I went into the living room and arranged myself into what I thought would be a relaxed position. Molly came in a few minutes later, went to the kitchen and emerged with a bottle of ginger ale.

"I wish this was champagne," she said with a grimace. She poured the ginger ale, put something wonderful and classical—Mozart's 21st, I think—on the stereo, then sat down beside me on the couch.

We drank three toasts—to each other and one to the Teddies.

Then she put her glass aside, slipped her arm around me and kissed me very lightly on the lips. She withdrew from me just far enough to look into my eyes and whispered, "I think this is where we're supposed to make up for all the pain by making each other incredibly happy."

We had a wonderful necking session that went on for ages. I couldn't believe I was in the arms of this vigorous, young Valkyrie, that those wonderful hands were exploring my body—politely but absolutely insistently.

"Shall we go into the bedroom?" she whispered into my ear.

Up to this point I was totally confident, passionate, aroused, boldly responsive to her exploration of my most intimate parts. I was also fully clothed.

If I had felt embarrassed about showing myself to Val, the reality of stripping for Molly put me into a state of mild panic.

"I want you to know one thing," I said. "There's something you need to know about me before we—before I—"

"Yes?"

"I'm forty years old, Molly. I've got a forty-year-old's body..."

She looked at me very seriously, then a smile spread slowly across her face, stretching out to include the dimples in her cheeks. "I've heard a lot of forty-year-olds have them," she said softly. "People who know tell me that's one of the nicest things about taking a forty-year-old to bed."

She stood up and held out her hand. "May I?"

"Yes."

She took my hand. We looked at each other for a long moment, then walked together into the bedroom and closed the door.

CHAPTER 27

Spring has come and gone. Summer is upon us once again—hot lazy days of softball and warm cricket-filled nights in Landlady's back yard. A lot of things have changed and a lot of things have remained the same.

Joy Drinkwater has left the Teddies to coach the O'Brien's. "Jack's an old goof," she says, "but he's good to work for."

She and Sharon were united in a public commitment ceremony in the MCC in Toronto. "I don't want the big teddy bear to feel too much like a bachelor while we're apart," she told me on the phone one day. Sharon and Joy have a house in town and a cottage on the lake. They built it themselves.

Anne just had her second baby—another girl. Ingrid told me Val once showed up for a game in Hamilton with a blob of Pablum on her lapel. She'll never live that down.

Nomi and Dorsey are halfway through another year of mutual aggravation. As for me, I still live at Landlady's. I still throw a football for Mandy on bright, lazy afternoons. But every Sunday—and quite a few days in between—finds me in Molly Gavison's bed. I love being there but I especially love being there on Sundays. We take things very easy then. We drink coffee, read the newspapers and make love for a very long time.

I'm sort of famous now. I believe the things I say. Best of all female athletes are starting to believe them. The Lambs wear regular uniforms now. No one would dream of interfering with our helmets. There's progress to be made on the calendar—there's always something. The best news is, Mandy's playing for an all-girls team. Molly's influence, I guess. She's the new hero. I should be jealous.

I still live with Landlady but I won't always. The house next door is coming up for sale. Molly and I are interested.

AFTERWORD
A Brief History of Women's Hockey

1892—the first organized women's hockey game was played in Barrie, Ontario, Canada.

1916—a Canadian women's hockey team played at an invitational women's hockey tournament in Cleveland, Ohio.

1930s and 1940s—women's hockey fell into decline, a consequence of war, depression and a growing professionalism in sport that focused on promoting men's sports.

1956—The Toronto Minor Hockey Association discovered that eight-year-old Ab Hoffman, a player in the Tyke division, was actually Abigail Hoffman. Although she was good enough to be selected to the all-star team, Abigail was not allowed to play the next season. Girls, the league said, were not welcome to play hockey with boys. The case received national media coverage, revealed the lack of opportunities for girls to play hockey and opened the door to discussions that eventually led to the establishment of leagues for girls. In the meantime, Abigail turned her attention to other sporting endeavours— swimming, then track and field. She went on to represent Canada in four Olympic games and later served as a sports administrator.

1969— women's ice hockey started in Sweden.

1970—women's ice hockey started in Finland. A women's hockey league consisting of four teams was organized under the auspices of the Ontario Minor Hockey Association.

1973—the first women's hockey team established in Japan.

1974—women's hockey started in West Germany.

1975—Michigan-Ontario Ladies' Hockey League commenced play with six teams.

1976—Gail Cummings of Huntsville, Ontario, was denied the right to play hockey with a boys' team in the Ontario Minor Hockey Association. Gail went to court and won but lost on appeal. She eventually went on to Temple University on a lacrosse scholarship.

1977—a women's professional hockey league was proposed to operate out of Southern California. The league folded without playing a game.

1980—the first women's hockey team established in Switzerland.

1987—after a two-year court battle, Justine Blainey won the right to play on a boys' team in the Ontario Minor Hockey Association. Prior to this, girls were allowed to play only if no women's team was available.

1987—Ontario Women's Hockey League hosted an international tournament for six countries in Toronto, Ontario, Canada.

1990—the first internationally sanctioned women's world hockey championship was held in Ottawa, Ontario, Canada with teams representing Canada, Finland, Japan, Norway, Sweden, Switzerland, The United States of America and West Germany. In the gold-medal game, Canada defeated the United States 5-2. The players in this historic event were: Team Canada—Geraldine Heaney, Denise Caron, Cathy Phillips, Teresa Hutchinson, Dawn McGuire, Shirley Cameron, Michelle Patry, Judy Diduck, Diane Michaud, Brenda Richard, Heather Ginzel, Angela James, Kim Ratushny, Laura Schuler, Vicky Sunohara, Stacy Wilson, France Montour, Sue Scherer, France St. Louis, Margo Verlaan, Susana Yuen.

Team USA—Lauren Apollo, Beth Beagan, Lisa Brown, Tina Cardinale, Heidi Chalupnik, Cindy Curley, Shawna Davidson, Maria Dennis, Kelly Dyer, Kimberly Eisenreid, Cammi Granato, Mary Jones, Sue Merz, Kelly O'Leary, Kelley Owen, Judy Parish, Yvonne Percy, Julie Sasner, Jeanine Sobek, Sharon Stidsen.

Team Finland—Liisa-Marie Sneck, Leila Tuomiranta, Ritva Ahola, Kati Ahonen, Katri Luomajoki, Paivi Halonen, Kirsi Hirvonen, Jaana Rautavuoma, Anne Haanpaa, Marianne Sulen, Leena Pajunen, Marika Lehtimaki, Tiina Pihala, Marianne Ihalainen, Johanna Ikonen, Katri Javanainen, Liisa Karikoski, Riika Neiminen, Katja Lavonius, Tiia Reima, Sari Krooks, Tea Repo, Leena Majaranta, Minna Honkanen.

Team Japan—Tamae Satsu, Kaori Takahashi, Michiko Hatakeyama, Rika Hasegawa, Tamami Nishida, Yoko Suzuki, Yasuko Masuda, Cheiko Tanaka, Hiroko Mabuchi, Kayoko Miuri, Yumiko

Tsukamoto, Yoko Kurihashi, Misayo Shibata, Shiho Fujiwara, Rie Satoh, Masako Satoh, Chihomi Ishii, Ayako Okado, Sairi Honda, Yumiko Itoh.

Team Norway—Mary Olaug Ansnes, Kari Berg, Lena Bergersen, Anne C. Eriksen Moseby, Inger Lise Fagernes, Liv Kari Fjellhammer, Marianne Gomsrud, Jeanette Hansen, Camilla Edj Hille, Hilde Johansen, Nina Johansen, Tonje Larsen, Marit Larssen, Gina Marie Moe, Tone Oppegard, Anne Therese Petersen, Christin Smerud, Eva Stromsborg, Kristina Soderstrom, Christine Wennerberg.

Team Sweden—Agneta Nilsson, Annika Ahlen, Marie Jonsson, Ann-Sofie Erikson, Susanne Morne, Pia Morelius, Karin Andersson, Helena Nyberg, Tina Bjork, Linda Gustafsson, Petra Wikstrom, Lisa Plahn, Pernilla Hallengren, Anette Jarvi, Kristina Bergstrand, Annika Persson, Camilla Kempe, Malin Persson, Asa Elfving, Christina Mansson.

Team Switzerland—Christine Bischofberger, Tanja Mueller, Nicole Andermatt, Claudio Blaetter, Barbara Wolf, Daniela Maag, Cornelia Ochsner, Andrea Schweizer, Kim Urech, Nicole Walder, Sandra Gruetter, Doris Wyss, Mireille Noethiger, Cornelia Tanner, Iris Holzer, Edith Niederhauser, Leila Zaech, Regula Stebler, Monika Leuenberger, Mirjam Baechler, Nicole Schumacher.

Team West Germany—Karin Berlinghof, Aurelia Vonderstrab, Claudia Haaf, Cornelia Ostrowski, Claudia Patzold, Karin Obermaier, Sandra Kinze, Kira Berger, Ines Molitor, Beate Baert, Karin Korn, Silvia Schneegans, Natasha Schafrik, Stefanie Putz, Elvira Saager, Bettina Kirschner, Birgit Lisewski, Christina Oswald, Maren Valenti, Monika Spring, Silvia Hockauf, Petra Lutz.

1992—Manon Rheaume became the first woman to play in a National Hockey League game when she played goal for the Tampa Bay Lightnings against the St. Louis Blues in an exhibition game. Manon currently plays goal for the Atlanta Knights, Tampa Bay's farm team.

1998—women's ice hockey will be included in the Winter Olympics at Nagano, Japan.

HEROES

Angela James of the Missassauga Warriors may be the best woman hockey player in the world. She has represented Ontario in five Canadian National Championships, winning most-valuable player awards in these tournaments both as a forward and as a defender. The high point of her career came in 1990 when she played on Canada's gold-medal-winning team in the first sanctioned women's international hockey championships. Canada was to repeat its championship performance in 1992 and 1994 with Angela as an integral part of the team.

What makes Angela's impressive career all the more remarkable is that she is a Black woman participating in a predominantly white sport. In the 78-year history of the National Hockey League, just three Black athletes have played on NHL teams. The first was Willie O'Ree. He was followed by Tony McKegney and Grant Fuhr, the latter an accomplished goalie rated by Stan Fischler as one of the best one hundred players in the history of the game. The paucity of Black athletes in the sport is the result of a number of social factors not the least of which is the absence of role models. Angela James' high profile in women's hockey is sure to encourage other young Black women to get involved in the sport.

Angela James, Willie O'Ree, Tony McKegney, Grant Fuhr: paving the way.

Bobbi Rosenfeld (1903-1969) excelled in every sport she played and she played them all—softball, hockey, golf, tennis, basketball. At one time she held the Canadian record in the broad jump and discus and also competed in the hurdles and javelin. She won two Olympic medals in running. If women could have played hockey then, she would have been the best female hockey player of the half-century.

Her greatest moment, though, didn't come in the winner's circle. At the 1928 Olympics she was entered in the 800 metres to encourage a young Canadian runner. Bobbi didn't run this distance, didn't even train for it. Her specialty was the 100 metre dash. Nevertheless, as the race took form, it appeared she might have a shot at a medal. She might have won. Instead, she stayed behind to support her teammate. Bobbi Rosenfeld, a genuine sporting hero.

Hockey—Sid Abel, Bobby Baun, Jean Beliveau, Justin Blainey, Toe Blake, Carl Brewer, *John Brophy, Butch Bouchard, Eddie Chadwick, Lorne Chabot,.Bob Gainey, Wayne Gretzky, Doug Harvey, **Gordie Howe, ***Tim Horton, Elmer Lach, Ted Lindsay, Harry Lumley, Jim Morrison, Lester Patrick, Pete Peeters, Rocket Richard, Larry Robinson, Terry Sawchuck, Anatoli Tarasov, ****Orvil Tessier,

*John Brophy—rightly or wrongly, John Brophy was the most maligned coach in the history of the Toronto Maple Leaf franchise. During his tenure with the Leafs, he was blamed for everything that went wrong with the team if not with the entire city of Toronto.

** Gordie Howe is considered to be the greatest player in the history of professional hockey.

*** Tim Horton was not only a great hockey player but a good businessman. The Tim Horton donut chain is named after its founder.

****Orvil Tessier was the best hockey player never to make it to the NHL. He made the big time as a coach instead.

Baseball—Jim Palmer.

Figure Skating—Brian Orser, Katarina Witt.

Judith Alguire lives and writes in
southeastern Ontario, Canada. She
is keenly interested in animal welfare
issues and has a hopeless passion for
sports of all kinds. Her personal
sport is running which she does with
enthusiasm.